Praise for P

"Goddard opens her Rocky Mountain Courage series with this thrilling romance set amid an investigation into a smuggling ring. This will be a great entry point for those new to Goddard's high-octane inspirationals."

Publishers Weekly

"Readers will definitely enjoy puzzling over this story. The pacing is perfect; continuous, mind-boggling action, with plenty of time for unfinished business."

Interviews and Reviews

"*Present Danger* starts with a bang and never lets up. Goddard's fast-paced romantic suspense will have your pulse pounding as you turn the pages. Hold on to your seat and your heart as you enjoy this thrill ride!"

Rachel Dylan, bestselling author of
the Capital Intrigue series

"A plane crash, a dead body, and two people who decide that justice and love are worth fighting for all add up to a riveting read you won't want to put down. I highly recommend this book!"

Lynette Eason, bestselling, award-winning author of
the Danger Never Sleeps series

"A riveting beginning to the new Rocky Mountain Courage series, *Present Danger* takes readers on a wild ride filled with family tragedies, long-buried secrets, ancient relics, and broken hearts. Goddard has crafted a page-turner that takes off in the first nail-biting chapter, weaves through unexpected twists and shocking revelations, then culminates in a whirlwind of betrayal and redemption. I couldn't read the final chapters fast enough!"

Lynn H. Blackburn, award-winning author of
the Dive Team Investigations series

"I was captivated from the very first scene of *Present Danger* to the shocking conclusion. You can always count on Elizabeth Goddard to bring you dramatic action and adventure scenes that put you on the edge of your seat!"

Susan Sleeman, bestselling author of
the Homeland Heroes series

"Elizabeth Goddard starts her brand-new Rocky Mountain Courage series with an opening that sucks you in from page one and doesn't stop until the heart-pounding conclusion."

Lisa Harris, *USA Today* and CBA bestselling
author of the Nikki Boyd Files

"*Present Danger*—another edge-of-the-seat story by Elizabeth Goddard that will keep you turning pages to the end."

Patricia Bradley, author of *Standoff*,
Natchez Trace Park Rangers series

DEADLY
TARGET

Books by Elizabeth Goddard

UNCOMMON JUSTICE SERIES

Never Let Go

Always Look Twice

Don't Keep Silent

ROCKY MOUNTAIN COURAGE SERIES

Present Danger

Deadly Target

ROCKY MOUNTAIN COURAGE
· BOOK 2 ·

DEADLY TARGET

ELIZABETH GODDARD

Revell

a division of Baker Publishing Group
Grand Rapids, Michigan

© 2021 by Elizabeth Goddard

Published by Revell
a division of Baker Publishing Group
PO Box 6287, Grand Rapids, MI 49516-6287
www.revellbooks.com

Printed in the United States of America

Library of Congress Cataloging-in-Publication Data
Names: Goddard, Elizabeth, author.
Title: Deadly target / Elizabeth Goddard.
Description: Grand Rapids, Michigan : Revell, a division of Baker Publishing
    Group, 2021. | Series: Rocky Mountain Courage #2
Identifiers: LCCN 2021009089 | ISBN 9780800737993 (paperback) | ISBN
    9780800740580 (casebound) | ISBN 9781493431885 (ebook)
Classification: LCC PS3607.O324 D43 2021 | DDC 813/.6—dc23
LC record available at https://lccn.loc.gov/2021009089

Scripture quotations are from The Holy Bible, English Standard Version® (ESV®), copyright © 2001 by Crossway, a publishing ministry of Good News Publishers. Used by permission. All rights reserved. ESV Text Edition: 2016

This book is a work of fiction. Names, characters, places, and incidents are the product of the author's imagination or are used fictitiously. Any resemblance to actual events, locales, or persons, living or dead, is coincidental.

Baker Publishing Group publications use paper produced from sustainable forestry practices and post-consumer waste whenever possible.

21 22 23 24 25 26 27   7 6 5 4 3 2 1

To my oldest son, Christopher.
Your unwavering faith and trust in the Lord,
along with a heart that listens,
will carry you through and take you far!

//////////////////////

The steadfast love of the LORD never ceases;
his mercies never come to an end;
they are new every morning;
great is your faithfulness.
                    (Lam. 3:22–23)

ONE

PUGET SOUND

For a few hours every Saturday morning, Erin Larson could forget that evil existed.

And usually, only on the water.

She dipped the double-bladed paddle into the sea, then again on the other side—*left, right, left, right, left, right*—alternating strokes in a fluid motion to propel her kayak across the blue depths. Her friend Carissa Edwards paddled close behind.

Left, right. Left, right. Left, right.

On the water she was close to nature and far from the chaos and noise of the city even though she and Carissa paddled along the shoreline and could see the cityscape in the distance. The quiet calmed her mind and heart. The rhythmic paddling mesmerized her. The exertion exhilarated her. Cleansed her of the stress and anxiety acquired after a week of forced labor.

Okay, that wasn't fair. Her suffering certainly wasn't physical in nature.

Water. Mountains. Sky. She took in the sights and once again . . . forgot.

Beautiful snowcapped Mount Baker—the Great White Watcher—loomed large in the distance to the east.

Left, right. Left, right. Left, right.

The slosh of paddles along with the small waves lapping against her boat soothed her and were the only sounds except for seagulls laughing above her—*ha, ha, ha.*

To the west, the impressive Olympic Mountains begged for attention. Erin couldn't wait for Mom to join her out here, when she finally convinced her to move.

A salty ocean breeze wafted over her as peace and beauty surrounded her.

She couldn't ask for more.

She shouldn't ask for more.

But God . . . I need answers.

Carissa caught up with Erin and paddled next to her kayak. "Thanks for coming with me today. I needed this."

"The exercise or the scenery?" Erin had just broken a sweat despite the early morning cool.

"How about a little of both? And the company makes all the difference, I'm not going to lie."

"Yeah," Erin answered with reluctance. She and Carissa had an understanding between them. On their kayaking excursions, peace and quiet were supposed to reign.

"By the way, I listened to your podcast last night," Carissa said.

Maybe she'd forgotten their unspoken pact. "Oh?"

Erin wanted to know Carissa's thoughts, but at the same time, she didn't want to hear the criticism. Nor would she trust any praise.

"Why keep it anonymous?"

"It could get complicated."

Carissa's laugh echoed across the water. "In my case, I'd probably want the dean of the college and my students to know. But then again, I wouldn't be talking about crime or missing people. I'd be talking about history. So, what took you so long to tell me?"

Erin lifted a shoulder, opting for silence. Maybe it would be contagious.

Now she wished she hadn't told Carissa, but letting her friend in on her secret was a step toward opening up. She kept too much hidden inside. Erin had never been good at letting others in. Although as a psychologist, she was all about learning what made people tick on the inside.

Erin breathed in the fresh air, listened to the mesmerizing ripple of the water, felt the warm sun against her cheeks, and chased away thoughts of crime and work.

"Cold cases. Do they ever get solved?" Carissa asked.

Left, right. Left, right. Left, right.

"Some do." Few.

"Why do you do it?"

"I need a hobby, I guess." Erin couldn't begin to explain the complex events that drove her to talk about missing-person cold cases in hopes that answers could still be found.

"I've been thinking." Carissa's kayak inched ahead.

Erin remained silent.

"We do this every Saturday," Carissa continued.

Left, right. Left, right. Left, right.

"It's been a lifesaver," Erin said. "Thanks for inviting me along."

After a week working for the State of Washington, the endless hours spent researching and writing reports for forensic evaluations, she needed the break. The job wasn't what she had dreamed about when she'd become a criminal psychologist. Still, she hoped it was a means to an end. In the meantime, she'd started the cold case crime podcast.

"How about we switch it up? Go hiking. Mountain trails and lush forests all around us."

"This is close. We don't have to drive far. Plus, I really love the water." *And have an aversion to dense forests.* Carissa didn't need to know that, as a psychologist, Erin was a walking oxymoron.

"I thought you might enjoy a change."

"No, I'm good with this." Erin's shoulders and biceps started burning. She was relieved they would soon turn around and head back.

"I hope you'll think about it. I'd love for you to join me next weekend. I'm hiking in Mount Baker National Forest, and I'm inviting you to join the group."

"What? You're ditching me to go hiking?"

"Um . . . Is it just me, or is that boat heading directly for us?" Panic edged Carissa's voice.

Erin glanced over her shoulder in the direction of Carissa's wide-eyed stare. A thirty-foot cruiser sped toward them. She and Carissa had strayed a bit from the shoreline. Regardless, that boat shouldn't be approaching them in this area or at that speed.

"Hurry." Erin quickened her pace. "We can get out of its path."

"We won't make it." Carissa stopped and raised her paddle, waving to get the boater's attention. "Hey, watch where you're going! Kayakers on the water!"

Arms straining, Erin paddled faster and propelled the kayak forward. Her friend hadn't kept up. "Carissa, let's go! Just angle out of the path."

Carissa renewed her efforts and joined Erin. Together they paddled toward the shoreline that had seemed so much closer moments before.

Carissa screamed. Heart pounding, Erin glanced over her shoulder. The boat had changed course and was once again headed straight for them.

Fear stole her breath. "Jump! Get out of the kayak and dive!"

It was all she could think to do.

"Now, now, now!" She sucked in a breath and leaned forward to flip the kayak until she was upside down in the water for a wet exit. Holding her breath, she found the grab loop and peeled off the skirt. Then she gripped the sides and pushed the kayak away from her body as she slid out. Instead of heading for the surface, she kicked and dove deeper. She was grateful she was wearing a manually inflatable life vest over her wetsuit because a normal life vest would drag her back to the surface, which was normally a good thing.

But today that could get her killed.

She pushed deeper, deeper, deeper . . . away from the surface.

We're going to make it.

Erin twisted around to glance upward. The water was murky and visibility was only about ten feet, but she could still see her friend struggling to get free of her kayak. Terror stabbed through her. Erin swam back to Carissa to help her, even as the boat raced toward the kayaks and was almost on them.

Her eyes wide, Carissa pushed forward, freeing herself.

The hull of the speeding boat sped right over the top of the kayaks, breaking Carissa's in half—the stern of her broken kayak propelled toward Carissa. Her head jerked forward.

All the bubbles of air burst from her lungs, then her form floated—unmoving. Unconscious? Or was she lifeless?

Her pulse thundering in her ears, Erin swam toward Carissa, grabbed her, and inflated their life vests. They rose quickly to the surface. Erin broke the water and gasped for breath as she held Carissa. The water remained disturbed from the speeding boat's wake and crashed over them.

Erin confirmed what she already feared. Carissa wasn't breathing. Adrenaline surged through her. She had to keep moving. Holding on to Carissa, Erin started swimming them back to shore.

She spotted the errant boat making a big circle.

Coming back? Had someone lost control? She had to make it to shore to give Carissa CPR. And maybe even to save them both.

Stay calm. Panic wouldn't help either of them. The water was cold, but not so cold that she needed to worry about hypothermia. At least not yet. The whir of a boat from her left drew her attention, kicking up her already rapid heartbeat. As she took in the slowly approaching trawler—a far different boat from the speeding cruiser—relief eased the tension in her shoulders. Three men and a couple of women waved.

A silver-haired man in a Seahawks cap shouted, "Do you need help?"

"Yes! Hurry!"

The boat edged slowly toward her, and she swam to meet it. The men reached down and pulled Carissa up into the boat.

Erin used the ladder on the side. "She needs CPR. She's not breathing!"

When she hopped onto the deck, she saw that one of the men had started administering CPR.

A redheaded woman wrapped a blanket around Erin. "Oh, honey, are you okay?"

Hot tears burned down her cold, wet cheeks. "No . . . no, I'm not okay." She dropped to her knees next to her friend.

Carissa coughed up water and rolled onto her side. When she'd finished expelling seawater, she sat up and looked around.

Erin hugged her and spoke against her short, wet hair. "I thought you were done for."

Carissa held on to Erin tightly, then released her to cough more. Erin took in the group standing around them, their watchful eyes filled with concern.

"I'm Vince. And this is my wife, Jessie." The man with the Seahawks cap gestured to the redhead, then made introductions. John, his son, and Terry, John's friend, and Mavis, John's girlfriend. A family affair.

"I'm Erin, and this is Carissa."

Jessie placed a blanket around Carissa. "Why don't you have a seat? I'll get you something warm to drink."

"Thank you." Erin sat with Carissa on the cushioned bench and took in her friend. She looked shell-shocked, and why shouldn't she? Was she going to be okay?

Carissa closed her eyes. Was she in pain or thinking back to what happened? Jessie had disappeared below deck to grab warm drinks. Mavis, Terry, and John were trying to recover the kayaks and bring them onto the trawler.

Vince remained standing, his arms crossed as if he were a sentinel sent to protect them. And at this moment, Erin needed that reassurance.

"If you hadn't come when you did," she said, "I don't know what would have happened. I can't thank you enough." She searched the waters around them. "Is that boat . . . Is it gone?"

"What boat?" Mavis approached and glanced at Vince.

"You didn't see that?" Erin got to her feet and pulled Carissa with her. She searched the waters. "A boat came right for us. Ran over our kayaks and almost killed us. They must have lost control. Maybe they were drunk or something."

"I saw a boat heading west," Vince said, "but I didn't connect that to seeing you in the water, swimming to shore. Kayaks and canoes are hard to spot sometimes. I'm sorry that happened. But I'll contact the Seattle Police Harbor Patrol and let them know. In the meantime, is there somewhere we can take you?"

"Back to the marina at Port of Edmonds. We could talk to the police there and tell them what happened," Erin said.

Vince eyed Carissa. "I'll let SPHP know we're on the way and to meet us there. Should we get you to the hospital?"

Erin shared a look with her friend. "She sustained a hit to the head. Maybe an ambulance could be waiting for us when we get to the harbor."

Carissa nodded but said nothing. Erin ached inside. She'd almost lost Carissa. She was grateful that her friend had survived. They had both survived.

Erin replayed the events in her mind. Had the boat deliberately veered toward them or had she imagined it? These boaters who'd helped them had simply been out enjoying the day when they spotted Erin and Carissa in the water, their kayaks floating, Carissa's in two pieces.

I can't believe this happened.

The water had been her place of peace and tranquility.

But no more.

Erin pulled her ringing cell from the plastic bag tucked in a pocket on her suit. She didn't recognize the number, but it was a Montana prefix. Her heart jackhammered as she answered, "Erin."

"Dr. Larson . . . Erin." The familiar male voice hesitated. "This is Detective Nathan Campbell."

Dread crawled up her spine. Nathan would never call her without a good reason. "Nathan . . . what's going on?"

"It's . . . your mom. She's okay. But she tried to commit suicide. I'm so sorry."

A few heartbeats passed before she could answer. "Wha . . . What?"

Nathan apologized again and repeated the words.

The air rushed from Erin. She couldn't breathe and stood. She headed for the rail and hung her head over the water, gasping for breath.

"Erin! Erin, are you there?" Nathan's concerned voice shouted over the cell loud enough she could hear him despite the boat's rumbling engine and rushing water.

Carissa joined her at the rail. "Erin, what's happened?"

The darkness closed in on her all over again, but this was different from before. Why hadn't she seen the warning signs? She had to fix this.

Squeezing her eyes shut, she lifted the cell to her ear again. "I need details."

Nathan relayed that her mother was in the hospital and in stable condition.

Ending the call, she stared at the cell. Mom was in trouble. The fact that the awful news had come from the man she'd left behind compounded the pain in her chest. This, after she and Carissa had barely survived a boating accident.

Evil wouldn't let her forget that it existed, even for a few hours.

TWO

Fishing. Rock climbing. Fishing. Baseball. Fishing.

Nathan Campbell hiked down the trail toward the Gray-back River, following his dad—a man he hadn't seen in person in seven years, when he was twenty-five. Nathan wasn't entirely sure how he felt about Dad suddenly showing up today. Memories crashed over him. Sure, Dad had been there for him when he was growing up, teaching and coaching him in outdoor activities to fill his schedule so he never got into trouble. But he left Nathan and Mom twenty-two years ago. Nathan didn't blame either of his parents, but it was a life-changing event that had blasted a big hole in his heart.

And now as he traipsed behind his detective father, Nathan considered that he'd become a detective too. He had literally followed in his father's footsteps—unintentionally, of course. How had that happened? He didn't need the man's approval, or even his respect. Still, Dad had given Nathan a good foundation.

"Almost there," Dad huffed over his shoulder.

At fifty-seven, Newt Campbell was still in great shape and only a little out of breath. Nathan was probably in the best shape of his life. He had to be since he was a search and rescue technical climber as well as a member of the evidence dive team.

They approached the river at the point where it calmed after spilling from the old dam created by a series of buttresses built decades ago. Boiling rapids echoed from the narrow part of the canyon over a quarter mile downriver.

Memories gushed over him like the rushing water.

Why'd you come back? Why had Dad brought him here to fish after sharing a few phone calls here and there over the years? Was he sick? Did he have regrets and this was his way of trying to make some new memories or revisit old ones? Nathan needed to stop trying to figure it out and let his father explain.

"What about this spot?" Dad smiled, but he couldn't hide his troubled expression.

"It's perfect." This had been their spot to fish back when Dad and Mom were still together. Nathan hated that he chafed at the memories—good memories of a solid family and a good father. Those had all been dashed. He shook off his growing agitation.

Dad opened up the bait box. "I fished here when I was growing up. Funny thing about life. When I was a kid, I never imagined I'd bring my son here." He gestured to his right. "And that dam's been here even longer than that. I'm surprised they haven't replaced it already. I thought we could fish here today before everything's ruined."

"What are you talking about?" Nathan baited his hook.

"That new copper mine they're putting in upriver."

"They're using a new method, Dad. Environmentalists and new laws won't let them otherwise."

"Whatever you say. We'll see."

"You came all the way here just to fish on the river before it gets ruined?" Nathan's laugh leaned toward incredulous.

"Nope."

Didn't think so.

They stood on the bank, baiting their hooks. Nathan was struck by the fact he had dreamed of this moment for far too long since Dad left. It was like the little boy in him came running back, filling his thirty-two-year-old self with the old feelings and creating new ones. He had more "dad issues" than he wanted to admit.

Dad cast his line out ahead of Nathan, then gave Nathan a questioning glance as if to offer his help. Yep. Just like old times. Still, he could bask in the comfortable silence and enjoy this moment, despite the questions that remained. Life had a way of shifting so quickly, so suddenly, almost like a river could twist and turn and the rapids could boil underneath you and suck you under. Erin had come back too. Like that could change anything and he could somehow erase the last five years without her or the hurt she'd caused him.

Even if neither Erin nor his father stayed in Big Rapids, the secret dream he thought would never come true had happened this week. Suddenly and without explanation.

If he was admitting things to himself, he might as well go ahead and admit that he hoped Dad had come back to see him. Yep, Father-Issues-R-Us.

Dad's pole suddenly arched and bobbed.

"You got one!"

Dad reeled it in easily enough, crouched, and lifted the cutthroat trout. He pulled the hook from its mouth and tossed it back in, then grinned up at Nathan. "I love to fish, but I'm not much for cleaning them up anymore."

He reached into a small cooler he'd brought and grabbed two sodas, then handed one to Nathan. They popped the tops, and Dad lifted his in a toast. "To old times," he said.

"To old times. It's good to see you, Dad. You look good, maybe a little grayer at the temples, but no worse for the wear."

Dad chuckled. "Glad you think so. Henry thought the opposite."

"So you saw the sheriff?" Sheriff Henry Gibson was Nathan's boss—directly, now that Sergeant Aaron Brady had moved on and they never filled the captain position. Budget cuts could be brutal.

"We had coffee this morning. Just catching up. He was a detective here when I was, you know."

"Yeah." Nathan had heard plenty of stories.

"He had good things to say."

"That's great." About what? The department? Nathan's work? "I'm sure he was glad to catch up with an old friend."

"Speaking of old friends, how is Celia doing? Have you heard anything?"

"She was released from the hospital and is home. Erin came to town to stay with her, but I don't know for how long."

And Nathan doubted Erin would be sharing her plans with him. He'd only stopped by as a courtesy to check on them. After all, he'd been the one to inform Erin that her mother had tried to commit suicide. He could still hear the shock and pain in Erin's voice when she heard the news, and that rolled through him now. His insides shook a little at the raw memory.

"I called her last week." Dad tossed out his line again.

Now that was interesting. Why would Dad call Celia? Sure, her husband, Dwayne, and Dad had been best friends until Dwayne died on that SAR mission. But Dwayne hadn't been married to Celia long before Dad moved to the Boston area, so it wasn't like he'd known her that well. Or was Nathan missing something? Had Dad had an affair with the woman, and that's why he left? Why was he calling his deceased best friend's widow when he hadn't even called his own son?

"Listen, son." Dad cleared his throat. "I should have come back to see you before now. I'm . . . I'm sorry about that."

"It's okay. I understand." Not really. What was he saying? He'd seen Dad a few times on the holidays when he was a kid. Twice in his twenties, and that was it.

"I debated telling you this."

Oh no. Nathan braced himself. Dad was sick—cancer. Something terminal. That had to be it.

"Keep this to yourself. No one can know."

"What's going on? Why can't anyone know?"

"Lives are at stake."

"What is it?"

"I'm looking into a cold case. On my own."

"A cold case brought you back to Montana?" Disappointment lodged in Nathan's gut. Of the possible reasons, that had never entered his mind. And yeah, he was that kid again, that little boy on the inside who wanted his dad's attention. Pathetic.

Dad's features twisted, and the frown lines deepened as if he considered how much to share.

Nathan's breaths came quicker, his patience reaching its limit. "What cold case, Dad? What's this about?"

"Remember. No one."

Nathan reeled in his line all the way and set his fishing pole aside. "Yeah, sure. Whose lives are in danger?"

"Years ago, Dwayne asked me to look into something. He'd found some old newspaper articles, copied them, and gave them to me. Only I was in the middle of the divorce and moving, and I forgot all about them."

"Until now?"

"I've been investigating a murder back in Boston, and it reminded me of the articles. I felt so bad that I never looked into them. Even though he's gone now, I decided to follow through on his last request. As it turns out, I think there might be a connection between the case I was investigating in Boston and the cold case Dwayne wanted me to look into. But my boss, Lieutenant Sullivan, shut me down on digging into it. He didn't buy the connection. I took some time off, and I'm following up on my own."

Interesting.

"I feel bad that I didn't help Dwayne resolve this before he died, and in that way, I let him down." Dad leveled his gaze at Nathan. "When I started looking into it, I got strange vibes from my boss, if you catch my meaning."

"Are you saying your boss doesn't want you digging into this for a different reason than he shared? As in, you think this is a cover-up?"

"Something feels off. All these years, I've learned to trust my gut, and now I've pulled on dangerous threads."

"But you're going to keep pulling."

"I can't let go. If I can find answers to a cold case and bring closure, then I'm going to do that. If I don't look into it, then who will?"

"What about your job? Are you risking losing that?"

He shrugged. "I hope it won't come to that, but if anything happens to me, you'll know why."

If anything happens? Nathan's chest tightened. He didn't like the precarious situation his father was in and was putting Nathan in as well. "What about Henry? Did you tell him?"

"No. Right now, the only person I trust is you, son."

Seriously? Why him? Nathan wanted to tell his father that he didn't even know him. He bit back those words but opened his mouth to ask more about the case—

His father cut him off. "In case something happens to me—"

A shot rang out in the distance and Nathan stiffened. A hunter probably.

Dad fell forward, his upper body splashing into the river.

"Dad!" The shock of the moment kept Nathan cemented to the ground.

Blood colored the water near Dad's head. Heart pounding, Nathan stepped into the river and pulled his father out and carefully dragged him onto the bank. Nathan dropped to the ground and supported Dad's head. Shock gripped him as he looked at the gunshot wound. Nathan pressed his shaking hand against the hole in Dad's head, blood gushing between his trembling fingers. Sobs broke from him as he checked Dad's pulse. It was weak, but Dad was still alive.

A gunman. A shooter out there.

If this had been intentional, Dad could still be in danger.

"If anything happens to me, you'll know why."

Nathan dragged Dad behind a boulder to prevent another bullet if someone had been aiming to kill. If so, they might already think he was dead.

Nathan's whole body quaked. He couldn't lose his father this way. He didn't want it to end this way. *Please, God, help me!*

Pull yourself together, man! He yanked out his cell and held it up in the air, still behind the boulder, until he got one bar.

One lonely bar.

Then he called for emergency services—a life-flight helicopter was the only way to save Dad's life.

If it wasn't already too late.

THREE

issing Children: Deadly Rabbit Trails, Episode 1

On the evening of Sunday, September 14, 1998, police received a 911 call from a woman claiming her daughter had been abducted. Dispatch struggled to understand her through the sobs but kept her on the phone while police headed to her home, but they took an extraordinary amount of time because the only bridge for seventeen miles had collapsed.

Erin hit the Pause button and removed the headphones that hadn't quite muted the noisy lawn mower outside her window. She'd been listening to the first episode in the latest season from her *Missing Children* podcast. Before recording the next episode, she needed to get her mind back into the flow. A thousand listeners would earn her twenty-five dollars from the popular insurance advertiser she promoted. She wasn't even close to that number yet, but she wouldn't give up on the podcast, even though she'd had to put the rest of her life on hold, taking leave from her "day job" to stay with Mom in Big Rapids, Montana.

As for Carissa, she'd recovered from the boating accident

and was already back at her job as a history professor, according to her email this morning. Erin would miss Carissa, but her friend understood that Erin had to focus on her mother.

She had no choice but to stay in Big Rapids for now, since Mom refused to move to Washington. A pang ricocheted through Erin's heart. She still couldn't believe she'd missed the signs that her mom was struggling, or maybe it was that there simply hadn't been any.

Though Erin was a psychologist, she didn't specialize in depression or suicidal ideations. Her concentration was in criminology—Erin wanted to understand the criminal mind.

While she figured out how to best help her mother, she would keep up with the podcast for her own sanity. Through the window, she spotted Mom's neighbor Delmar Wilson still mowing his grass.

She grabbed a few Cheetos and crunched on them while she waited until he finished mowing. The man peered at Mom's house now and then. He came across as kind of creepy to Erin, and she wasn't sure if there was any basis for that or if it was more that he eyed her mother with interest. And that concerned Erin. On the other hand, at least Mom seemed to have friends who cared about her.

But that was another anomaly. According to Mom's friends, they hadn't noticed anything off with Mom either. No obvious signs of depression. Nadine, Mom's closest friend from church, hadn't noticed anything either. She'd been eager to confirm with Erin that Mom never talked of killing herself. She hadn't seemed hopeless at all. On the contrary, she was a happy volunteer at a local nonprofit benevolent organization. Main Street Thrift Shop was much more than the name implied and offered assistance to people who'd fallen into unfortunate circumstances. They provided clothing, bedding, and necessities, as well as a scholarship or two every year to high school seniors.

Their motto? "By our work we are known."

"Amen," Erin muttered.

If anything, Mom had been thriving. And Erin had been stunned at the news Nathan had delivered. Erin was in Big Rapids to support her mother in her time of need—and to solve the mystery of her attempted suicide. An attempt her mother had no memory of. A good network of friends was important, but Erin wouldn't trust anyone else to take on the responsibility of suicide watch. Hence, she had moved back for the foreseeable future.

She glanced out the window when she heard the mowing stop. Delmar wiped his forehead with a rag. Once again, he eyed the house. Erin opened the mini blinds completely and waved at Delmar. He waved back. Good. She wanted to re-mind him she was here to take care of her mother. Instead of starting up the lawn mower, he left it there and headed to his front door.

Erin started listening to the podcast again, eager to get started on the second episode. Uncertainty about opening up this case for close perusal weighed on her. But talking about cold cases on a podcast was one of many ways answers could be found, in addition to television commercials and newscasts. And recently, revisiting DNA and running it through genealogy databases solved cold cases. *Missing Children* was Erin's contribution.

Forty-five minutes later, she'd finished listening to the epi-sode and stared at the script she'd written for episode two, contemplating recording it now.

Glass shattered somewhere in the house, startling her. She tore off her headset and raced through the house. "Mom!"

Her mother stood in the kitchen, staring down at a broken platter—roast and carrots were scattered across the floor, along with fragments of the dish. Erin took it all in, her gaze finally landing on her mother's feet.

"Oh, Mom. You're not wearing shoes. Carefully come my way and try not to step on anything. I'll clean it up."

"I'm not a child! Do not treat me like a child." Her angry face shifted into one of a tortured soul. "Oh, Erin."

Mom covered her face with her hands.

Erin didn't think the new medication was working well. She stepped across the mess on the floor to hug her mother. "It's okay. I've dropped a plate of food plenty of times myself. Everyone does it."

Mom stepped away and stared at the floor. "But now our dinner is ruined."

"I'll order takeout. In fact, I'll order it now so it will be on the way while I clean up."

"I'll clean it. I dropped it, after all."

Erin took her mother's hands. She breathed in and out, slowly and calmly, hoping her mother would do the same. "We'll do it together. But get shoes on first."

Mom finally smiled. "I'm glad you're here, Erin. I missed you."

Mom carefully stepped around the visible platter shards. On the other side of the dinner disaster, she turned. "Oh . . . Did I interrupt your podcast? I'm sorry if I did."

"I had just finished listening to the first episode. In fact, you could say it was perfect timing. Now, get your shoes on while I call for takeout, and we'll clean up together."

Mom's shoulders dropped as the tension eased from her. When she headed down the hall, Erin grabbed her cell and ordered pizza. Then she picked up the largest pieces of the platter and tossed them in the trash can. Mom returned and showcased her stylish athletic slip-ons, and together they cleaned up.

"If it's any consolation, the roast smelled good," Erin said. "I've missed your cooking."

"That's nice to hear." Mom crouched to wipe the floor. "But I just hate wasting food like this. I wanted to make you something special."

Erin had to keep her mother looking at the positive side. "You can always make another roast. But tonight, we're having pizza. That sounds good, right?" Erin felt like she was walking on eggshells around Mom, trying to stay upbeat and keep things positive, when really, if she hadn't been told, she would never have known that her mother had taken an entire bottle of Valium, a benzodiazepine, and one of the most commonly prescribed drugs in the country. She didn't know how long she could keep this up, or if she even needed to.

Erin washed her hands, and Mom tugged the plastic garbage sack filled with broken glass and their meal out of the can. She exited the back door to place the bag in the bigger garbage container outside.

Erin moved to the hallway and looked up at the attic door. Nadine was the one who found Mom on the floor in her room, the empty pill bottle next to her. Nadine claimed the attic ladder had been down. Erin wanted to search the attic to see if Mom had come across something that had disturbed her. In the meantime, she would encourage Mom to get back to her Bible study and prayer group—more spiritual activities that were good for her soul to go along with the medication prescribed by her doctor.

Mom came back in from outside as Erin entered the kitchen again, and together they worked to finish sweeping and mopping up the mess.

Erin had just put the broom away when the doorbell rang.

"I'll get it." Erin and her mother spoke the words simultaneously.

Erin chuckled and headed to the door. "I bet it's the pizza. Go ahead and get some dishes out."

Mom nodded and reached for the cabinets. Erin opened the door and surprise filled her. Her best friend, Terra Connors, stood in the doorway, holding a pizza box.

Erin gasped out the words. "What? How did you—? Oh . . ."

Terra laughed. "I intercepted the delivery guy. Tipped him too."

Erin opened the door wider. "Since you're bringing dinner, come on in."

Terra stepped inside. "Are you saying I couldn't come in if I wasn't bearing gifts?"

"You're welcome any time of the day or night, with or without gifts." Erin hugged her longtime friend. When she released her, Erin took in Terra's appearance. Erin's eyes were blue-green, and she wished she had bright blue eyes like Terra. And since she was wishing, she might as well wish for Terra's long, dark mane instead of her own dirty-blonde mess. Then she realized something. "You're letting your hair grow out?"

Terra shrugged. "For the wedding. Jack likes it longer."

Erin set the pizza box on the table and glanced over at Mom as she went into the kitchen to grab another plate.

Terra leaned in and whispered, "Are you staying for a while?"

Erin had seen Terra only briefly since coming back to town and took this chance to explain that she'd made the decision to live here at least for a while. Most of Erin's things remained at her apartment in Snohomish, for which she still had a lease, but she had a feeling she could very well be making this her permanent residence.

Erin's mom returned to the dining room and set out another plate. They gathered at the table, and Terra said grace. Erin took a bite of the Hawaiian pizza and savored the combination of sweet pineapple and Canadian bacon. Her shoulders rolled forward as tension drained out of her. "This is so good. I needed this." She quickly eyed Mom. "But your roast and carrots would have been just as good, Mom."

Mom grinned, then shoved a slice toward her mouth and took a bite.

Terra leaned back and sighed as she chewed. Erin was glad for the extra company.

She and Terra first became close when their loved ones died in the same tragic accident. All SAR volunteers, Erin's stepfather, Terra's mother, and Alex Knight's father died in an avalanche while trying to save someone stranded after a plane crash. Plaques now memorialized the fallen SAR team at the Rocky Mountain Courage Memorial that rested at the base of Stone Wolf Mountain. Since then, Terra, Erin, and Alex had forged a special bond. In fact, Terra was more like a sister to Erin. Alex, a brother, though he had also left Montana for a job that took him far from them.

"Tough day in the forest?" Erin asked.

"You could say that." Terra suddenly stopped chewing and averted her gaze.

"All right. I know that look. You can't fool me. What happened? Or are you not allowed to talk about it?"

Terra pressed both hands on the table. "There's no easy way to say this. Nathan's father was shot. It happened down by the river while he and Nathan were fishing."

Erin's pulse filled her ears as she let those words sink in. "Is he . . . ?"

Terra's brow furrowed, and she shook her head. "He was life-flighted to the hospital in Bozeman, but I don't know his current condition."

Erin stared at the slice of pizza on her plate. Concern for both Nathan and his father vanquished her appetite. "What happened?"

"As a USFS Special Agent, I was called in since it happened in the national forest. I left to come here to tell you, but I was waiting for the right moment. Jack is still at the scene, but I'm not sure he'll be investigating either since he and Nathan are close. It could be the new guy."

"The new guy?"

"Trevor West is the new detective. Jack suspects Henry will give him the investigation."

Erin nodded and wished her stomach would settle down. She glanced at Mom. They didn't need this news right now. Mom got up from the table and tossed the rest of her half-eaten slice into the trash.

Terra looked from Mom back to Erin, and realization seemed to dawn in her eyes that talking about this in front of Erin's mother, who'd recently left the hospital after swallowing a bottle of Valium, wasn't the best idea. She mouthed the words, "I'm so sorry."

Erin needed to change the subject. "How's Jack doing?"

Grayback County detective Jack Tanner and Terra had gotten engaged last fall, and Erin couldn't be happier for her friend. The two had split up years ago and found their way back to each other. The thought reminded her that she and Nathan had split up five years ago before she'd left for Washington. They'd known each other growing up, but it wasn't until college, when their majors centering around crime caused their paths to cross now and then, that Nathan had finally asked her out. Given her issues, she never should have let herself fall for him. And she'd tried to stay away. They had danced around their attraction for years, and then finally she agreed to that first date that turned into a year-long serious relationship.

If she'd ever wanted a chance with the right guy, she'd blown it.

And she didn't see them getting back together. Terra didn't answer Erin's question, but her intense gaze pulled her back to the moment.

And what had happened. Erin's heart seized in her chest. "Poor Nathan. He hadn't seen his dad in years, last I heard. Did his father move back?"

Terra shrugged. "I think he was visiting for a few days."

Mom slid back into her chair at the table and pressed her hand over Erin's. "You should go to the hospital and be there for him."

Still staring at her plate, she shook her head. "Mom, we're not together anymore. That was years ago. He wouldn't want me there."

"He's such a good man. A good detective. He stayed with me, waiting at the hospital until you got there. Nadine told me." Mom offered a compassionate but tenuous smile, as if almost begging Erin to go.

Thanks for the guilt trip. When Nadine found Mom and the empty bottle of pills, she called 911, then contacted Jack, her detective nephew, but Nathan showed up first. Jack was on a call across the county. Nathan then called Erin with the news. He'd been supportive and checked on things every couple of days since Mom was released from the hospital. Mom was right. Nathan was a good man.

"I think you should go too," Terra said.

They were ganging up on her now.

"My presence would only be an intrusion." Then again, if she could return the favor or help in any way . . .

"How about I hang out here while you go?" Terra asked.

Erin glanced at Mom and then Terra, who subtly nodded, conveying that she understood Erin wouldn't leave her mother alone. Not yet. Not until she was sure Mom was no longer a danger to herself.

"How about that, Mom?" Erin asked. "You and Terra could watch some old episodes of *Hawaii Five-O*."

Mom shrugged, clearly not liking the idea they wouldn't leave her to stay alone. Still, she didn't argue or try to win a losing battle. "That sounds fine. If Terra staying with me is what it takes for you to go to the hospital. Or, if you're busy, Terra, I could call Nadine or even Delmar next door to come over."

"Terra's here, Mom." While Nadine would be fine, Erin didn't know how long she would be gone. And she still didn't like creepy Delmar.

An hour and a half later, Erin rushed into the hospital

in Bozeman, the nearest trauma center, and asked for Newt Campbell. She was directed to a waiting area.

What am I doing here? A simple call would have been enough. After the way she'd hurt Nathan before, when she walked away from a future with him, she had no right to step back into his life. But they'd been close once, and when he called her about Mom, she knew they were still connected, though painfully so.

Another step and she was in the waiting area. Across the room, Nathan held his mother, Elisa Campbell, in his arms as she cried. Though Nathan's eyes were closed, Erin could see the raw pain etched in his features, and her heart stuttered to see him like this.

Oh no. His dad couldn't be dead. *Please, Lord, let it not be so.*

She swallowed the knot swelling in her throat and took in his rugged face. The scruffy jaw and thick, black hair that she'd once loved to weave her fingers through. The memories flooded her and almost took her breath away.

When he glanced up, his dark-brown gaze hung on Erin. At the agony spiking through his eyes, she almost took a step back. She wasn't sure what to do. Join them? Sit in a chair and wait? Why had she come?

When a doctor approached, Nathan released his mother and turned to hear what news the physician would deliver. Then he glanced over his shoulder at Erin and gave a subtle nod, a simple acknowledgment that he knew she cared, before he entered a set of double doors with his mother. ICU.

Erin gathered that his dad had survived but was in critical condition.

Nathan knew she'd come and she cared. Was it truly enough? *By our work we are known . . .*

She would go home now. But as she walked away, she had the odd sense that the earth shifted and rumbled beneath her, and all the stability she'd fought for and gained was crumbling away.

FOUR

Nathan remained in Dad's room with his mother and encouraged her to eat the tuna sandwich he'd grabbed from the cafeteria. She refused to leave Dad's side. If she still felt so strongly for him, Nathan couldn't fathom why his parents had divorced. Again, his thoughts went to Dad and his call to Celia. Maybe the blame was on Dad.

Still, Nathan supposed some connections never died, and maybe that explained Erin's appearance in the waiting room last night. She'd rushed into the room and then stopped at the sight of him holding Mom. He was distraught over the events and was trying to remain strong for his mother, but he'd seen the concern in Erin's eyes. No matter they'd broken up five years ago. No matter the way she'd left him when she left Montana. She'd been there for him last night, however briefly.

He scraped a hand across his face. He wasn't coherent enough to think through the implications or how any of it mattered. Staring at his own tuna sandwich, he realized he wasn't hungry, but maybe if he ate, then Mom would eat too. Several family friends had come by to visit, and she'd had to go out and speak to them since Dad wasn't yet out of the ICU, but she always returned and sat next to him.

For Mom's sake, Nathan finished off the sandwich that tasted like cardboard. "You need to eat and keep up your strength for Dad."

The words seemed surreal since Mom and Dad hadn't been together for twenty-plus years. He moved to stand by the bed and stared at his father's black-and-blue face, most of his head wrapped from the surgery to remove the bullet. A deep ache clawed his insides, and he couldn't shake it. He couldn't stand to see his father like this. How long had he been praying for the man? Finally, he got the chance to spend a few moments fishing with him at the river.

Were those the last moments he would ever have with his father? Was that a gift from God? He should be grateful, thankful he got to talk to his father. Go fishing with him, of all things, one last time.

Please, God, don't let that be our last time together. Please let him survive.

It seemed impossible that Dad had lived long enough for the helicopter to swoop in, rescuers to stabilize him in the hoist and lift him, then fly him to Bozeman.

A miracle, really. Still, Nathan didn't understand any of it. Why had this happened?

His cell buzzed, and he glanced at it. Henry. His boss, Sheriff Gibson. *I'm in the waiting room. Are you able to see me?*

Henry was thoughtful to come all the way here to check on Dad. Nathan worked to pull his thoughts together. He'd given his statement to the newest detective, Trevor West, who'd been assigned to investigate.

What would Nathan say to Henry? Dad had told him not to share about their conversation regarding the cold case—the reason Dad had come back to Big Rapids.

"Lives are at stake."

Dad's or someone else's?

What do I say, Lord? How much do I tell him? Or how little? How did being a detective suddenly become impossible? He scraped both hands through his hair, exhaustion and indecision pressing down on him.

"Mom, the sheriff's out in the waiting room," Nathan said. "Will you be okay?"

"Sure. I'm not going anywhere."

Nathan exited the ICU area. They would move Dad to another room soon, where he might shrivel away for years if he never woke up.

Nathan found the waiting area and spotted the sheriff. A few others occupied the room—a middle-aged couple spoke in low tones. An older man, maybe in his seventies, sat in a chair alone and hung his head.

Nathan slowly approached Henry. Hands in his pockets, Henry stared out the window. Nathan joined him, looking out at the parking lot, the town of Bozeman, and the mountains beyond. Henry angled his head to Nathan, concern evident in his features as he thrust out his hand. When Nathan took it, Henry pulled him into a bear hug. Since Nathan joined the county sheriff's department, Henry had been a mentor to him. Nathan did his best every day to both please the Lord and avoid disappointing *this* man.

Henry leveled his gaze on Nathan. "How is he?"

Henry had been friends with Dad back in the day when they both worked as detectives for Grayback County. Dad had moved on to bigger-city investigations, and Henry had moved up to become county sheriff. Nathan's throat grew tight. He shrugged, searching for the words, forcing his mouth to move past the painful emotions. "The doctor took the bullet from his head. Swelling is expected. He'll wake up when he wakes up. More than that, I don't know."

Henry remained quiet for a few moments as if he, too, were

trying to find the right words. Then he said, "And what about you? How are *you* doing?"

Nathan shrugged. "I'm here."

"You want to talk about it?"

He didn't know where to begin and he might explode trying to, so he shook his head.

"Anything I can do, you let me know. In the meantime, we'll find him, Nathan. You leave the investigation to us. We'll find the man who shot your dad."

Nathan was glad for the opening. "At least let me ride shotgun. Be part of it. Something. I can't just sit here and do nothing while a shooter is out there."

"Doing nothing is exactly what you're going to do. You can't expect me to let you get involved. You can't think clearly after an incident like this, especially since it involved your father. You were there, and you're still processing through the shock of it. I can see that well enough in your eyes." Henry gripped Nathan's shoulder and squeezed. "Don't you worry. I won't let this go. He might be your father, but he's also my friend."

"Let Jack investigate instead of Trevor. He's too new at this."

Henry scratched his chin. "I spoke with your father's boss back in Gifford. Newt moved over from Boston PD about three years ago. We might want to look at his past cases. See if someone from one of them targeted him."

Nathan's heart pounded. Dad's words came back to him. Dad was digging into a cold case and had pulled on "dangerous threads," he'd called them.

"Right now, the only person I trust is you, son."

Why couldn't his father trust his old friend Henry Gibson? Sheriff of Grayback County.

"Do you think someone targeted him? Followed him all the way to Montana to take him out?" Nathan couldn't wrap his mind around it—if only Dad could have shared more, but it sounded like that's exactly what Dad had been trying to tell him could happen. He squeezed his fists. He was torn about what to do. How much to say. He thought he could even hear the ripping sound in his chest. Henry would take notice if Nathan didn't calm down. He forced his breaths to slow.

Henry scratched his ear. "I suppose time will tell. Could be someone here, someone who had a bone to pick. After all, your dad was a detective here before he left."

Nathan studied the sheriff. Could that be the reason his father left to begin with? To protect his family? Or was Nathan imagining ghosts where there were none? Grasping at too many nonexistent straws? "What else did Dad's boss say?"

Henry pursed his lips and shrugged. "Nothing important."

"I hope you'll keep me in the loop on the investigation."

Henry eyed Nathan. "An old phrase comes to mind when I look at you and listen to you. Like father, like son. You sound just like him."

Though Henry's lips remained flat, Nathan caught the smile in his eyes. Guilt suffused Nathan.

"You got something on your mind, son?" Henry called him *son*. Now he'd turned mentor instead of boss.

"Before he was shot, Dad was telling me a story. He asked me to keep it to myself. But now I don't know what to do." Why would he have asked that of Nathan, knowing it could put him in such a predicament? Or maybe Dad hadn't fathomed this would happen. But it had.

How would Henry react if Nathan shared that his dad said he couldn't trust anyone, not even Henry?

The man crossed his arms, and wisdom seemed to flood his eyes. "If he asked you not to share, he must have had a good reason. Because you're bringing it up to me, I take it that you're battling whether you should keep what he told you a secret."

Nathan nodded subtly and could no longer hold Henry's gaze. Instead, he stared out the window at an older large sedan struggling to park in the slim spots. What could he say?

Henry tapped his chin and studied Nathan. "He put you in a tough spot."

Shoving his hands into his pockets, Nathan frowned. "That's why I need to look into a few things."

"You do what you want in your free time, because I'm giving you a week off. Spend it here with your father. Or spend it getting your head together. Trust your gut on how much to share. That's all the advice I can give you, son. Sometimes being the best law officer you can be means listening to your instincts. Newt didn't share whatever it was with me. He shared it with you. Now you carry that burden alone. I'm going to give you the benefit of the doubt here, some leeway, let's say, because you've earned my trust. I'll be here if you decide you need help carrying the burden."

Nathan couldn't have asked for more from Henry, and his words only increased Nathan's confusion about Dad not telling the man.

Trust your gut. Dad had said that much as well.

Henry squeezed Nathan's shoulder again. "I'm going to head back to my county. Take care of yourself, Nathan, and keep in touch."

Henry turned and walked down the hall toward the elevator. Nathan released a long, hollow breath. His world had been turned upside down, and he was struggling to claw his way back to a standing position.

Nathan had wanted a chance to crack the case of his life. This . . . *this* was the case of his life. His father's shooting. A case he wasn't allowed to investigate. Only now did he realize that deep down he wanted to crack a case to get Dad's attention. He'd never realized how deeply he craved that until this moment. How deeply he wanted Dad's approval, even after all these years. Now with his father's life hanging in the balance, it all seemed trivial.

"Like father, like son."

Maybe Nathan would look into his father's cold case. He would take up his father's mantle. And he wouldn't tell anyone because . . .

"Lives are at stake."

FIVE

Missing Children: Deadly Rabbit Trails, Episode 2

When police finally arrive at the home, they find the woman, Angela Gardner, with her mother, Shelley Woodley, the abducted child's grandmother. They learn that neighbors, family, and friends are already searching the woods for the missing child who is lost in the dark. Officer Felisha Farley later reported that she remained hopeful and tried to encourage the recently divorced Mrs. Gardner that her daughter would soon be found, but that she'd spoken too soon when Mrs. Gardner shouted at her that a man had taken Missy.

Officer Farley needs to confirm that an abduction has taken place before she can issue an Amber Alert, which are mostly reserved for "stranger" abductions, and Farley has questions regarding Missy's father. She radios for additional law enforcement to be dispatched to Cliff Gardner's home. While further questioning Mrs. Gardner, Officer Farley learns that the missing child, nine-year-old Missy Gardner, hadn't been alone when she went into the woods. Missy had gone to the woods with her best friend and neighbor, Erica Weeks, who allegedly could confirm the abduction. Officer Farley radios for one of the officers who is searching in the woods to return and remain with Mrs.

Gardner so that Farley can go next door to take statements and question Erica and her mom.

In the next episode, we'll listen to the 911 call, and let me warn you, it will give you chills. Your assignment? For those who lived in Kenosha, Wisconsin, or the surrounding region in 1998, think back to the night the bridge went out. Talk to family members and show them Missy's picture. If you have any information on this missing person, please call the Wisconsin FBI field office or the local Kenosha police.

Erin wrapped up the podcast episode and shot out the door for a desperately needed run. Her escape from the reminders of the evil in this world. The podcast gave her purpose, but it drained her in a thousand ways. In lieu of kayaking, she'd taken up jogging. Twenty minutes in, sweat dripped down her back and gathered at her temples as she pushed herself along the sidewalk near the city park. The last couple days here in Big Rapids had left her more scattered than she wanted to admit.

The fresh air and exertion would clear her head. She hadn't had a chance to breathe, much less think clearly, since her carefully planned life had imploded.

She could probably say goodbye to that promotion she'd been hoping for, if she even had a job to return to. She had to face the facts—she might not ever go back to Seattle. Once Erin was certain her mother was well and truly mentally healthy, she would try once more to convince Mom to move out to Washington. After all, there weren't nearly as many job opportunities for her line of work here in Nowhere, Montana.

Her cell buzzed, and under normal circumstances she would ignore it, but since this could be Nadine or Mom, who were having coffee together when she left, she needed to check. Erin slowed her jog and glanced at her cell—it was the Seattle Police Department detective she'd spoken with before leaving Montana. But she'd missed the call and it had gone to voice mail. She would listen after her run and continued on.

But it buzzed again. Terra. Erin jogged in place and answered. "Hey, what's up?"

She hoped her friend had news for her.

"What's with the breathing? Is something wrong?"

"Calm down. I'm on a run."

"Oh, phew. Okay, well, I called to let you know that Jack learned Nathan's father is still unconscious. He made it out of another surgery to relieve some hemorrhaging, but he remains unconscious as his brain heals."

Erin stopped running in place and bent over her thighs to catch her breath. Heartfelt pain engulfed her. "I'm so sorry. That's . . . just awful. I'm glad he's alive, but still . . ."

"Yeah."

"Have they found the shooter yet?"

"Not that I've heard."

"Thanks for letting me know." Erin had informed Terra of what happened last night at the hospital, and that she didn't feel comfortable returning today. Besides, she was more or less anchored to the house. She needed to think about Mom right now.

Terra remained quiet.

"Are you still there?" Erin asked.

"Yes. Just making a turn on a bumpy road here. Before I lose my signal, let me get to the main reason I called. Nathan isn't at the hospital, even if you changed your mind and decided to make the drive over there."

"Thanks for the intel. I won't be changing my mind." Erin straightened and tried to decide if she should resume her jog or if she was done. "Anything else?"

"Yes."

She thought so.

"Jack is worried about Nathan. Says he's in a bad way."

"Who wouldn't be?"

"Jack can't find him. He's not answering his cell."

Smart man. "He probably needs time alone to think."

"Maybe, but it's been a few hours."

Erin turned to walk back to the house. "I'm sorry. Jack will figure it out. Nathan will be okay."

"Is this the psychologist talking?"

"Um . . ."

"Just what I thought."

"What?"

"I just meant you weren't really giving it much thought. Okay, that was harsh. I'm sorry."

"I know you're worried," Erin said. "The first thing that popped into my head was the crime scene. The Nathan I know, or knew, would be trying to solve this crime."

"Listen, you're right in that he wanted to be part of the investigation, but the sheriff told him to take a week off. So he can't go there. Jack was at the scene earlier with Trevor, the lead investigator, and Nathan wasn't there."

Terra wanted something from Erin, that much was obvious. "I'm sorry. I don't know what you think I can do." She hadn't meant to sound so cold.

"You can help us figure out where he is. Jack is actively trying to find him."

Erin swiped her arm over her forehead, anxiety building in her chest. "Terra, really. I don't know why you would think I can help. I don't know him anymore. I don't know where he would be. He's a big boy. He just needs to process through it."

Please don't ask me to get involved like this. I have enough on my plate.

But she couldn't ignore her own growing concern for Nathan or forget how her heart reacted to seeing him again. All the more reason to stay out of it.

"Jack and I were both thinking that since you're his ex *and* a psychologist, you could think about it from that angle. You know, work your forensic criminal psychology magic."

"He's not a criminal," Erin said.

"He doesn't have to be for your magic to work." Terra must have stopped driving—her cell signal was crystal clear, and no road noise came through.

Erin sighed.

"Will you please help? Can you think of where he might go?"

Erin crossed the street and headed up the sidewalk to Mom's quaint little house—the home Erin grew up in, at least for part of her childhood. "Nothing more than what I've already offered is coming to mind, but I'll let you know if that changes."

When Terra didn't respond, Erin said, "You still there? Or did I lose you?"

She glanced at her cell to confirm that the call had dropped. At the porch, Erin entered through the front door, and as she passed Nadine and Mom playing cards at the kitchen table, she gave a small wave. They barely lifted their heads to acknowledge she'd returned. She headed to her old bedroom, showered in the adjoining bathroom, and dressed.

Though she tried not to be overly concerned about Nathan's whereabouts, she couldn't let it go. Nathan could be in trouble or need someone to talk to. If anyone should have caught subtle signs Mom was in trouble, Erin should have been the one, but everyone had missed those signs. Erin couldn't ignore that Nathan could be in trouble too and could need help.

Getting out of the house and driving around might be one way she could find him, or at least that would give her some ideas. Her hands were filled up and overflowing at the moment, and she couldn't offer much more help than to simply find him.

Lord, please just let Nathan be okay.

Purse over her shoulder, she stopped in the kitchen. Nadine was putting away the cards alone. "Where's Mom?"

"She's changing into her gardening clothes."

"I need to run an errand, and I'm not sure how long I'll be."

"You go right ahead." Nadine smiled. "I'll be here. Celia and I were just going out back to plant some pansies I brought."

"Pansies?"

"I thought they might liven the place up a bit."

"And I agree," Mom said as she entered the kitchen. "Once we're done, we're going to sit in the lawn chairs and soak up some sun before the rain comes back."

Her mother smiled and seemed full of life and love. Except for . . . Wait. Something flashed in her gaze, then it was shuttered away behind Mom's smile. What was it? Anguish? Fear? *Oh, Mom.*

Erin pressed her hands on Mom's shoulders, then leaned in to give her a peck on her cheek. "Love you, Momma."

She left her mother with Nadine and walked outside. Delmar was in his front yard watering his grass and waved at Erin. Was he watching for a chance to get her mother alone? *Wow, Erin, give it a rest.* The guy wasn't committing a crime, for heaven's sake.

In her vehicle, she leaned forward and pressed her forehead against the steering wheel. She had the distinct impression she was getting sucked into a quagmire, and she didn't have a clue how to navigate it.

Where would you go, Nathan?

She'd hurt him before, when she pushed him away and left him behind. What had she been thinking to ever fall for the guy when it could only end in hurt? The secrets she'd held for years prevented her from letting him get too close. From taking that next big step in their relationship. She'd done the right thing, breaking it off. He would never understand because no one else, not even Nathan, could ever know what happened before.

Unbidden, the past rushed at her.

She'd made a mistake and trembled in fear. Mom shook her. "Look what you've done!"

A knock on her windshield startled her, pulling her back to the moment. She calmed her ragged breaths and stared up into Delmar's smiling face.

Erin started the vehicle and lowered the window.

"Hi, Delmar. What can I do for you?"

"I just wanted to make sure you're all right."

Oh. She'd been pressing her head against the steering wheel. "Yes, I'm fine. Thanks. I was just thinking through something." She'd said too much.

"Anything I can help with?"

"Nothing you need to be concerned about."

He glanced at the house, longing in his eyes.

"Mom has company today. She's doing fine, by the way."

He turned his attention back to her, and her skin crawled. She rubbed the goose bumps.

"I'm glad to hear it. You need anything at all, you let me know." Delmar turned and walked back to his yard. The high school science teacher and his wife had lived next door when Erin and Mom moved in. Then Mom married Dwayne, Erin's stepdad. Delmar's wife died and then, eventually, Dwayne died too. Both widowed, maybe there *was* something going on between Mom and Delmar.

Delmar waved toward the backyard. Mom appeared between the houses and gestured for him to join her and Nadine in the back. Oh, great. Then again, Erin's aversion to the man was probably just a personal thing. Mom would be safe with her friends planting pansies and enjoying the sunshine.

Erin should concentrate on finding Nathan. *Where would you go, Nathan?* He'd always been driven to prove himself—to what or whom, she could guess. His father. Nathan couldn't see it himself, back then at least, but it was plain as day to Erin that he longed for the man's approval and had become a detective to be like his father. Erin didn't understand that—the man had abandoned his family, after all. The human mind, human nature still confounded most of psychology, and that made sense considering that psychology studies didn't take the sin nature into account. But her thoughts were getting off track.

She pushed them back on task—Nathan wanting to be like his father. Thinking along those lines, Erin believed he was probably at the river—just like she'd suggested to Terra—the place where his father was shot, especially if Nathan felt left out of an investigation this important to him. If he wasn't supposed to be there, he could have waited until after the other detectives left the scene.

There was only one way to find out.

Erin headed out of town and toward the Grayback River to the place where Nathan had taken her once before. She'd never been able to shake her fear of the woods, but back then she was in love with Nathan and would have done anything for him.

The fishing spot had meant something to Nathan, and now that memory had been destroyed with the worst kind of violence. Painful though it was, she imagined Nathan's shock at seeing his father shot in the head. A shudder crawled over her.

Twenty minutes later, she spotted the trailhead that led down to the Grayback River where Casper Creek ran into it, near that old dam. She recognized Nathan's old Jeep Cherokee and parked beside it. He hadn't come in his unmarked county vehicle. Had the evidence team and the investigators already finished with the crime scene, or was Nathan lurking in the woods, waiting for the moment when he could enter the area without concern? Erin tried calling Terra to let her know she'd found Nathan's vehicle at the trailhead to the crime scene. But her call wouldn't go through.

Still, finding his vehicle didn't mean she'd actually found him.

She got out of her car and moved around, holding her cell up just right. There. Two bars. She called Terra and got her voice mail, so she left a message. Then she called Jack and also got his voice mail and left him a message. Then she texted both her friends in the same text.

> Found Nathan's car at the Casper Creek Dam trailhead.

Erin leaned against her car and waited for a response. She listened to the forest sounds. Insects buzzing. A squirrel crawling up a nearby pine tree. Birdsong filled the air and eased some of the tension. She breathed in the scent of evergreens and fresh mountain air. She could make out the sound of the river echoing in the canyon down a ways.

The minutes ticked away and the sun rose higher in the sky as a dark thunderhead built up—another round of storms. She tried calling her friends again, then climbed back into her vehicle. She'd done what she could. But she didn't shift into reverse or drive away yet. What if Nathan truly was in trouble, mentally and emotionally? Look what happened to Mom when Erin hadn't been quick enough to respond to her cries for help. She got out of the car and locked it. Erin wished she had thought to bring a backpack and water—like Terra always told her—but hiking wasn't her thing, and so she hadn't planned for this.

She wouldn't turn back now. Thunder rumbled in the distance. Erin just hoped she found Nathan before the storm hit. And *if* she did find him, what exactly would she say? She'd better figure that out—and soon. Or maybe she only needed to listen, and he needed to talk.

Would he open up to her, someone who had hurt him before?

Ignoring the mounting tightness in her chest, she continued hiking the trail. The woods weren't going to kill her. The forest wasn't dangerous. She repeated the mantra in her head as she maneuvered the path and then veered from the trail at the familiar boulders. She remembered this shortcut from her past off-trail experience, compliments of Nathan. Next, the path led her downward until she reached an area previously submerged before the dam controlled the flow of water. She hung back at the edge of the forest where the trees thinned out. Up ahead, she spotted the riverbank.

And there on a boulder next to the river crouched Nathan. Here, in this natural setting, he looked more ruggedly handsome. Handsome and . . . forlorn. Her heart rate kicked up at the sight of him. Erin pushed back the sudden surge of emotion and focused on the reason she'd come.

She didn't see crime scene tape, and maybe none had been placed in such a remote area. She wished Terra or Jack would call or at least respond that they had received her messages. It would be even better if Jack would show up. She didn't feel comfortable leaving Nathan, though he might not appreciate her intrusion at this, one of his most brutal moments.

Lord, what do I do?

Nathan rose and then angled around to look right at her as if he'd sensed she was there.

He did not look happy to see her.

SIX

The river roared behind Nathan, spilling from the dam up-river and boiling in the canyon downriver. But here next to him? The river flowed peacefully, without turmoil, and in complete contrast to the emotions stirring inside him.

Erin lurked in the trees—and looked as skittish as ever. Like if he took one step toward her, she would bolt. Yep. That was the Erin he'd known before. Her psychology degree, distinguished title, and fancy job hadn't chased away her inner demons. But she was more beautiful now than when Nathan had fallen for her. Unfortunately, he thought he might still be susceptible to her special brand of charm. There'd always been something about her that drew him. He'd been helpless before, vulnerable, and yeah, more than a little stupid to have believed for even a minute that she would marry him.

He trusted that he wasn't that guy anymore.

Her blonde hair was pulled back in a ponytail, and she wore jeans that left no doubt she was thinner than she used to be. Along with the jeans, she had on hiking boots and a pink T-shirt. He was impressed that she'd made that hike through the woods alone, though she still hung back as if unsure of herself.

He should be flattered, or at least more appreciative of the effort she'd made. How long had she been watching?

ELIZABETH GODDARD

"Are you just going to stand there all day?" He waved her over.

The way she hesitated, he wondered if he'd figured it all wrong. She almost seemed surprised to find him here, but then again, he couldn't imagine her coming on her own. Unless . . . Wait. She was Dr. Erin Larson. A criminal psychologist. Someone in his department could have asked her to view the scene and give her take on things. Except she was alone out in the woods, and that would be something new for Erin. He processed all these thoughts as she hiked gingerly toward him.

The ground shivered with a slight tremor—a mild earthquake, just one of many that had occurred over the last few weeks. Erin's eyes widened, her surprise evident as she stumbled. As she lost her footing, her body shifted toward the boulder next to Nathan.

He rushed to catch her in his arms. "I got you."

His reflexes cost him, though. He found himself much too close, staring into her wondrous blue-green eyes that often changed colors. Her soft breaths caressed his face.

And suddenly his heart pounded at her nearness. Not good. He released her, and she quickly stepped back.

"Thanks." Her gaze held his for a few heartbeats before shifting to the river. "What's with these earthquakes?"

She stepped closer to the river, and Nathan inched closer too.

"You lived here. You know this region has a lot of them. But I hear you . . . the last few weeks it's been worse. Who knows? Nothing to worry about, I'm sure."

She stuffed her hands into her pockets, and her elbows hung out at her sides. "I heard they're digging a new copper mine up the river. Is that the reason? You know, with all the explosives they use, maybe that can create a few small quakes?"

He shrugged. "All I know is that you get a different answer with each person you ask. Except for me."

"Why not you?"

"Me? I haven't got any answers." He attempted a grin, but his heart wasn't in it.

Erin's gaze roamed over his face. His heart jumped. And here he thought he wasn't that guy anymore—the man who could crush hard over her.

Her lips flattened.

"I'm sorry about what happened." Erin looked into his eyes—searching, analyzing, offering help? He wasn't sure.

"Did Detective West ask for your help?" Nathan asked. "Send you out here to the scene? I'm surprised he didn't come with you. Or is he going to meet you here?"

Nathan stared at the place where Dad was standing when he was shot. That image rocked through him again. The report of a rifle echoed, ricocheting through him. He inwardly groaned, squeezed his eyes shut as he stepped forward—an almost stumble.

"Are you okay?" Her soft voice penetrated the flashback.

"I . . . I don't know." He stared at the water. Didn't want to look at her, fearing what he might see in her eyes. Pity? Accusation?

"To answer your question, no one asked me to help with the investigation. My experience lies more in forensic evaluations to learn if someone is able to stand trial, and I research, that sort of thing."

Then why are you here?

Good to know that the department hadn't hired her, because that freed her up to talk to him about what happened. He kicked a pebble into the river and watched it disappear in the dark-green flowing water.

"I sat with your mom a bit in the hospital until a few friends got there." But Erin already knew that. He wasn't sure what else to say.

"I don't know how to thank you," she said.

What was he going to say? It was all in a day's work? That wasn't really it. "You're welcome. I brought that up because while I was there, we chatted, you know, to kill the time."

Erin angled her face, her brows furrowing. "Did she seem all right? I mean . . . right after it happened."

"I'm no mental health counselor, but if anything, she seemed disturbed that she was in the hospital. She denied that she had tried to kill herself and said she couldn't remember what happened. But beyond that, when the conversation lightened up, she seemed happy enough. You can't blame yourself if you're thinking you missed the signs. All her friends missed the signs too."

"I'm the psychologist, remember?" Erin's shoulders bunched around her ears, then dropped as she also stared at the water.

A safe place to look. A person could let the sound of the rushing water, the sight of it carry their anxiety far away— except in his case, where right now it reminded him of his father's shooting.

He wanted to reach out to her. Find a way to reassure her. But he doubted he was the best person to do that. So he changed the subject. "She told me that you have a cold case podcast."

Erin's face tightened, and she lifted her gaze from the water to him—he could swear her blue-green eyes were the same colors of the Grayback River as it reflected both the sky as well as the tree-covered mountains around which it flowed. "No one's supposed to know. I mean, only a few people know."

He offered a grin, hoping to disarm her. "I gathered. I couldn't find anything about your podcast on the internet, but I started with your name."

"I use pseudonyms for all the players—writers, editors, narrators."

She still hadn't shared the name of the podcast. "Pseudonyms so you can keep it anonymous."

"It was a little complicated to set up, but doable."

"Why so secretive?"

"Why so many questions?"

"It's intriguing, that's all."

Her eyes narrowed as she looked at him, and he wasn't sure if it was because the sun had broken through the approaching storm clouds and hit her in the face, or for some other reason.

He had a feeling she was onto him. "What?"

"I think there's more to your questions."

Yep. "You're as sharp as ever." Didn't mean he was ready to tell her his reasons, though.

That earned him a laugh, a sound he hadn't heard in far too long. *I've missed you.* He shook off the unwelcome emotion.

He wanted to know more about her endeavor into exploring cold cases. Erin could be a resource for him. That is, if he continued along this precarious path. If Nathan told anyone what Dad had said, it should be Henry—so why was he leaning toward talking it through with Erin?

He'd been advised by both his father and Henry to go with his gut, and since the stakes were high—he'd seen that for himself firsthand—he would continue until he figured it out. He might need Erin's help.

What am I doing?

The ground trembled—just barely—but he felt it in his toes. In his bones. Or was that just him quaking, shivering through with anger that his father had been shot, and on top of it, he was left with the burden of a volatile secret? Since Nathan couldn't be involved in investigating his dad's shooting, withholding what he knew was treading into dangerous territory. Was there a way for him to skirt around the edges without technically interfering? Henry had given him some "leeway," as he put it.

"So why'd you come here today? Really?"

Erin turned her back to the river. "Terra called. She and Jack are worried about you. They couldn't get ahold of you," she continued, "and asked me if my psychology experience might tell me where you would be. Imagine that."

He angled his head and couldn't help the hint of a smile, even in the midst of this tragedy. "And did that help you?"

She gave a slow shake of her head, along with a small hitch in the corner of her mouth. "It wasn't necessary."

"You knew where I'd be."

"I told them you would be here, but I was informed you aren't to investigate this crime. Jack had been here earlier and said you weren't here, so they didn't believe you would return to the crime scene."

"And yet *you're* here."

"It's not rocket science or even psychology." She held his gaze, her blue-greens penetrating.

That she knew him so well scared him.

"After what's happened, if you weren't with your dad, then you'd be here, your favorite place to be with him."

"That's right." Erin remembered. She knew him too well. A big emotional knot lodged in his throat. He wouldn't be able to speak until he steadied his emotions.

He moved closer to the river, close enough to stick a foot in if he wanted, and Erin stayed near him. Strange how her presence here disturbed him in some ways and soothed him in others. His dad's shooting had scrambled Nathan's brain more than he thought.

"Look," she said. "I should probably go. You need time alone. I just . . . I came to make sure you're all right."

As in that he wasn't going to try anything like her mother had. He would ask how Celia was doing, but that seemed like an inappropriate response to her comment.

"And also find me for Jack and Terra."

She chuckled. "True. I'm not going to lie."

Erin stepped from the riverbank and started for the trail-head.

"Wait," he said.

She turned around, her eyes taking him in as if gauging his condition. But something more, something deeply personal, flashed behind her gaze. "What is it?" She took one step toward him. "I'm here to listen if you need to talk."

"I thought you weren't that kind of psychologist."

"I'm not." A soft smile emerged. "But I'm here to listen anyway."

She didn't add "as a friend." And for some reason, he was kind of glad.

"Then stay, because I do need to talk, after all."

"Okay, then."

Nathan eased onto a big, flat boulder, and Erin sat on the other side. He eyed the thunderhead that looked to pass them to the west. Good. He needed this moment. The evidence techs didn't take long to look over everything because a rain shower had come in the night, and they'd had to work quickly, including up in the area from where the shot must have been fired. Fine with him. It would give him more time to look around here and think. Decide if he was going to go against his own rule book, which gave no instructions for situations such as the one his dad had placed him in.

God, help me. He couldn't figure this out on his own. He needed an outside perspective, and yet the simple act of telling someone else would be blowing it. But his gut told him that Dad was onto something that was not going to get solved. Or was he simply justifying his own wants and needs? His own actions, should he actually go forward.

Nathan squeezed his eyes shut, opened them again, and took a deep breath. "I need to tell you something. I've been asked not to speak to anyone at all. But I don't know what I'm doing. Erin, I need help."

The way she looked at him—

"Not therapy. Not that kind of help." Well, yes, maybe. "My father put me in a difficult situation. He asked me not to tell anyone. That lives are at stake."

"And you want *me* to advise you on this?" Erin watched him.

"He said I was the only one he trusted. The problem is that it's connected to his shooting. If I keep it to myself, then I'm edging close to withholding evidence and possibly obstructing justice, but I don't know that yet. I do know that Dad made it sound like he was afraid to even trust his own people."

Erin blew out a long breath. "I understand about keeping some pieces of truth under wraps. There can be a purpose behind it."

That surprised him. "You do?"

She nodded. "Did you mention any of this to Sheriff Gibson?"

"Only that Dad had told me things he didn't want me sharing. In a way, I offered up to Henry that I knew something and asked what I should do. Henry told me to listen to my gut."

"Well, then there you go. He isn't forcing you to tell him. He trusts you that much."

"The thing is, Dad was with him, he could have told him. But he didn't."

"Nathan, why are you talking to *me* about this, really?"

Because it started with her stepfather, and more than that, Nathan didn't know. "You have some insights into cold cases. And this is a cold case. Will you hear me out? Just keep it between us?" *Can I trust you?*

"Why not talk to Jack about it? He's your friend."

"I'm talking to you because you're not associated with the county sheriff's office. Okay?"

Erin shrugged. "Go on."

"I came here fishing with Dad just like old times. He told me about a cold case he was working. It was why he'd come to Big Rapids." Nathan cleared his throat, then continued. "It would seem that your stepfather, Dwayne, found some old newspaper articles he'd wanted Dad to check into. Well, Dad and Mom divorced, then Dad moved to Boston and took his detective job and forgot all about the articles. That is, until the last few weeks. He has been working a case that reminded him of those articles, so he looked into them. He thinks there's a connection between the articles—the cold case—and the case he's working now. He also said his boss shut him down. Didn't want him pulling on that thread. So Dad took time off and came here."

"Wait. Are you saying he came here for a vacation or to pull on the thread? And if the thread, then why come here?"

"Before I tell you the rest, I need to know if you'll help me."

"And I'll need to know more before I can agree. Like what brought him to Big Rapids?"

"Looks like we're at a standoff. I honestly can't tell you more. Dad was about to tell me when he was shot."

Erin tossed a pebble into the river, and Nathan waited for her to process all he'd told her.

"What exactly are you asking me?" she finally asked.

Nathan stared at her. "What do you think I should do?"

"Hmm. Well, I know you trust the people you work with. You have each other's back. Your father knows that too, so his words and actions lead me to think you need to know more before you can make a decision. If you can find a solid reason to go along with your dad's request, that would make a difference."

"A solid reason beyond the simple fact Dad asked me to tell no one and that he only trusted me."

The ground shuddered again, coupled with a deep, thunderous rumble this time. A sharp crack he felt to his bones reverberated through the trees and echoed in the canyon.

His lifted his head and looked upriver. Disbelief twisted with dread in his gut. "The dam! It's breaking."

SEVEN

The river exploded, bursting from the sides, breaking through the already weakened structure. A terrifying force tumbled, rolled, sped toward them. Erin stared at the astonishing sight. Heart racing, she gaped at certain death, the shocking scene gripping her. Fear cemented her feet on the ground.

I have to move. We have to run.

A wall of water sped downriver, gathering speed and debris. Though her mind told her what must be done, her body wouldn't cooperate. She tried to lift one leg, then another. Her limbs refused to respond. Her life was in mortal danger if she didn't move. A scream fought to escape, but terror had squeezed her throat. She couldn't even breathe.

Nathan gripped her shoulders and shook her. "We have to get out of here. Come on!"

He tugged her hand, pulling her out of her stupor. She stumbled forward. Her limbs finally responding, she joined him. He gripped her hand and towed her along with him as hard and fast as the terrain would allow. But it was no use. Nathan had to release her hand to navigate the pebbles and boulders as they made their way toward the trees. Beyond that, the land rose sharply.

Erin veered away. "Wait! The trailhead is this way."

Nathan paused and stretched out his hand, reaching for her again. "Forget the trailhead. We have to get to higher ground!"

Erin wouldn't argue. He waited for her to close the distance and took her hand as though he feared they would get separated and he would lose her. The roar closed in around them, growing louder.

Another crack resounded. More of the dam collapsing? Her pulse thundered in her ears, almost louder than the deadly force racing toward them. She risked a glance over her shoulder.

That was a mistake. A big mistake.

"Erin!" Nathan pulled her along, and she ran with him toward higher ground. He urged her forward with such powerful strength that she had no choice but to move with him if she wanted to keep her arm.

Her breaths quickened as she hopped over boulders and rocks, propelling her body faster . . . *faster* . . . as a cacophony of violent sounds echoed around her.

We're not going to make it. Oh, God, I don't want to die . . .

She yanked her hand from his grip. "I can't move as fast as you. Just go on. I'll catch up!"

Time seemed to slow. Nathan glanced over his shoulder at her, then shifted his gaze to what lay beyond her. His eyes widened. His horror-stricken face told her that he knew the truth. What she'd finally admitted to herself.

"We're not going to make it!" A cry ripped from her tense throat.

Nathan reached for her, catching one hand in his, tightening his grip as the flash flood tumbled over them. The force ripped her from Nathan's grasp and pulled them apart, then tossed her around.

"Erin!" Nathan shouted her name even as his face disappeared when the monster caught him and dragged him under.

Cold, jagged fingers of water pressed her down, down, down in a rush of shocking violence. Spun her around. Over and over. With her lungs screaming and her eyes shut, the force rolled her, tossed her, pulled her deeper, and pushed her forward as though she were nothing more than debris. In this moment in time, Erin had absolutely no control over her life—if she'd ever had any.

Her heart cried out repeatedly. *Please don't let me die . . .*

Sheer terror gripped her. Her heart pounded, consuming the limited oxygen in her lungs.

God, help me. Help Nathan.

This was it, then. She should prepare for death, but how did one do that? Images of her coming demise accosted her. At any moment would she just lose consciousness? Or hit her head on a boulder or be impaled or drown?

Though it seemed impossible, she couldn't let go of hope that she would survive. She and Nathan would both survive. Pain ignited in her back as her body was dashed against the rocks. Pressure built in her lungs until Erin was sure her head might explode. What could she expect next? She fought the whimpers that tried to escape.

These were truly her last moments on this earth.

Suddenly her face rose above the tide. She exhaled. Opening her eyes, she gulped in more air. It could make the difference between life and death. Water rushed over her and into her mouth. She swallowed too much, spewing and coughing as she forced her head above the rush of the flood. Up ahead the canyon narrowed, rising tall and lofty with rock walls on both sides that turned the water into rapids.

Trees on each side of the riverbanks reached for her as the water spread out for a few hundred yards before entering the canyon. Water continued to spew from the broken dam and pushed her forward much too fast. But she had made it this far. Maybe there was hope. Still, Erin was at a loss for how to save herself.

God, you've helped me through so far. Please show me a way out of this. Help me!

And what about Nathan? Her heart screamed, burst with pain at the thought of him trying to save her and being ripped away. Was he struggling like she was? Or was he already gone?

"Help!" she cried out in case someone would hear. Maybe Nathan had survived and was out there somewhere.

Her muscles burned, and her strength was quickly fading. She knew to float feet first and go with the flow, but this was no normal river that had swept her away.

Ahead she spotted a small calm pool between the rocks. It was coming up quickly to her right. With the last of her strength, she swam toward it. This was her chance to make it. *Please, God, help me.*

The initial rush of water had flowed over the small pool, but now the water level had dropped as it spread out and rushed forward. She swam toward the calmer water and used the current to her advantage, allowing it to carry her forward. With one last push, she found herself heading straight for a thick branch wedged against a boulder. If she could just grab on to that, she could pull herself over to the safety of the pool and then out of the water.

She let the current carry her. Just a few more feet. Wait for it . . . Wait for it . . .

She grabbed hold of the branch. The violent river tried to push her, rip her away from the branch. She dug her fingers, her nails even, into the wet bark. This was her lifeline.

Thank you, Lord, for sending me help.

She put one arm over another as she clawed her way toward safety.

Almost there. Almost there.

Groaning with the effort, she put all her strength into it and pushed forward against the current. Holding tightly to the tree, digging her fingers into the bark as she went, she pulled herself toward the calmer pool sheltered from the violence. She had no idea if the dam would collapse more, so there was no time to lose to get to higher ground.

The powerful tug of the current eased off. She'd made it to calmer waters. She couldn't relax yet, but she exhaled slowly, letting renewed hope infuse her. She'd come this far.

Her feet touched the ground covered in smooth pebbles. Moving forward, she gained traction and pushed herself through to the calmer water and beyond that, toward the bank.

Suddenly her foot was caught. Stuck. She pulled and tugged, but she'd somehow stepped between two small rocks in an awkward position. Erin sucked in a breath and held it as she thrust her head beneath the water's surface, then reached down to free her foot. She tried to move the rocks pinning her in place. Pulled on her leg. It was no use. Lungs screaming again, she rose above the water and sucked in another breath.

Erin looked around and took in the rushing river that still poured from the dam as the reservoir released its contents. At some point, it had to even out, didn't it? She searched for Nathan. He was somewhere out there too. Or across on the other side. *Nathan, where are you?*

Her heart tried to stay afloat on top of the ever-rising dread and the possibility that he was already gone.

Another crack resounded, reaching to her bones and echoing between the trees, mountains, and canyon farther down. *Oh no.* Her gaze jerked upriver. The dam was too far for her to make out much, but she suspected the sound meant it was giving way even more.

Erin prepared for the worst. More water could rush over her and flood the pool, her momentary safe place. Even if it did, it might not last, and she could hold her breath for that long.

"Erin!" Nathan's welcome voice found the terrified places in her heart. She looked around for him. "Erin, over here!"

There, a few feet away, he swam diagonally toward her across the floodwaters. He lifted a hand. "Here!"

"I see you! Be careful!" She pointed at an even greater volume of water. "Hurry. It's coming directly for you."

And I'm stuck.

Tears surged. Erin could do nothing but watch the wall of water race for her again. Engulf her. Take her under. If she somehow survived, this would become the new recurring nightmare to replace the old one, though both were filled with terror and darkness.

Still, her mother's voice from long ago broke through her thoughts, a constant reminder of that night and her mistake. But this was no time to think on the past. The secret could die with her today.

She held her breath. The force slammed into her and freed her from her prison but . . . swept her away again. She couldn't breach the surface, no matter how hard she tried.

Her lungs spasmed as she breathed in the river.

EIGHT

Holding on to Erin's limp form, Nathan rode the river until he could gain his freedom and break away from the current. His limbs ached with the effort of fighting the torrent, but he was almost there, and this could be his last chance to save them.

No, it definitely *would* be his last chance. Fighting the river had sucked away his energy, and he couldn't last much longer, even though he prayed hard and willed himself to keep going.

He aimed for that good stretch of safe, dry land that jutted out right before the canyon narrowed. He had to make that or they would both die. Erin had drowned, but he held on to hope that he could revive her. He couldn't consider any other outcome. With the last burst of strength in his limbs, he swam them toward the bank until his feet finally touched the bottom. He groaned with the effort to keep himself anchored to the rocks. Legs cramping, Nathan carried Erin out of the flood field and onto higher ground to a patch of wild rye. He kept going in case another wave rushed at them. But he believed the dam had released all the trapped water, and the flow now would be even and steady.

What destruction the breaking dam had caused downstream he couldn't know.

And right now, he didn't care.

He cared about only one thing. One person.

God, please, help me.

After finding the first decent spot to gently place Erin on the ground, he immediately administered CPR.

"Come on, baby. Come on . . ."

God, please don't let her die on me. Don't let this happen. You brought us this far. We're here now, and I could sure use your help.

"Erin, come on. You can do this. Wake up. Fight, honey, fight for it. We need you." *I . . . need you.*

His cell phone hadn't survived the torrent, so there was no calling 911 to rescue them or revive Erin if Nathan failed. He continued performing the cycles of chest compressions, and then breathing for Erin, and he wouldn't stop.

He couldn't stop.

Quitting would be giving up on her. He sure hoped she hadn't given up on herself.

Then . . . movement. A breath on her own. Her chest rose.

Nathan's own breath hitched.

A cough.

More coughing and choking. Erin rolled to her side and released all the water that had been trapped in her lungs, then she dragged in a ragged breath.

His heart jumped to his throat, apprehension and relief both swelling in his chest.

Nathan watched and waited. He sucked in oxygen too—now that she was breathing, he could breathe. Even now, his heart jackhammered as hope flooded his soul.

He held out his hand, wanting to touch her, to reassure her, but he kept his distance. "You're safe, Erin. You're safe now."

She sat up and leaned back on her arms. Mud, branches,

and debris clung to her hair. A few scratches ran across her cheeks, mingling with the grime and dirty river water.

Tears streaked through the muck on her face.

The pain of his own tears ached behind his eyes. "I thought . . . I thought I'd lost you."

He realized the words held a deeper meaning for him than he'd intended. Had she caught that meaning? Certainly he'd already lost her long ago. They were over. Or so he had thought, but looking at her now, he admitted a small part of him hoped what they'd had before wasn't completely gone.

The desperation of the moment must have taken hold, and Nathan shook off the errant thoughts.

"What happened?" she finally asked, her throat sounding scratchy.

How far back did she need him to go? "The dam broke."

He'd heard a loud rumble just as the earth quaked, and then a crack. "Maybe all the earthquakes, over time, had weakened it. Dad had commented"—the thought of his dad sent a pang through his chest—"that he couldn't believe it hadn't been replaced. It's been around for decades."

Bridges and other infrastructures had failed in recent years because they hadn't been fortified or replaced. They simply couldn't last forever. Erin and Nathan had been in the wrong place at the wrong time.

Together they watched the river swollen with floodwater begin to slowly even out and die down, settling into its previous course. But it had left a path of destruction in its wake.

Across the landscape *and* his heart.

"What now?" Her voice still sounded raspy. He took her in again, concerned for her emotional state.

Shoot, he was concerned for his as well. He wasn't likely to get over that experience anytime soon, especially since it came on the heels of his father being shot. The Grayback River would never be the same for him again.

He dug his cell out of his pocket and shook the water out of it. "Well, we're not calling for help unless your phone is waterproof."

"You know, I think it's advertised as water resistant, whatever that means." She pulled hers out. "But the screen is cracked." Erin pressed the power button, but the cell didn't come to life.

"You must have hit something." Nathan studied her. "Are you hurt anywhere?"

She moved her arms and shoulders around, then twisted her ankles and winced. Erin brought her right foot toward her to examine it more closely. "I feel like I got battered, but nothing's broken."

"What about your ankle? Is it bothering you?"

"I was almost safe, then my foot got caught between some rocks. My ankle is a little sore and bruised, that's all. What about you?"

He had a plethora of aches and pains to go with the scratches, for sure. "I'm good."

Good enough to get moving, because they definitely couldn't languish next to the raging river that had almost taken their lives.

Now that they had taken a few moments to catch their breath, Nathan stood and offered his hand. "We need to get out of here."

Erin slowly got to her feet. "Thank you, by the way, for what you did back there." She averted her gaze, a V forming between her brows, then looked back at him. "You saved me, Nathan. I could have died. And you could have died trying to save me. You risked your life."

Her mouth turned down as she shook her head, and her eyes welled with tears.

"Come here." Nathan pulled her to him. She shivered and his body shook as well—adrenaline rushing out of him. That, along with the fear that had gripped him.

He closed his eyes. *Thank you, Lord. Thank you for saving us.*

Stepping out of his arms, Erin used the edges of her T-shirt to wipe off the mud on her face. "Better?"

He shook his head. "It's going to take a lot more than that. I wouldn't worry about it. After all, it's just me here."

"Right. And now you can truly say you've seen me at my worst."

He brushed a clump of mud from her cheek. "I can say the same of you. You've seen me at my worst. It'll be our secret." He winked. "And now we should get going."

Erin pointed. "We're on the far side of the river. How do we get out of here? Isn't this a wilderness area?"

She brought up a good point.

"You said that Jack and Terra were looking for me. Did you get a chance to tell them you found me?"

"I tried, but I had bad reception. I texted them and left voice mails too. I hope those messages made it through, and then maybe they will learn what's happened and know to look for us."

Nathan eyed the river and turned to the wilderness terrain behind them. "Our options are limited. I know I said we should get out of here and get help, but we could actually wait here for a rescue. The problem with that is we don't know how long it will be before the dam break is reported." He didn't want to tell Erin what she was probably already thinking, fearing, but he doubted they would make it back to civilization before dark.

NINE

E rin followed Nathan's gaze. Rocky cliffs edged the small meadow alcove as the river narrowed into a canyon up ahead.

"I don't want to wait around here for a rescue," she said. "It's not like we're lost or have to survive in the wilderness. I mean, more than a night." And it would be one long night.

"Surviving in a wilderness area in the dark with no protection and no shelter, food, or water isn't on my bucket list, though I know some people pay for the experience."

"Not something I would pay to experience unless I had a tent, shelter, and everything I needed."

"So, what's your plan?"

"We'll have to climb out. It's not so bad over there." He gestured at the rising rock wall as opposed to the sheerer cliffs.

Easy for you to say.

Her shoulder ached. Her legs hadn't stopped shaking. Even her ankle and foot were now starting to cramp in rhythm with her pulse. Every part of her throbbed. But she wouldn't complain. She had survived.

"What are the odds they will look for us here?"

"If your message got through, they could already be headed

to what's left of the fishing hole. Eventually they'll figure out something is wrong." He sighed. "Bottom line, I'm not sure how long it will be before someone comes to look for us. We should head back toward the dam. Once authorities hear about the break, someone will come to the dam. Of that we can be sure."

"Okay, so we're in agreement." Erin eyed the cliff they needed to climb and pushed back the fear lodging in her gut. What was there to be afraid of? She'd just been revived and got a second chance to live her life. A life apart from this man she had loved and walked away from. Or would she get a second chance with him too? She shook her head at the errant thoughts and glanced at him. He deserved better.

"Lead on."

He studied her long and hard. The setting sun broke over the mountain to the west and hit him right in the face, so he squinted. She had the distinct feeling he was deciding if she was even capable of the climb. Erin pressed past him, ignoring the pain in her body and hiding her slight limp. She'd kind of been hoping she wouldn't have one, but there it was.

Erin was a survivor. She could survive the night in the wilderness with cuts and bruises and a throbbing ankle. What else could go wrong?

"You're more hurt than you let on." He caught up to her. "You said your foot had been caught. That's it. I'm carrying you."

He reached for her and she stepped back, tripping over a branch. He caught her much like he'd done when she first arrived. "Thanks, but I don't want you to carry me. How about I ride piggyback as far as the cliff, then I'll climb on my own."

He nodded. What else could he do? And unfortunately, what else could *she* do? She closed her eyes for a moment. It could have been worse, so much worse. Like nearly getting killed by an errant, crazy boater and then hearing that her mother tried to commit suicide—all in the same hour. Oh yeah . . . She could check that off the list of bad days she had experienced.

At the bottom edge of the cliff, she climbed off Nathan's back and favored her injured leg.

"We'll take it slow and easy," he said. "You go first and make your way up. I'm right behind you to support you in case you slip."

Erin eyed the terrain of rocks and dirt. Up close, the cliff looked higher than she had thought, though honestly, it looked doable. She saw places she could gain solid footing and rocks to hold on to, even a few tree roots. She would be thankful for the small things.

A thought crashed into her. "Oh no . . . Mom. Nathan! Mom . . . I left Nadine with her. I've been gone much too long. I can't leave Mom alone."

"Erin." Nathan gently gripped her arms. "Nadine won't leave her. And in fact, maybe she'll even call the police to look for you. It's the silver lining, Erin. You have to look for the silver lining."

"You're right. I need to see the positive in the negative situation." Erin shook off the cascading negative emotions. "I promise, I'll focus on getting to the top."

Nathan took her hand and pressed it against a rock, showing her where to start. She lifted her foot and pulled herself up with a grunt.

"Remember, I'm right behind you," he said. "It's not El Capitan. You'll be fine."

Right. She had thirty or more feet to go. She wouldn't give in to the fear and instead focused on each next step until finally, the cliff sloped inward, changing into more of a steep hill. Her wet clothes and hair had almost dried when she started, but now she was drenched all over again, only this time in sweat rather than river water.

When she finally climbed over the edge where the earth

flattened out, she fell into the reeds on her back, though the soil was still damp from recent rainstorms. Relieved to have come so far, she closed her eyes and savored the feel of victory over the flash flood and now this cliff. And without too much effort, she could actually fall asleep there in the tall grass. Sleep forever.

"I knew you could do it." Nathan's words came out breathy. He crawled next to her, crushing the reeds beneath him, but she didn't open her eyes. She felt the warmth of his body, breathed in the scent of sweat and earth and something entirely wild and masculine.

Whoa, hold it right there. She could not go down this road with Nathan again. She couldn't go through breaking his heart again. Or breaking her own.

"Nothing seems to get you down," she said. He'd pulled her out of the river, revived her, and coaxed her up a cliff, all on a positive note.

"I'd love to be that guy, but I have my bad days just like the next person."

"Thanks for the warning," she said. As if she'd never caught Nathan in a moment where he was dark and disturbed.

She opened her eyes to look at him. He rolled to his side and propped himself up on his elbow. His dark eyes looked down at her, and his equally dark—almost black—shaggy hair was a tangled mess. She reached up and ran her fingers through it to . . . um . . . pull the debris out. But she was lying to herself. That wasn't the reason at all.

Something feral flashed in his gaze, then he climbed to his feet and offered his hand. "Come on, Erin. It'll be dark soon. There could be something we can use at the dam. Maybe even shelter. Someone might be there tonight, but definitely the authorities will be there by tomorrow to check the infrastructure and see what happened." He smiled. "And we'll be there when they do."

"You're doing it again. You're sounding positive and encouraging. But I get the feeling it's for my benefit."

"What's the harm in that?" He shifted, turning his back to her, then crouched for her to get on.

Erin climbed onto his back and held tight. Dusk had fallen. From here, she could make out some of the damage the river had done as it surged over the riverbank, grabbing dead trees and pulling new ones from the ground along its deadly path. Now, though, the water sounded peaceful, less angry.

Her thoughts returned to those moments before the dam had broken. Nathan had asked her to help him. It seemed nonsensical to help him look into something so dangerous and that could potentially cause him trouble with Sheriff Gibson. But if she didn't help him, then who would? If Erin were in the same position, she would have no qualms about finding the truth about a loved one. Still, it was a bad idea all around. Nathan shouldn't investigate his father's shooting.

Erin shouldn't help him do it.

"Silver lining," he'd said.

Digging into cold cases had been her thing—albeit a way to make recompense for the past.

Nathan stumbled, and she gripped him tighter.

Being carried piggyback style was efficient but awkward. She felt the toned muscles in his back ripple with his movements. Nathan was strong and dependable and . . . the best person she knew. She'd been a fool to push him away. But that was Erin—a fool when it came to love.

She had only been protecting him, but he could never know that.

TEN

*L*ord, guide me. Help me get us to safety.

He was pretty sure it was nothing less than a miracle that had allowed him to grab Erin and carry her to safety, then revive her. Considering that, he had to believe they would be okay on the other side of this harrowing night.

Lightning flashed in the distance, rippling through a massive thunderhead. Thunder clapped a few seconds after the flashes. Still, the storm remained far from them.

He hoped he would find some sort of outbuilding at the dam or someone who'd come to check on it. Or see the searchlights of a SAR team. He had no flashlight to guide the way and was relying solely on his excellent night vision and the fact that the sky wasn't completely overcast.

Erin shifted on his back.

"You okay? You need to get down?"

"No, I'm fine. I wouldn't want to mess with the pace you're keeping. But I do have a few questions. Can we talk? Or do you need to focus?"

"We can talk."

"Before the dam failed, you were sharing what your father

DEADLY TARGET

had told you. You said he was about to tell you more when he
was shot."

This was as good a time as any to have this conversation.
"Yeah."

"It sounds like you have a lot of questions with no answers.
Are you sure that you should look into your father's shooting?
Into that cold case he mentioned?"

"Given what little I know and since I've been charged with
keeping it to myself, I don't see how I can't look into at least
the cold case." The pressure built on his shoulders again and
had nothing at all to do with carrying Erin. "I'll circle around
the edges of things and offer help. See what's what. I'm hoping
Dad will wake up and talk and clear things up."

"As I mentioned before, you need to know more before
you can know what to do." Erin blew out a soft breath, and it
warmed his ear. "I don't want you doing anything without me."

Nathan cringed inside, wishing he hadn't asked her. What
had he been thinking?

The image of her body floating on the river like a dead log
knifed through him again, and he almost stumbled.

He really wanted to kick himself. Again. "I know I asked
you before, but now . . . after what's happened today, I don't
think I could take it if something happened to you because
you were helping me."

"Stop," she said.

"I just can't, Erin. I can't risk it." Nathan kept moving.

"No, I mean stop hiking."

Oh. He stopped walking. Erin released her hold on him
and hopped down. He knew what was coming next and turned
to face her. How much could she actually see of him in the
dark, with only the stars and the sporadic lightning flashes to
light his face?

Her eyes were fire. At least he could see that much.

"You think it was easy for me to come to this decision?" She fisted her hands on her hips. "To decide to help you? You think I *want* to work with you? I mean, it's hard enough just being here with you, Nathan."

Oh, shoot. He wasn't entirely sure how to take her words. He thought they'd been getting along fine, under the circumstances.

He caught the faint shimmer of moisture in her eyes and pursed his lips. What did he say in response?

"I didn't want to hike through those woods to find you at the river, but I did. And I . . ."

"*Why* did you?" They were going to do this now? Be honest about everything?

"Because my mother tried to kill herself. Because I wasn't there for her. I kept putting her off, and I could have lost her. Jack and Terra thought you were in a bad place, and I couldn't . . . I had to check on you. To see you. And then you told me about your father." She pressed a hand over her eyes. One hand on her hip. "Why did you tell me any of something you weren't supposed to share with anyone? I can't unhear it."

She dropped her hand to pierce him with her shadowed gaze. He couldn't quite see the fire in her eyes now, but he could certainly feel it.

"Now you can't stop me," she said. "I'll look into it anyway. I'm all about cold cases, remember?"

Erin marched ahead of him, limping a little, but not much, determination in her stride.

Despite the odd circumstances, he felt a smile coming on. He caught up to her. "Okay. I hear you. You're in this with me now. Thank you. I just don't want you to get hurt. Someone tried to kill him. I don't know why I would invite you into that."

"Because you need help, Nathan. You can't do this alone. Now that it's decided, let's talk about what happened." She blew out a breath. "Someone tried to kill him because they knew he was looking into something and had possibly learned something. But no one has to know that *we're* looking into it."

He scratched his scruffy jaw. "Just help me with the cold case, and then maybe I can offer it up to Henry, from a different angle." Or he would tell Henry everything, despite what Dad had said. *God, what do I do?*

"The big question—what cold case was he looking into?" she asked.

Light drew his attention, and he almost stumbled. "See that?"

Erin looked forward. "Yeah, I see lights at the dam."

Nathan and Erin rushed toward the light, weaving around trees, fallen branches, and underbrush until they finally reached the dam. Nathan paused to catch his breath. Solar-powered floodlights were set up on the other side of the dam, but whoever had set them up was gone.

"We missed them!" Erin groaned.

"But they know about the dam. This is great news."

The familiar sound of a helicopter resounded, and Nathan spotted a searchlight. The copter swooped low along the river, shining the searchlight everywhere—the riverbanks, the water, the forest. It continued on a path that took it away from the dam and downriver.

Nathan waved his arms. "No, wait! We're here."

That's where they would focus the search. Understandable. Since the lights had been set up, he held on to hope that someone would be back to the dam soon.

Erin sagged, then dropped to the ground on her rear. "Well, that's just great. We were late to our own rescue party."

ELEVEN

Early morning light cut through her dreams. Oh, wait. She hadn't been dreaming that she'd slept in Nathan's arms. They'd needed to generate body heat. She and Nathan had snuggled in the corner of an old concrete tower originally built along with the dam decades ago. No one had returned to the dam.

Erin shifted, and instantly the aches and pains from yesterday's fight with the flash flood returned. The shock of hard, cold concrete against her back fully woke her, and she shivered. Opening her eyes, she saw Nathan standing a few feet away near a big opening at the tower along the edge overlooking the failed dam. His appearance was rough against the backdrop of the mountains. Stubble thickened along his jaw. And her heart bounced around erratically.

Nathan looked so good. Nathan *was* good—on the inside and out. She wished she hadn't walked away.

No choice. I had no choice.

She stretched and rolled her neck to get the crick out and chase the dangerous thoughts away. She hadn't been cold in his arms last night and had slept hard. Licking her lips, she rubbed her eyes, then started to climb to her feet. Nathan had closed the distance and reached down to assist her.

"I'm okay. I can get up on my own."

"I know you can. I didn't want to be a jerk and just stand there and not offer to help." He grinned down at her.

"Fair point." She took his hand, thinking that would make him feel useful.

His thick hair was especially mussed this morning, even compared to yesterday's tangle of sticks and debris and mud. She must look a mess too, and probably looked worse than she felt.

He held on to her hand a moment longer than necessary and stared down at her. Erin couldn't move if she wanted to. Just when she thought she might figure out what emotion surfaced in his eyes, he released her hand, then returned his attention to what was left of the dam and the river flowing freely from what had been a small reservoir. The day wasn't anywhere near being warm enough yet, and in fact, early morning was the coldest part of any day. She subtly leaned closer to soak up some of his body heat.

Catching on to her plight, Nathan wrapped an arm around her and pulled her close, where she settled in to fit nicely against him. If only she hadn't noticed.

"I didn't want to leave you sleeping in the cold," he said, "but I heard activity. Trucks or big equipment. A search helicopter. So I got up without waking you."

He didn't mention that she snored in her sleep. Phew.

"They'll find us today, don't worry," he said. "I almost wonder if they gave up the search last night because, well . . ."

Nathan hadn't finished that sentence. He didn't have to. "They'd switched to recovery. Believing we were already gone, they planned to search for our bodies farther downriver." It sickened her to think of what their friends and family were going through. "I wish we could have done more to alert them."

"I'm sure they searched as long as they could," he said. "The terrain is much too hazardous for searching on foot at night."

"I hope no one else was hurt," she said.

"I have a feeling no one ventured too close to the area because of news that a shooter was on the loose."

"Our disadvantage was that we were much too close to the dam when it gave. You probably could have made it to higher ground without me." Erin leaned her head against his shoulder, not caring at the moment that she was getting too comfortable.

"No. We were both goners. But we're here now." His voice was thick with emotion.

"I know. That silver lining."

"Not really a silver lining this time."

"Oh?"

"More the grace of God."

Okay. "I need coffee." She couldn't consider the differences without strong, black coffee. Spending the night with him under such intolerable circumstances had left her feeling far too familiar with him—all over again. She was in dangerous territory, yet desperate times called for desperate measures.

They were in survival mode.

Her heart was definitely shifting into a survival mode of its own. And hadn't it taken her much too long to get him out of her system before? Even the smell of him now—that outdoorsy, woodsy scent mingled with masculinity—sent her heart and head tumbling back, only she wasn't in the past, she was in the present. And caring much too deeply for him as if no time had passed.

"Look!" Breaking his hold, Nathan gestured toward the ravine.

Relief whooshed through her on multiple levels.

A helicopter flew straight up the river toward the dam—searching for bodies, no doubt. But they were very much alive.

Erin and Nathan stepped out of the concrete tower and onto a railed overhang that appeared structurally secure and unaffected by the collapse. They jumped up and down and waved their hands.

"We're here!" Erin shouted. She almost couldn't believe they were near the end of this catastrophe.

The copter approached, then hung in the air near the dam above the river. Terra waved at them from the opened door, her smile beaming! Erin could sense the sheer joy and relief coming off her friend. Jack leaned over her and gave them a thumbs-up.

The helicopter slowly approached, careful to land in a space free of trees or any obstruction that would disrupt the landing or cause harm. Once the copter was on the ground, Terra jumped out and ducked beneath the spinning rotors and ran to Erin. Grabbing Erin up in a bear hug, Terra almost bowled her over.

Erin clung to her friend a few moments, soaking up the warmth and relief that she and Nathan had been found. Rescued.

Terra finally released Erin, shouting over the rotor wash. "I was so worried! I didn't want to give up, but I was afraid you were gone."

Caught up in Terra's tears of joy, Erin let hers flow too.

Erin backed away but gripped Terra's arms. "What about my mother?"

"We've already radioed in that we found you alive and, I hope, well."

Erin nodded. "I'm well."

"We searched downriver, but Jack had the brilliant idea—albeit a little late—that if you had survived, you guys would have tracked back to the dam, the closest structure. I'm so sorry we didn't think of that until early this morning. It was still dark, and by the time we got a pilot and were in the copter, the sun was already up."

"It's okay, Terra. You found us." Erin was running on fumes. "Can we go now?"

Terra laughed and pulled Erin toward the helicopter that remained powered up. Erin and Nathan climbed in. After she buckled in, Erin rested her head against the seat and closed her eyes. She was safe, and she'd once again survived a near miss.

She had never doubted that Terra—a US Forest Service Special Agent and SAR team member—would not give up until she found her. The smallest of smiles lifted the corners of Erin's mouth. In the midst of this horror, there was a silver lining—Nathan. Her head told her that kind of thinking was dangerous. But her heart warmed at the thought. What would he think if he knew Erin considered reconnecting with him the bright side of their shared trauma?

Still, though she agreed with him that every cloud had a silver lining, some clouds carried violent storms with them.

And she could feel one raging toward them in her bones.

TWELVE

The helicopter flew over the river, and Nathan was able to see much of the devastation, noting it mostly stopped with the narrowing canyon. He imagined the force of the releasing water had been slowed by the canyon, backing up the flash flood, and that had caused more turmoil for him and Erin as they tried to survive, as well as more widespread damage in the area immediately below the dam.

But it was over now.

He let the adrenaline completely drain out of him, because he had to prepare himself for what came next. As the helicopter flew them to the local hospital to have their injuries treated, Nathan pressed his head against the seat back and closed his eyes, his soul breathing an internal sigh of relief.

First Dad was shot.

And then the dam. And that moment. That horrible, terrifying moment when Erin was yanked from his grasp by the wall of water . . . it all rushed over him again.

Adrenaline had kept him alive and moving and on alert.

That, and well, he had no doubt God was watching over them. Otherwise, he had no idea how they had survived. Years ago, he'd been part of a search and recovery team after a flash flood decimated a campground located in a narrow gap between mountains.

The only survivor—a dog caught in a treetop.

Before yesterday, Nathan had seen firsthand how deadly things could turn, and now, of course, he'd experienced it himself. Except for the death. He struggled to believe they'd survived.

Unfortunately, he would also struggle to forget the feel of Erin in his arms as they both sought warmth and comfort.

Jack squeezed Nathan's shoulder. "You okay?"

He nodded mostly to reassure Jack but kept his eyes closed. Far too many emotions crashed through him, and he wasn't prepared to reveal to Jack or anyone else in the helicopter just how tormented he'd been. Though his friend probably understood. Still, he didn't trust himself to speak just yet and would wait until he had composed himself.

Just when would that happen? By the time they arrived at the hospital? Or would it take much longer?

Forty-five minutes later, he sat on the edge of a table at the small hospital in Big Rapids while Dr. Sato finished stitching up a gash in his back. He hadn't realized how badly he'd been hurt. He'd been too focused on keeping them alive for well over twelve hours.

The doctor looked at his eyes once more with his flashlight, sparking irritation. "You're bruised and banged up, but other than the laceration on your back, you're all in one piece." Dr. Sato leveled his gaze on Nathan. "You're lucky to be alive."

"I don't believe in luck."

"Fortunate. Does that work for you?"

"God had something to do with it, okay?"

"I can't argue with you there." Flashlight in the eyes again. "The fact that there was a shooting there the day before pretty much cleared out the campers and fishermen. So only you two were caught in the dam failure."

"What about Erin?" Nathan asked. "Is she going to be okay?"

"She fared better than you."

That news stunned him, actually. "I was afraid she might have internal injuries."

"Not that I'm supposed to talk about her injuries with you, what with privacy and all that, but you're a detective and the man who kept her alive, administered CPR, so I'll bend the rules. No internal injuries. She's doing well." The doctor winked, then grabbed a bandage from a drawer and Nathan waited for him to put it in place over his wound.

A male nurse entered to clean up after the doctor.

"Are we done here?" Nathan reached for the clean T-shirt that hung over a chair, courtesy of Jack. "I need to go see her."

The doctor pulled off his gloves. "She's down the hall, first door to the right."

"Thanks." Nathan dipped his chin and hopped from the table. Before he could exit, the nurse handed him some paperwork. Nathan quickly signed the discharge papers, then exited the room and went in search of Erin.

Outside the room, he peered through the small window and found a party. Jack, Terra, Nadine, and, of course, Erin's mother. Celia's expression was grim.

He pushed through the door and joined them. "I admit I'm a little jealous. Everyone's in here checking on Erin, but nobody came to see me."

"You were in a mood, dude," Jack said. "We thought it best to give you your space."

Erin gingerly slid from the treatment table.

"I'm free to go." She studied his face. "How are you doing?"

"I'll feel better once I get cleaned up." He glanced at Jack. "Thanks for letting me borrow the clean clothes. The doctor wouldn't let me put the muddy ones back on."

"I keep an extra set in my truck with me. Keep the shirt." Jack squeezed his shoulder.

Nathan groaned and shrank away. "Watch it. I got stitches."

Jack's eyes widened. "Oh, man, I should have known. I'm sorry. I didn't mean to—"

"It's okay." Nathan tried to hide that the aches and throbs were beginning to get to him.

"You got stitches too?" Erin asked. "How many?"

"Twenty-four."

"I only needed ten," she said. "Why didn't you say anything when we were out there? You acted like you weren't hurt."

Could he really tell them he hadn't realized he had a gash that needed tending? He'd been too focused on Erin and making sure they endured the cold night in the wilderness. On getting them to the dam, which might have been a mistake in that their rescuers hadn't searched the dam until this morning. But they were here and safe now.

"I get it." Jack held his gaze.

Nathan saw in his eyes that he truly did understand. It was only a few months ago that Jack sustained much worse to save Terra—a woman he loved. At the thought, Nathan buried the rush of emotion. He and Erin weren't a thing, and he couldn't afford to love her.

"Come on," Jack said. "Let's get you home."

Together the group exited the room. Erin stopped by the administration desk to provide insurance billing information. Terra had gotten Erin's purse with her wallet and ID from her vehicle parked at the trailhead and brought it up to the hospital.

"I can take you home," Jack said. "Terra will take care of Erin. Don't worry."

And Celia. Nadine had stayed with the woman through the night, and she'd been beside herself. Terra brought them both up to the hospital to see that Erin was all right.

And she was in good hands. Nathan could let go.

Jack hung back and waited for him. He felt as if he should

say something to Erin, like they had unfinished business, but Jack was right and Nathan shouldn't worry. For now, they could both use a few hours of rest and recuperation.

He turned his attention to Jack, who had been there for him today. Both Jack and Terra had been there for Nathan and Erin. "Thanks, buddy." He wasn't sure how people who didn't have friends and family survived in this world.

Jack was walking with Nathan toward the exit when Celia approached. "Nathan, I need to talk to you."

He glanced at Jack with a shrug. "Hold on."

Celia pulled him aside so they could speak in private. She leaned close and whispered, "Did they find out what happened to the dam? Who caused it?"

He studied the woman who only last week allegedly tried to commit suicide. She denied she'd done it and had him worried for her state of mind. Now she was asking him *who* had caused the dam to fail.

Not *what.*

THIRTEEN

erra had driven them home from the hospital. Both Terra and Mom had been adamant that Erin go to bed, and she hadn't argued with them. But first, she wanted nothing more than to take a long, hot shower to wash away the grime and mud—and maybe a few of the memories.

Erin turned on the shower, and unfortunately the sound brought unwanted memories. What was it with her and water now? She didn't think she would be kayaking anytime soon after what had happened back on Puget Sound, and now even the sound of rushing water—river or the shower, it didn't matter—which she should find soothing, tormented her. She pushed beyond her initial unwelcome reaction and stepped into the hot spray, then slowly relaxed as it flowed over her and rinsed away the last many hours.

Dirty water swirled around, then disappeared down the drain. Exhaustion pressed her to finish before she was truly ready to give up the warmth, and she dressed in a clean navy T-shirt and black yoga pants, then crawled into bed. She could sleep for a week.

With her head against the pillow, soft blankets covering her, and the shades pulled to provide the room with at least some semblance of darkness, Erin gave herself permission to crash. At first, the pain ricocheted through her, making her feel as if her whole body vibrated with it, but then she let go and gave in to the exhaustion . . .

And the nightmares . . .

Mom shook her. "Why didn't you listen?"

Erin jerked awake. The images of her nightmare from long ago hadn't been overcome by recent events like she'd expected. Maybe even hoped. The clock on the nightstand told her she'd been lost to the world for at least four hours.

Voices—Mom and another female voice she didn't recognize—spoke in low tones in the living room. Erin doubted Mom's friend would leave until Erin was up and well enough to be with her mother. Or rather, she hoped she wouldn't leave. She sat up and rubbed her eyes.

Before the dam broke—literally, and it would almost seem figuratively in terms of traumatic events—Nathan had been sharing his morbid story with Erin.

With her and no one else.

She couldn't let him down. If she focused on helping him, then she could rise above the trauma—and she needed that for her own mental health. Two people needed her help. Mom and Nathan. As for Nathan, she wanted to get into the attic to see if she could find the articles Nathan had mentioned.

She ran a brush through her hair, then left the bedroom. Mom and Aurie—pronounced like Laurie without the *L*, as she always said when she introduced herself—a woman Mom worked with at Main Street Thrift Shop, stopped chopping vegetables at the counter. Both looked up at Erin, stunned expressions on their faces.

Mom set down the small knife. "Oh, honey, you should be resting. Did you need something? I can bring you whatever you need. Are you thirsty or hungry?"

"No, I'm fine." Erin moved to stand between the women

and looked down at the vegetables—carrots, celery, onions, zucchini. "I need to work." But not necessarily chopping vegetables.

"You need to rest," Mom said. "Should I call the doctor and get a prescription for—"

"No." *Let me cut you off right there.* She didn't need more prescriptions in the house that her mother could potentially abuse—if that's what was going on. Mom was taking medication, but Erin was in charge of administering the antidepressant. And in her absence, Nadine had helped with that.

"We have plenty of veggies to chop here," Aurie said. "If you want to help."

"Yeah, what's up with that?" Erin grabbed a cut celery stalk and crunched on it.

"They're going into a big stir-fry for Sunday's church pot-blessing." Aurie grinned. "You know, pot-blessing instead of potluck."

"I get it." A small laugh erupted. Maybe she could truly get back to some normalcy.

"And Aurie was so sweet," Mom said. "She brought over a lasagna that we can warm up for later. She used to be in the catering business. Did you know that?"

Erin shook her head on the business, but on the lasagna . . . "Oh, thank you. That *is* sweet."

Erin appreciated the friends Mom had made over the years living here, and a sliver of regret skimmed through her heart. For months she'd been trying to get Mom to leave her friends to come out West to live with Erin. It took time to develop long-lasting and trustworthy friends, which Erin knew well because she'd yet to create a decent network of them in Seattle. Mom had built a life here. Even if Mom gave that up and moved out to be with her, Erin was working all the time. What had she thought she could offer?

None of that mattered now.

Aurie grinned and handed over the chopping knife, hilt first.

"Actually." Erin shrugged as she gave Aurie a sheepish grin. "I have my own work I need to get on top of. I'm behind as it is."

"Are you sure?" Mom asked.

"Yes. Working in my office will help clear my mind." Of far too much trauma than anyone should have to experience in one lifetime. Erin gave her mother a quick hug. Since she couldn't search the attic, her podcast was the next best thing.

When she pulled back, Mom held her arms and smiled, looking like her usual happy self and nothing at all like a woman who'd had her stomach pumped last week. Erin simply couldn't trust that look, because she had missed the signs before.

Oh, Mom. I almost lost you.

"Okay. After Aurie and I finish here, and when you're done too, then maybe you and I can have a cup of coffee along with some key lime pie I made for last . . ." Her mouth suddenly turned down.

And Erin would work to bring back her good mood. "Oh, good. I love key lime pie. Thanks, Mom.

"It's good to see you, Aurie. Thanks so much for hanging out." Erin wouldn't say more and hoped Aurie understood the depth of her gratitude. For now, at least, keeping Mom occupied and in good company was for the best.

She headed to her office and overheard Aurie asking her mother what job Erin was working on. Erin wasn't sure keeping her podcast anonymous mattered anymore. Then again, she might want to go back to her job at some point if it was still available to her.

She closed her office door behind her and sat in her chair at the desk, then shut her eyes. The world seemed to spin around her. She drew in a few calming breaths, then focused on getting out her next podcast episode. Opening up the script where she'd left off, she read through the next scene of the story and the words pulled her in. She hoped her listeners would be riveted as well. She longed to make a difference. She lifted her headset, pressed it over her ears, adjusted the mic, and began.

Her voice shook at first, but she kept going. She could edit and smooth things out, or worst case, do it all over again.

"Welcome to episode 3. If you recall . . ." She gave a recap of the previous episodes, then said, "And today, we listen to the actual 911 call made by Missy's mother."

Erin digitally inserted the recording that she'd obtained and listened to the frantic mother's call, feeling the woman's anguish to her core. Would her listeners?

Once the 911 recording was over, Erin continued. "We learn that the bridge had collapsed and police had to take another route, which was much slower. Dispatch remains on the call with Missy's mother, Angela Gardner, and even tells her about the bridge, but the details about the bridge have been redacted. Regardless, due to unfortunate circumstances, the police took an extraordinarily long time to get to the house. Still, neighbors and friends were already searching the woods.

"I can't help but wonder if police had arrived at the house within minutes of the emergency call, whether the missing child would have been found and her abductor caught. Next, we'll talk about the statement Erica Weeks gave to the police. Here's a teaser. Only Erica knows the full story of what happened up to the point that Missy was taken, and her story will make you shudder."

Erin ended the podcast before she read through the advertisements. After taking off the headset, she pressed her head on the desk. Maybe she should have rested a bit longer, because now she was completely spent.

A light knock on the door drew her head up as her mother opened it. Mom frowned.

"Hey." Erin offered a meager smile. It was all she could muster.

"We finished chopping, and Aurie's gone. I'm sorry to interrupt. I have a headache, and I'm going to take a nap. Wake me up when you're ready for the key lime pie."

"I will." Though this late in the day, they might as well save it for dessert after the lasagna. "I'll put the lasagna on in about an hour. Will that be okay?"

"Thanks." Mom's frown remained as she shut the door. Erin suspected it had to do with her headache.

Erin would take advantage of her mother's nap. She wouldn't have to wait until the middle of the night to search the attic. At the moment, Delmar was edging his grass, so that could help to cover any noise she might make. With Mom napping, Erin could search the attic for articles that Dwayne left behind. Mom had boxed up a lot of his stuff and stored it in the attic.

Nathan mentioned that Dwayne had given articles about a cold case to Newt to look into. Knowing what cold case he wanted information about would go a long way in helping Nathan. Beyond that, Erin could see if there was something in the attic that had triggered her mother to want to commit suicide. After all, Nadine had claimed the attic stairs were hanging down when she found Mom.

In the kitchen, Erin quietly grabbed a soda and popped the top. Mom would be settling in for her nap. Erin crept down the hallway. The trick would be getting the attic steps pulled down. Quietly, she tugged on the small rope, and springs squeaked as the stairs unfolded downward. She held her breath and waited.

Mom didn't come out of her room. Even if she did come out and catch Erin going into the attic, it wasn't like she was committing a crime, but she didn't want to trigger her mother again, if that was possible.

Erin crept up and into the attic, and at the top of the steps, she found the switch and flipped on the light, surprised the bulb worked. Dust and cobwebs filled the space like no one had been up there in decades, but Mom had been in the attic recently. That was, if she'd made it up the steps before taking those pills. If she had, then the dust had settled back into place quickly.

Old furniture, a cedar trunk, and plastic bins had been stacked against the wall along with numerous cardboard boxes. Erin would start with the closest box. The tape had been cut and she ran her hand over the top and found it reasonably dust-free. Mom must have been looking in this one.

What got you so upset you would try to commit suicide?

Then there was the issue of Mom not remembering that she'd self-poisoned. Erin had looked into it to confirm her suspicions. Studies showed benzodiazepines caused memory impairment, especially after the event. And of course, many people who suffer from depression or attempt suicide struggle to remember the exact details leading up to the moment, especially involving an overdose—so that wasn't so unusual. But in Mom's case, she didn't remember taking the pills and claimed she wouldn't have even tried to commit suicide. Erin feared she could even become more depressed over the sense of loss of control over her life.

Erin would need to do additional research into it. Talk to someone who might have more information about benzodiazepines, specifically Valium, and memory impairment. She put that on her mental to-do list. Having those answers would go a long way in helping Mom. A therapist might be able to answer her questions, but Mom was still waiting to get in to see one, and that appointment was weeks out. Erin wouldn't concern herself too much with the memory issues until she knew more.

She opened the box and peered inside to see stacks of photographs, old magazines, and yes, newspapers. Maybe she could find those articles. But why keep all this? She didn't think her stepfather had been a hoarder. Mom either. Nor was there a lot of family memorabilia to keep. Erin had never even met her grandparents on Mom's side. Her grandmother had died when Mom was born and her grandfather later, but before Erin was born.

It felt like Erin and Mom had lived on their own most of their lives together. When they moved to Big Rapids, Montana, before Erin was ten, Mom married Dwayne. They'd only been married a few years when he died in the SAR accident, and once again, Mom and Erin were on their own.

They had each other's backs. Erin went to the University of Montana for her bachelor's degree and continued through their clinical psychology PhD program. She stayed close as long as she could, even with her residencies, but eventually took the job in Washington, and Mom didn't follow. Why had Erin believed she could convince her, or even that Mom would be better off living with her there?

Erin released a heavy sigh and focused back on her task so she could make headway before Mom woke up. Plus, Erin needed to put that lasagna in the oven to warm up.

She pulled a stack out of the box and began thumbing through it. Maybe she could find something that would help Nathan *and* something that would help her understand what was going on with Mom. If she found a photograph, a letter, or an item that could have been the catalyst to Mom's suicide attempt, then she and Mom would have a serious talk later.

Over key lime pie.

FOURTEEN

Nathan sat in his vehicle in the parking lot at the county offices and stared at the doors.

Erin had suggested Nathan needed to learn more so he could make an informed decision about what to do, considering that his father had put him in an impossible situation. Having had some time and space away from the incident—okay, only two days—he decided, depending on the outcome of his conversation with Henry today, that he would tell him what Dad had said, which honestly wasn't that much. The simple fact was that if Henry talked to Dad's boss back East, he could probably find out as much as Nathan had been told. Dad's police department would know he'd been looking into a specific case and could reasonably assume the shooting might be related to this case, especially since Dad's boss had steered him in another direction. Still, if there had been a cover-up, someone could have deliberately concealed knowledge of the case Dad had been looking into.

And that's why Nathan couldn't let it go.

But he felt like he was going in giant looping thought circles and getting absolutely nowhere.

He hopped from his vehicle, strode across the parking lot,

then entered the county sheriff's offices. He ignored the looks of surprise as he weaved between desks on his way back to Henry's office. He found the sheriff with his back to the barely cracked door while he talked on the phone. Nathan could see him through the window, and unfortunately, he could hear some of what he was saying.

He hadn't intended to eavesdrop, and then felt more than awkward.

Nathan turned to walk away, but then caught a few words he couldn't ignore, so he lingered near the door.

"Nobody's going to dig into this, I can assure you."

Yep. *Now* he was definitely eavesdropping.

His heart pounded at the words. Nathan shut the door quietly, then knocked. Henry ended his call as he turned. His eyes widened when he saw Nathan. In two strides he was at the door and opened it, waving Nathan into his office.

Henry's left eye subtly twitched, irritation coming off him in waves. "I told you to take some time and get some rest. And what happens? You—"

"I what? Got swept away when a dam failed? How was I supposed to know—"

Henry held his hand up, signaling for Nathan to stop. Nathan didn't want to stop, so instead he ground his molars.

Henry sagged. "I'm sorry, Nathan. I shouldn't have jumped down your throat. I was worried when I got the news that the dam had failed. Jack had informed me that you might be there at the crime scene."

"I wasn't at a crime scene. The scene had been released by then, okay?"

Henry's frown was one of pain, and he moved behind the desk and eased into his chair. "I can't say that makes me feel any better. The fact you were there means—"

"That I wanted to be where Dad and I had fished ever since I was a kid. I had hoped that memory hadn't been destroyed, and now I'm not so sure it hasn't been replaced with . . . with . . ." Nathan couldn't finish the sentence. "The whole place is messed up now. First, he was shot right there in front of me, and then the torrent washed everything away."

Nathan hadn't come here to pour out his frustration. For that, he might need a therapist. Henry might suggest finding one, and Nathan didn't want that from him, even if it was department policy. He took the seat across from Henry, putting the desk between them.

Henry tapped a pen against his desk, then finally lifted his gaze to Nathan. "What's the latest?"

"We're still waiting for him to wake up." Nathan glanced at his cell. "Mom said she would call or text as soon as he does."

"It's nice of her to stay by his side like that."

Nathan shrugged. He still didn't understand his mother staying next to her ex-husband's side as if they'd remained married for the last twenty-plus years. But they'd remained friends over the years, and apparently, Dad had no one else. His cousin Ned was down in Ecuador on a mission trip. So if he did have other friends and family, anyone back in Boston, where were they?

"I take it you have something you need to tell me or you wouldn't have come in," Henry said. "Did you finally decide to share what your father told you?"

Henry's words on the phone still rang in Nathan's ears. *"Nobody's going to dig into this, I can assure you."* Who had Henry been talking to? Nathan bit back what he wanted to say.

"Actually, I was wondering if West has learned anything about the shooter."

Henry's head bobbed. "There was another guy out hiking in the area. He might have seen something. West is going to talk to him. I just got off the phone with your dad's boss—Lieutenant Sullivan, Gifford PD. As you know, one of your father's past cases could be connected to the shooting, though we have no indications that's the situation yet. Sullivan has someone looking into Newt's previous cases, and we'll let them do it. Obviously they're going to be more familiar with his investigations. They'll let us know if they identify any that need to be further examined." Henry dropped the pen he'd been tapping against his desk and leveled his gaze at Nathan. "I understand how hard this is for you, son. But can you trust your fellow detectives to do their jobs? After all, your father is one of us—an officer of the law—and we want that shooter as badly as you do."

Nathan wanted to question Henry about what he'd overheard. Why would Henry tell Dad's superior that no one was digging into his dad's shooting? And then turn around and ask Nathan to trust his fellow detectives? The office started to tilt. To anchor himself, Nathan stared at photographs and awards on the wall behind Henry. Before he could get a word out, Henry continued.

"Now do me a favor and drive over to Bozeman and hang around until your father wakes up. Get out of town, in other words." He hung his head. "When I heard you were down by the river when the dam broke, you almost gave me a heart attack, Nathan."

If people are in danger, Dad, then why not tell your friend Sheriff Gibson?

"*Right now, the only person I trust is you, son.*"

Nathan wanted to share the burden with Henry. If a past case was the reason his father was shot, then the more people on it, the better. But Dad had held it close for a reason. And apparently, Henry had promised Dad's boss that no one would go digging around. Nathan could only assume he was talking about Dad's case. Dad's past. What else could it be? Nathan wanted to confront the man now. But he would bide his time and find out what he could before it was too late. Funny how quickly his intentions reversed.

Henry rose and came around to stand next to Nathan. Nathan stood too.

"You've been through two traumatic events. That's more than most people experience in a lifetime, and they happened in the same week." Henry rested a hand on Nathan's shoulder. "Please get some rest. Do it for me, would you?" He offered a grin. "I don't want to see you around here for two weeks."

"What? You told me a week."

"And yet you're here." Henry eyed him. "Besides, that was before the dam failed."

Failed.

Celia's whispered words came back to him. *Did they find out what happened to the dam? Who caused it?*

"Are you sure it wasn't deliberate?"

Now Henry gave him the same look he'd given Celia when she'd said those words to him. Because, really, who would go to the trouble to take out an old dam in the middle of Montana for no good reason?

"Want to make it three weeks?"

FIFTEEN

Erin searched through a few boxes and found old newspaper articles stashed in a folder or simply embedded in the mass of junk. Mom had collected all of Dwayne's belongings, stuff from his drawers and files, and put them into cardboard boxes, which she stacked in the attic to go through at some point in the future when the items wouldn't cause so much pain.

It had been just over fifteen years since Dwayne had been called out on that SAR mission in which he'd been killed in an avalanche. Had that moment when Mom believed she could go through his things without the pain finally arrived last week and that's when Mom had climbed up to the attic?

Erin found herself getting caught up in looking through the old photographs that hadn't made it into the albums shelved downstairs or in digital form on Mom's computer. Finding a few pictures of her mother when she was young—a teenager or maybe early twenties, Erin smiled. Back then, Mom looked a lot like Erin.

The doorbell rang.

Oh no.

Mom might wake up.

And Erin hadn't found the articles Nathan had mentioned yet, though they might not be here. Regardless, she was done for now, whether she wanted to be or not. At least she'd given a cursory look, and she would try to come back later.

She hurried down the attic steps and returned them to the ceiling, then raced to the door. After looking through the peephole, Erin opened the door to Nathan. He'd shaved, and his dark hair was free of the river debris. She could smell the fresh scent of soap.

A smile shimmered in his dark-brown eyes.

Her heart pounded at the sight of him, the nearness. Erin shook off the unwanted reaction at seeing the man she'd spent the night with—under the direst of circumstances. But she couldn't forget how his sturdy chest had cushioned her, his arms had cradled her, and his body had warmed her.

"Hey." The simple greeting sounded a little too breathy, giving entirely too much away.

His eyes roamed her face as if he were trying to read it. "I hope this isn't a bad time."

Um . . .

"Erin, who is it?" Mom's voice sounded muffled. She was still in her room.

"Just a friend, Mom." Erin called over her shoulder. "Go back to your nap."

He visibly cringed, scrunching his face. "Sorry. I didn't mean to wake her."

Erin stepped out onto the porch and pulled the door shut behind her. "I would think you'd be at home taking it easy, either that or at the hospital. How's your dad?"

He shook his head. "No change."

Erin gestured toward the swing on the porch and almost immediately regretted it. They'd spent plenty of time on this same porch swing when they were an official couple. Erin slowly sat on one end and Nathan on the other side, yet it still felt too close. Being so close and comfortable with him last night—in his arms to keep warm and survive—only seemed to make this moment uncomfortable. And at the same time, her heart pounded as if she'd never gotten over him.

"I'd invite you in," she said, "but I have a feeling you don't want to talk in front of my mother."

He angled his head. "What gave you that impression?"

"The look on your face. You're kind of beat and desperate."

"Oh." He shifted back in surprise.

That elicited a chuckle, and it felt good to laugh. "Yes, and despite that, I also see a spark in your eyes." *And a few questions building there too.* "You really aren't following me, are you?"

He grinned and shook his head. "Not at all."

"You show up looking like you survived a flash flood and spent the night in the cold, but you're still here looking for all the world like you're onto something, and you welcome the challenge." Erin offered her own grin.

He arched both brows and bobbed his head. "Wow. You're good. I'm impressed."

Then his lips spread wide and his dimples appeared. Her heart skipped a beat or two or three. Though he was only teasing, the compliment sent warmth spreading through her. It took some effort, but Erin pulled her gaze away from his killer smile and stared at the bungalows across the street.

Nathan pushed and set them swinging, if only slightly. A good, tall glass of lemonade would set the mood and bring back the memories in a mad rush. Erin was done with mad rushes for the foreseeable future, so she stood and leaned against the post, crossing her arms.

"Nathan, seriously, what brings you by?"

"I have two weeks off now, instead of just the one. I'm supposed to rest and recuperate and watch my dad waste away in a hospital bed. I want to stay hopeful, but I have to prepare myself for the fact that he might not ever wake up. Even if he does, who knows if he'll be able to communicate." Nathan rose, fisted his hands, and paced the porch.

"And you need to know what cold case he was looking into when he was shot." She lowered her voice. "I was up in the attic earlier to see if I could find the originals or even copies of the articles Dwayne had given him."

"And?"

"Nothing yet."

"There's something else," he said.

"Go on. I need to know everything."

"Brace yourself." Nathan stopped pacing and stood next to her. He gently guided her off the porch and around the house to the backyard until they stood by the freshly planted pansies, away from anyone who could possibly overhear them.

"What's going on?" she asked.

He leaned closer and whispered, "Your mother suggested that someone could have intentionally taken out the dam."

Erin took a step back. "What? Are you serious?"

Nathan held her gaze. "Dead serious."

She pressed her palms against her eyes. Her mother was losing it. Either that, or she had already lost it.

Lord . . . help me.

Erin dropped her hands. "Are you dismissing her suggestion?"

"I saw Henry today and asked if he thought the dam breaking could have been deliberate."

Hugging herself, Erin waited for the rest.

"He threatened to give me three weeks. I mean, who under normal circumstances wouldn't want three weeks off, as long as they're getting paid?"

"Someone who wants answers. I think your father never got the chance to tell you the most crucial information that he wanted kept secret." Still . . . Erin measured her next words. "That said, when someone is under tremendous pressure, they often give something away. Hint at what's bothering them, or what they're hiding, without realizing it. So think back and try to remember everything he said. How he said it, that sort of thing."

Nathan stared through her as he swatted away a buzzing insect. "I considered telling Henry about what Dad said, then realized Dad didn't tell me much, and now they're already looking into his past cases to see if there's anything that could be tied to this shooting. But if Dad was right and there was some sort of cover-up, we might never know the truth, especially since I overheard Henry telling Dad's boss that nobody would be digging into things here."

Nathan's dark-brown eyes had grown even darker. Erin chewed on that information for a few moments. What could that mean? Sheriff Henry Gibson was one of the good guys. They had to be missing something.

Lord, how do I help him? "What are you going to do?"

"I'm going home to pack. I'm taking the first flight in the morning to Boston. Going to go into my dad's house. I have his key." He dangled the key ring from his finger.

The news shouldn't have surprised her. But fear for his safety squeezed her heart. After all, his father had been shot and possibly for what he knew. She'd even encouraged him in this quest. But now she regretted it.

"Nathan . . . I . . ." She stepped forward, intending to dissuade him.

"How's your mother doing? Is she okay?" He'd redirected the conversation, the look in his eyes a clear warning she shouldn't try to change his mind.

Erin shrugged. "I think so, but she has her moments. She still doesn't remember downing the bottle of pills. We don't talk about it because it disturbs her too much, and that's understandable."

"What are you going to do?" he asked.

"What do you mean?"

Nathan swallowed and stared at the grass, then glanced back up at her, myriad emotions surging in his gaze. "Are you going back to Seattle at some point?"

Oh. He was asking her if she would be staying. Why did he want to know? Her breath hitched at the possible reasons. A few heartbeats passed before she could speak.

"I took family medical leave. It's indefinite at this point." She hung her head, and her heart spoke . . . "I gave up a possible promotion." If only she could pull those words back. She hadn't meant to speak them.

"Oh, Erin. I'm so sorry."

"We do anything for family, right?" She swiped at the tears spilling onto her cheeks.

I guess this is where God wants me right now.

And she would turn the conversation back where it needed to be. Dwayne's articles had nearly cost Newt Campbell his life, and she wanted to know why too.

"So you're going to Boston. Are you sure you can leave your dad? What if he wakes up? What if he has something more to say?" She grabbed his hand, ignoring the sudden current that surged up her arm all the way to her heart. "Have you . . . have you made sure that his room is secured? A Bozeman cop or someone to watch out for him."

He nodded. "You sound like a cop."

She lifted her hand, releasing his. "Criminal psychologist, hello."

"Henry saw to the extra security. Mom told me earlier today when I called to let her know that I was okay. She hadn't heard about the dam or that I was in trouble." Nathan started walking toward the side of the house. Erin strolled next to him.

"While I'm sorry no one thought to keep her informed, I'm glad she didn't have the added burden of worrying about you," Erin said. "Especially since you came out on the other side with only twenty-four stitches." She smiled to inject some levity.

They hiked into the front yard until they stood next to Nathan's vehicle. "Oh, I forgot to mention that Henry shared that a hiker might have witnessed something, so Detective West will be interviewing him," Nathan said.

"And while he's interviewing the hiker, you're going to Boston to dig deeper." She sucked in a bolstering breath, then said, "You asked me to help, so I'm going with you." There. She wouldn't let him go through this alone.

Nathan opened his mouth. "You shouldn't—"

"Don't worry. Mom has so many friends, it's ridiculous. I'll find someone to stay with her for a night or two." She didn't imagine they would need longer than that.

If Erin didn't go, she might never learn what articles, what cold case, her stepfather, Dwayne, had been asking about. She needed to see for herself what had brought Nathan's father back here.

She wasn't sure if it was the unknown or the possible implications that left her unsettled. Either way, she'd learned well enough that the past, especially a cold-case past, could come back around to bite in unexpected ways.

SIXTEEN

The slight downward shift and pressure change on the plane alerted Nathan that they were approaching Logan International Airport in Boston, Massachusetts. He opened his eyes and blinked. Exhaustion had taken hold as soon as he'd buckled in for the hours-long flight, though he had never fully fallen asleep. He licked his parched lips and spotted the drink still sitting on the tray table. If he reached for it, he might wake Erin since her head rested on his shoulder. Her soft snores told him she was asleep, and he was glad. They were both probably pushing their minds and bodies to make this trip so quickly after what they'd been through. But there was no time to waste.

A measure of guilt corded his throat for letting Erin come with him. For inviting her into the investigation in the first place. Aurie and Nadine had agreed to stay with Celia while Erin took the trip. She'd told her mother that it was work related, and in a way it was. Erin said she could potentially add this cold case to her podcast—after the danger had passed, of course.

And that was just it. The danger was very real and present. Maybe Dad's boss—his captain or sergeant—had warned Dad away because of the potential danger, yet that's not how law enforcement worked. So now Nathan was stepping into the storm in his father's place.

Like father, like son.

Had he been selfish to share with Erin in the first place?

Yeah, he probably didn't think through that very well, but it was too late now. Fatigue chased him, and he had no time to give in to it.

Next to him, Erin's mouth hung slightly open. Her lashes fluttered, then she opened her eyes. A few breaths passed as she took in her surroundings, then moved away from him with a start. She cleared her throat as she stretched her arms as much as space would allow.

"We're landing." He reached for the water and finished it off. The flight attendant moved down the aisle to collect garbage.

With her fingers, Erin weaved her mass of light-blonde hair together and clipped it on top of her head. Nathan would love to get his hands into that. But that unbidden thought had no place in his mind. And he had a feeling such thoughts weren't going to stop anytime soon, so he would just keep pushing them aside as long as he had to.

He glanced at his watch. They'd had one stop in Denver, which had added time to their travel. "We'll be on the road by two thirty. Maybe three."

"Yay. I'm relieved we'll miss rush hour traffic, though just barely," she said. She handed her water to the flight attendant and pushed up her tray table.

"I keep thinking that if your dad's boss didn't want him looking into the cold case, but he continued and someone shot him to prevent that, then what are the chances someone has already been at your father's place and searched it?" She chewed on her thumbnail, a nervous habit Nathan hadn't seen before. "Maybe someone is even watching the house."

Even the police.

She *had* been thinking about this. Good. He needed all the help he could get. "I'd say the chances are good. We'll be careful."

She pressed her head against the seat and sighed. Nathan noticed she squeezed the armrest as well. "Don't worry. We'll be careful. I have every right to enter my father's house with the key he gave me and search for something he wanted me to find." Dad hadn't given Nathan the key, exactly, but Nathan had retrieved it from his things.

The jet vibrated and rumbled in response to the air turbulence, and he found himself gripping the armrest too. He covered Erin's hand with his right hand and squeezed. She sent him a small smile, and he caught himself lingering on her perfect lips. Nathan shifted to look out the window instead. In some ways, the forced proximity was brutal.

Erin . . . She'd been his everything before she'd destroyed him by walking away.

He'd been going to propose.

Propose.

A guy didn't just get over that. And apparently, he hadn't gotten over it even after five years . . . or her. That she was sitting next to him on this venture seemed surreal. Nathan struggled to push aside thoughts of what could have been between them and focus on the present and what mattered.

Finding Dad's shooter. He allowed those gruesome images to blast through his brain again and he was back on track.

Forty-five minutes later, they had landed, grabbed their luggage and Nathan's checked firearms, then taken possession of the rental car they had reserved. Nathan navigated the thick traffic as he headed to his father's home in Gifford, a suburb where he worked for the police department. Boston traffic seemed to close in around them. Digital boards as well as big green signs with arrows directed them, including one particular sign that directed traffic to the Charles River Dam.

"I know my mother is having issues," Erin said, "but is there any possibility someone destroyed the dam to maybe . . . I don't know . . . to cover up evidence?"

"That would be a lot of trouble to cover up evidence."

"What kind of evidence could someone want to hide?"

"Remember, it had rained that night. Rain could have already destroyed the evidence. Nobody needed to blow up a dam. I'm not sure it's as simple as a stick of dynamite. I heard a loud noise when the dam collapsed, but I thought it was just the dam breaking up. Maybe I'm wrong, but I brought the mention of someone taking out the dam to the sheriff's attention, and it's up to him to look into it. As for evidence, a bullet was lodged in Dad's brain, so we have that."

He squeezed the steering wheel even tighter at the thought. Would he get his father back? And even if he did, would he be the same? *God, help me to do this.*

Erin pressed her hand gently on his shoulder. "We're going to figure this out. I'm here to help however I can. Justice will never happen unless we dig where no one else is looking."

"You mean where no one wants us to look? Don't forget what happened to my father because someone didn't want him looking deeper."

SEVENTEEN

While Nathan drove, Erin texted Mom to check on her, then a call came through with a Washington area code. Erin's heart jumped. She quickly answered. "Erin Larson."

"Dr. Larson," a familiar voice said. "This is Detective Munson with the Seattle PD."

"What can I do for you?" She glanced at Nathan, tossing him an apologetic look.

He gave her a brief concerned glance before focusing back on the road. She hoped he couldn't hear the call, but sometimes voices carried in small spaces.

"I'm calling to give you information regarding the boating accident." She suddenly remembered that Detective Munson had called the day she'd gone in search of Nathan, and she never had the chance to return the call. Fortunately, she'd been able to quickly get a replacement cell with her same number before their Boston excursion.

Her heart rate kicked up. "I thought it had already been resolved."

"Not so much. In fact, I'm no longer sure it was an accident."

Her stomach knotted. She wasn't certain she wanted to listen to this while Nathan was sitting next to her, possibly able to hear the detective. Nathan already had enough to worry about. She considered offering to return the detective's call when she had more time to talk. And more privacy. However, she was anxious to hear what he had to say.

She angled away from Nathan. "Please explain."

"We had trouble tracking down the boat to start, and then we couldn't locate the owner. But we finally found him. It would appear he was physically separated from his boat before the incident."

Erin frowned. "I'm not following you."

"There's no other way to tell you, other than to just say it. The boat owner was murdered. We believe he was murdered so that his boat could be taken. Given this new information, I want to rule out the possibility that the boater intentionally targeted you and Miss Edwards."

Erin tensed and tried to wrap her mind around what he was saying. "I'm so sorry that someone was murdered. Are there any other leads you're tracking? Other possible motivation for the murder or other targets? I can't think of any reason why Carissa and I would be targeted."

"I agree it was probably an accident, and you and Miss Edwards were simply at the wrong place at the wrong time. But I think it prudent to be certain and to rule out that the boating incident was deliberate."

Erin cracked the window for more air. "Thank you for your thoroughness. Have you spoken with Carissa? Does she know?"

"Yes. And I'd like to talk to you in more detail. Miss Edwards shared that you're in Montana. Can you come back to Seattle for additional questioning?"

"At the moment, I'm on the East Coast on a business trip. What else can I do to help? I'm happy to speak with you over the phone or even a video chat for the time being."

"Just answer a few questions for me now. Can you think of anyone who would want to harm you?"

"No. There's . . . just no reason."

"No ex-boyfriends?"

Erin glanced at Nathan. "I can only speak for myself when I say there are no past boyfriends who would want to harm me."

Nathan stared straight ahead and worked his jaw.

Erin kept her breaths even. "I can't speak for Carissa, though. But I can't believe anyone would try to hurt her. Still, I think you're right to cover all the bases." *God, keep Carissa safe.*

"She'll be coming in to talk to me this afternoon. What about someone connected with your job as a forensic evaluator for the State of Washington?"

Erin squeezed her eyes shut and racked her brain. Had someone been unhappy, displeased with the outcome of a case due to something she'd written in a report? "I'm behind the scenes. I review criminal and civil information, write up relevant history for those who struggle with mental health issues. I've . . . I've never been called upon as an expert witness even. As far as I know, I have no enemies."

"I've been looking into this. Your report is what tells the court if someone is competent to stand trial, isn't that correct?"

She cleared her throat. "Um . . . well . . . yes. But the outcomes of the reports are in the hands of legal professionals. As for my job, I haven't been working in this position all that long. In fact, I'm working under a more senior evaluator. I can't think of anyone who would target me."

"Well, keep thinking on it, and please contact me if you remember something."

"I promise I'll get back to you if I think of anything that could help."

"I would appreciate it, but one more thing."

"Yes?"

"Miss Edwards shared that you have a crime podcast."

Erin closed her eyes. "Yes."

"And no one could have targeted you for that?"

"The podcast is anonymous, in that I use pseudonyms."

"Why keep it a secret?"

Nathan slowed as he drove through a neighborhood. Erin really wanted to focus on the moment, their joint investigation into this cold case. At the moment, they didn't even know what cold case Newt had been looking into.

"Detective Munson, as I mentioned, I'm traveling and I'm just about to go into my meeting. As I told Carissa, I don't want to cause any disruption or complications with my job with the state even though my *Missing Children* podcast has nothing to do with the cases I dive into there."

"Right. You focus on cold cases."

"So, you listened?"

"Yes. I'm listening to the current episode and can't wait for the next one."

Because she had a new fan? Or he was fishing?

"I'd like to chat some more. Can you call me tomorrow?"

He was persistent, she'd give him that.

"I'm not sure because of the nature of my current business trip. Let's try for ten a.m. I'll confirm with you tomorrow."

"You're on the East Coast. That'll be seven my time."

"You're not an early riser?"

"Tell you what, I'll call you at ten my time, and that'll be one for you. We can play phone tag for a bit, and then eventually, I'll come see you in Montana if we don't connect."

Erin couldn't help but smile. "I appreciate your hard work, Detective. We'll connect one way or another. I hope and pray you find the murderer." *And that it has nothing at all to do with me or Carissa.*

How could it?

Nathan parked the vehicle against the curb under a sprawling old oak tree and let the engine idle. "I'm afraid to ask what that was about, though I did get the gist of it. Let me get this right. Someone tried to kill you in Seattle and you didn't tell me?"

"First, I don't know that's what happened. I was in a boating accident. In fact, you called me on the cusp of that. I was still standing on my rescuers' boat with a blanket wrapped around me when you called to tell me about Mom. Carissa was the one to suffer the most. Her kayak was broken in half, and she got knocked out and drowned. They had to revive her. We thought . . . The boat seemed to veer toward us. I thought it was just a freak accident."

"I heard something about the boat owner being murdered, and now the detective wants to know about people who might want to harm you. Erin, what's going on?"

She read the other question, the silent question, in his eyes. *Why didn't you tell me?*

"I don't know what's going on, and Nathan, really, we both have so much on our plates. I wanted to push that incident to the far recesses of my mind." She covered her face. *Just hold it together a little longer.* Erin dropped her hands. "Can we just focus on one thing at a time? We're here, and we need to get this over with before something else happens, okay?"

"Sure. But we're talking about this later."

"Okay. Let's go see if we can't find those articles Dwayne gave your dad and figure out what cold case he was looking into."

He stared at her. "I remember you always wanted to study criminal minds."

While she considered his statement, she noted the house numbers. Newt's home sat back from the road. A tree with purple blooms blocked the view, but she could still make out black shutters against white siding and the red brick along the basement. "I thought that's what I wanted. But now I spend too many hours reading about, interviewing, and diving deep into those minds."

A shudder crawled over her.

"Then why do you do it?"

She studied him. Why did he want to know? "To find the answers, Nathan. It's the same for cold cases. Answers bring closure. And that's what we're hoping to do today." She pushed the car door open, but he grabbed her hand and prevented her from stepping out.

"Erin, wait. Promise you'll tell me everything about Seattle when we're done here."

She nodded but didn't voice promises she might not keep. Nathan released her hand, then he got out too and joined her on the other side of the silver rental sedan.

"I'm worried about you," he said.

"You have enough to worry about with your father and this case." She crossed her arms and glanced at the neighborhood houses and the old trees that lined the street, spreading out their branches to give shade.

Nathan jammed his hands into his pockets and stood next to her. She released a slow breath and relaxed. She was glad she'd been with Nathan when she got that call. Standing next to him now, she felt safe and protected. And really, through all of it, even in the face of his own trials, Nathan had been there for her.

But she shouldn't start depending on him too much, not like she was at the moment, because, well, Nathan deserved better than her. He deserved someone who didn't carry the weight of a dark past.

EIGHTEEN

Tension gripped Nathan's shoulders and crawled down his back, spreading through his whole body, as he stood next to Erin across the street from Dad's house.

Breathe in. Breathe out.

He inched closer to Erin. After what he'd just overheard about an incident she experienced in Washington, his protective instincts had kicked into overdrive. Erin had tried to hide that the call had upset her, so he wouldn't press her for more information now. She was right—they were here and needed to focus on the task at hand. The sooner they figured out a few things here in the Boston area, the faster they could focus on what happened back in Washington as well as in Montana.

"Are you ready?" He glanced at her.

She nodded.

Together they crossed the street, then walked up the side-walk to the front door. Palms sweating, Nathan paused. Erin turned to the side, watching the neighborhood.

Would he find answers here? He tugged his father's key ring

out of his pocket and thrust the key into the keyhole, holding his breath as if there was any doubt it would work. It clicked, and he turned the knob and cracked the door open, hesitating before pushing it all the way. The back of his neck prickled.

"What are you waiting for?" she whispered.

He didn't want to give onlooking neighbors cause for concern, because after all, he was simply stopping by his father's house to check on things while Dad was in the hospital. Still, he slipped his gun out of its holster, glad he'd brought the weapon along.

"I'm just listening to my gut. Stay right behind me." He opened the door and slipped inside.

Erin kept close on his heels, then stepped to the side against the wall. "Oh my . . ."

His sentiments exactly.

Furniture had been overturned. Lamps broken. Pictures ripped from the walls and thrown on the floor. Shattered glass covered the area rug.

Erin sucked in a breath. Nathan's heart pounded at the sight of the living room. He flipped the lights on to get a better look.

"Should we call the police?"

"You call them while I check out the rest of—"

A thump sounded from somewhere in the house. Nathan stiffened and glanced at Erin. Her eyes widened.

He lifted his weapon, prepared to clear the house. "Stay here."

"Be careful," she whispered and bent down to pick up a fallen brass lampstand. She held it like a bat, then shrugged. "I need a weapon too." In the other hand, she held her cell and called 911.

He hated leaving her alone, but he wouldn't take her with him to face off with whoever remained in the house. He crept forward across the space and tried to avoid stepping on glass or anything else that might make a sound. He'd only visited the house twice since Dad had moved here, and tried to remember, to visualize the layout in his head. Three bedrooms down the hall at the back of the house. The master at the front. Dad used one of the bedrooms for an office.

A clank resounded from the back.

Whoever had wrecked the house was still there. Nathan's pulse kicked up as he quietly approached the back bedroom, his gun raised. He stopped in the doorway to watch a muscular guy with red hair pulling books from a shelf against the far wall, too focused on his task to realize that someone else had entered the house.

"Police. Hold it right there." Nathan spoke through gritted teeth. "Lift your hands where I can see them."

Instead of complying, the man whipped around and threw a heavy book toward Nathan's head. He dodged it as Ginger Man shifted to grip the shelf, groaning as he rocked it forward, then he shoved the whole bookshelf over. It came toward where Nathan stood watching. Books filled his vision as they spilled out everywhere. Nathan stepped back so he wouldn't get trapped under the shelf as the man scrambled over the top, using it as a jump point to dive right into Nathan.

Ginger Man's body slammed into Nathan, and they both crashed to the floor. The added weight of the man on top knocked the breath from Nathan. And the gun from his hand. Pain ignited in his back where he'd gotten the stitches. A hefty fist came toward him and he twisted, then kicked the man completely off. Nathan scrambled to his feet, climbing over books and broken shards of glass littering the floor.

His gun had slid under the one shelf that remained standing. Nathan dove toward Ginger Man while dodging another punch. He landed his own smack in the man's face. Blood burst from the man's nose, but he didn't seem to notice as he kicked Nathan in the gut, then jabbed him in the solar plexus.

Doubling over, Nathan pushed past the pain. He couldn't let

Ginger Man get away. Reaching under the shelf for his gun, he wrapped his hand around the weapon and jockeyed to stand in the doorway, blocking Ginger Man's escape.

The man's lips twisted into a smirk as he lifted a chair and tossed it through the window. He jumped through the opening before Nathan could reach him. The man appeared to be a hardened criminal, experienced at avoiding the law, and knew Nathan wouldn't shoot him.

At the window, he watched the redheaded man race across the backyard and jump the fence. If Nathan was going to catch him, he'd better go now. He eyed the shards still lining the window frame and prepared to jump through.

"Nathan!" Erin's voice pulled him back from the edge.

He couldn't leave her alone in this volatile situation. What was he thinking? He worked to catch his breath and turned to face her. She still held the brass lamp as if she wasn't afraid to use it.

Concern filled her eyes. "Are you okay?"

He nodded as he caught his breath, glancing outside again. Ginger Man was long gone. Nathan backed away from the window, stepped over the books, and skirted the shelf. He stood near the doorway next to her and looked at the mess.

"What happened? Or should I bother asking? It seems obvious." She touched his face.

He shrank away from the pain.

"You're hurt."

"It's nothing."

"You're bleeding. I wouldn't call it nothing. I hope you don't need more stitches, only this time in your face." A flicker of amusement danced in her eyes. She was trying to lighten the mood.

He bit back his frustration so he didn't direct it at her. Still . . . "I let him get the best of me. I had a gun on him, but he wasn't afraid of it. Didn't think I would shoot."

"Because you wouldn't."

He shrugged. "He wasn't threatening my life by throwing books at me."

She looked him up and down. "Are you sure?"

"Hey, I gave as good as I got."

She held up her cell. "I called the police. They should be here any minute."

"It's taking them too long." His stitches throbbed, and he hoped he hadn't torn them, but he would worry about that later.

"It's only been a couple of minutes."

It felt like a lifetime.

Navigating this strange situation with the police district for which Dad worked would be interesting. For Nathan's part, he hadn't known the house would be ransacked when he got here, though a small part of him had suspected it. "Dad's house is a crime scene now."

"Should we leave?" Erin tucked her hair behind both ears, her expression somber. "This feels awkward."

"I'm not leaving before I look at Dad's crime board." Nathan gestured to the wall behind Erin.

She angled her face over her shoulder, then turned to face the board. "Oh. Now we're talking. This might actually make the trip here worth it."

Names and pictures and photographs edged around a big white space. Lines were drawn connecting the images and information. "Looks like some missing information."

Erin approached and lifted her fingers to hover over the clearly demarcated empty space, though she didn't actually touch it. "Do you think the articles that Dwayne gave Newt were here?"

"I'm not sure. He said he was working on a case that reminded him of the articles. I would think they wouldn't be the center of his investigation." Sirens finally blared in the distance. "They're almost here. We should look around to see if we can find the articles before it's too late."

"You don't think the man who was going through the office got them?" she asked.

"No."

"Why not?" Erin asked. "It seems the cold case is important and could be the catalyst for everything that's happened."

Nathan took in the names scribbled on the board. *What were you working on, Dad?* He leaned closer and pulled tape off one edge of the empty white space to examine it. A small sliver of paper was stuck to the tape. "You could be right. The articles could have been at the center of this crime board. Whatever was there, I'm guessing that Dad took them down before he left."

"I'd say it's a good guess," Erin said. "He was told not to continue looking into that case, so he took down the articles as a show of compliance, while . . . um . . . he continued his investigation." She reached into her purse and lifted out her iPad to take pictures. "We can use this. Do you think the man in here was looking for the articles too?"

While she took pictures, Nathan glanced around the office. "I'm not sure what the guy was looking for. I can't imagine he would tear the place up for an article or two about a cold case. Articles can be found in newspaper archives online. The advantage he has is that he probably already knows the cold case. So again, why was he here?"

"He could have wanted to remove the articles so the cold case your father was working on wouldn't be discovered." She shrugged. "It's just a thought. As for us, we can go online. We don't necessarily *need* the articles Dwayne gave your father anymore."

"What are you talking about?" he asked.

"With the crime board, we can work backward. Look at how all these notes and names connect and then cross-reference everything." She put her iPad away in her purse. "Sure, that will take more time, but it's something to work with."

Why hadn't he thought of that? Henry hadn't wanted him investigating because he was too close. Understandable. Maybe being too close truly did mess with his ability to think clearly. He pinched his nose as he squeezed his eyes shut. And sensed the moment Erin moved closer. His breathing hitched at her proximity, and he opened his eyes. Her blue-green gaze held his, and he had the sudden urge, the sudden need to pull her into his arms—for no reason and for a thousand reasons all at the same time.

Erin had always scrambled his mind, ignited his heart, and it looked like nothing about that had changed.

Before he could reach for her, she took a step back and smiled.

"Don't worry, Nathan. Remember, you *hired* me to look into this, and you've come with me to both protect me and offer your insights." Her eyes grew intense—the blue seemed to explode with color. "Do you understand?"

"Yeah. You've got my back."

Erin wasn't a private investigator, but she was privately consulting as a criminal psychologist in case the authorities grilled Nathan about his activities here.

What would I do without you?

NINETEEN

Erin glanced around the floor of the office—books all over. Photographs of Nathan with his father. Awards. Newt with Dwayne years before he died in the SAR incident. "I wish we had time to look. This could be our last chance, at least for a while."

"Let's go welcome the police." He gestured for her to follow and they stepped carefully around the ransacked office, down the hallway, and into the living room.

Erin followed Nathan out onto the porch as a cruiser pulled up to the drive, and two patrol officers—one stocky and in his midforties and the other looked all of fifteen—jumped out and rushed up to the yard, their weapons drawn.

Nathan stepped off the porch. "Hello! We called you. I'm Nathan Campbell, and this is Dr. Erin Larson. This is my father's house."

Nathan produced his identification in addition to his law enforcement credentials. The officers put away their weapons. Erin stepped from the porch and approached them.

"I'm Officer Lincoln," the stocky, older officer said. "And this is Officer Cruise."

"My father's in the hospital in Montana," Nathan said. "I

came out here to check on the house, and we found it ran-sacked and the intruder still inside. He was in the office, look-ing through my dad's things. When he saw me, he attacked me, then jumped out the window and fled on foot through the adjoining yards."

Officer Lincoln wrote in his notepad. "Can you give me a description of the man you claim was inside the house and attacked you?"

Nathan described the man in detail. "And I gave him a bloody nose."

"I'll secure the scene." Officer Cruise swiveled on his heels, then marched toward the home.

"Good," Nathan said. "You guys will call in your forensics unit to get prints and search for evidence, right?"

"I don't know how things are done in Montana, but here in the city, a break-in is a low priority." Lincoln snapped his notebook shut.

Erin couldn't tell if the words were meant as an insult to Nathan, who worked law enforcement for a low-crime region in the country, or maybe she was being too sensitive, feeling defensive on Nathan's behalf.

"I don't think you understand," Nathan said. "My father is *Detective* Newt Campbell of the Gifford PD. You might know him. He was shot while visiting me in Montana. This break-in could be related to his shooting."

Officer Lincoln nodded and might have responded, but his attention was drawn to another cruiser pulling up to the curb. Out stepped two men, one of them in plain clothes, though a badge hung around his neck. A detective.

Erin distanced herself from the growing contingency of law enforcement and stood back on the edge of the lawn, taking in the picture. Absorbing everything about the house and the neighborhood. A few neighbors and passersby had slowed or stood nearby to watch. She didn't see the redheaded intruder among them. Was he watching them from somewhere else—behind a bush or a window somewhere—right now? Perhaps the police had not taken an interest in Newt's home before, but now they certainly would.

Erin glanced at their rental car across the street and noticed a thirtysomething man in a Red Sox cap walking on the sidewalk. He turned around and walked back again. Nothing unusual about that until the third time. Maybe he was simply watching the unfolding scene regarding a neighborhood home—a cop's home.

She returned her attention to the house, where still-in-high-school Officer Cruise had finished securing yellow crime scene tape, cordoning off the house. It certainly looked like they were making the house break-in a priority. Nathan stepped away from the officers and started toward her, his expression grim.

He approached and stood next to her, his frustration palpable.

"Well, what now?" she asked.

"I have a feeling I should expect to hear from Henry, and he's not going to be happy. My presence here at the home is going to go to the top, and Dad's boss will probably call mine."

"But like you said, you were here to check on your dad's home, nothing more."

"Yeah. True. But nobody is going to fully buy that story now. Remember what I told you—Henry assured Dad's boss, Lieutenant Sullivan, that no one would dig into it. I'm not exactly sure what he was referring to, but here I am, digging."

He shifted his gaze to look across the street. She followed and spotted the same man walking back and forth. "That guy. He's been watching us and pacing. He isn't the guy you fought in the house, is he?" Maybe his hair was red under the cap.

"No. He's probably just a curious neighbor. If he's so curious, he might have seen something."

Nathan crossed the street, and Erin joined him. They passed

the rental car and walked toward the man. When he saw them heading his way, he immediately turned to walk in the opposite direction, changing up his pattern a bit. That told her something.

Nathan picked up his pace at the sidewalk. "Hey! Hey, buddy. Can I talk to you?"

The man took off, sprinting down the sidewalk, and raced around the corner at the intersection.

"Go after him!" Erin slowed. She was a runner, but not a sprinter. Her bum ankle wouldn't stand the stress of chasing after the guy.

Nathan hesitated. "I don't want to leave you."

"I'm here with the other cops. Just don't pull your stitches, okay?"

But Nathan had already taken off, and she wasn't sure he'd even heard her cautionary words.

Lord, please protect him! And help us get answers.

Erin wished Nathan had left her the keys to the rental car now. She leaned against it, then spotted a small slip of paper tucked under the windshield wiper. Erin didn't reach for it. Not yet. She remained in place next to the car.

A van pulled up to the curb in front of Newt's house—the GPD evidence team, she assumed. Either they'd gotten a warrant or Nathan had power of attorney and had given permission. She and Nathan certainly hadn't expected things to unfold this way. Still, maybe walking in on an intruder had been a good thing, because now the local police would be examining the house too. And from the sounds of it, they hadn't searched the house—at least not extensively—before this moment. This could have lit the required fires to get answers.

However, the way Nathan had explained things, his father had been nervous about others, including his own fellow officers, knowing what he was up to. Erin watched the house and law enforcement faces involved. A figure drew her attention from the house—Nathan strode down the sidewalk toward her, gasping for breath like he'd been on the chase of his life.

He stopped in front of her. He leaned over, hands on his thighs.

Erin waited for him to catch his breath, then finally said, "I take it you didn't catch him."

"He just . . . disappeared." He pushed off his thighs and rose to full height.

His brown eyes—usually warm and inviting—had grown dark.

"I'm going to give you permission now. Next time, please leave me. Or I'll give chase with you." She glanced across the street at the activity. "Looks like they're taking the break-in to the next level."

He dipped his chin, his eyes on the house across the street. "Let's get out of here."

"Wait, don't you want to hang around? Or even watch them to see what they find?"

"I think we have all we need at the moment. Besides, they're not going to let me any closer."

He started toward the door, then paused as he noticed the slip of paper stuck in the wiper.

She stared at the note too. "I saw that but was waiting for you to open it. I wonder if it's from our friend, the one you chased."

"Let's find out."

He glanced around, making sure no one was watching, before he snatched the paper free of the wiper as he clicked the key fob. Erin got in on the passenger side while Nathan slid into the driver's seat. He turned on the vehicle, along with the air conditioner—the day had grown warm.

"Are you going to read it?" She was surprised he hadn't opened it the instant he took hold of it.

"Yes." He unfolded the paper and held it so that she could read the scribbled words along with him.

8:00 P.M. Cooper Hill Burying Ground.

"A cemetery?" She crinkled her nose. "Why a cemetery?"

"I don't know. But my guess is the guy I chased left the note."

"When I first spotted him, he was moving away from our vehicle, so that's my assumption too. And if that's the case, he obviously didn't want to talk to you out here in the open and in broad daylight. But I'd prefer meeting him at a diner or something. Not a *burying ground*. You can't get creepier than that, especially in the dark."

"It won't be dark at eight. Maybe he wanted to meet before dark, but when the cemetery will likely be completely empty."

Nathan folded the paper and handed it to her. She pulled out a small Ziploc baggie and stuck it inside.

At Nathan's surprised look, she shrugged and said, "In case we need to get prints later."

Steering the rental from the curb, Nathan drove slowly down the street and left the police contingent at his father's house behind. "Let's go check in to our hotel and grab something to eat."

"I'd like to look at the pictures I took of the crime board before we go meet this guy."

"You're not going. It's too dangerous. I don't know what I'm walking into."

"Exactly why you need me along. You asked for my help, so let me do it." She had three hours to make him see reason.

TWENTY

fter checking in to their ridiculously priced hotel in downtown Boston, Nathan sat across from Erin at Biryani's Italian Restaurant a couple of blocks down. He'd opted for a hotel with more security. The price was worth it.

The restaurant afforded a good view of the street with tables near the window, but under the circumstances, he wouldn't make them an easy target and chose to sit at a small booth in the back corner. He wished, too, that the circumstances of their dinner together were altogether different.

Just two old friends catching up would be preferable to this scenario.

Then again, he wasn't sure he could ever think of Erin as nothing more than a friend. They had too much history. Too many shared memories. Even now her soft smile captured his heart, making him wish for so much more with her. A second chance.

That would never happen, but what did he know? He couldn't have predicted these circumstances under which he would find himself eating at a fancy restaurant with Dr. Erin Larson again.

But this was not a date.

She skimmed the menu, and her gaze flicked up. Tonight her ever-changing blue-green eyes were a little greener. The lighting and the earth tones must have something to do with it. But he had a feeling her changing eyes—a color he could never quite pin down—were a mere reflection of Erin. She was hard to read, hard to pin down, maybe even hard to truly know.

But he didn't want to think about their past and focused again on her eyes. Gorgeous eyes that had always drawn him in. At the sudden pounding of his traitorous heart, he perused his own menu.

A thought hit him. "You know, we could just get out of here and grab some bags of Cheetos. I saw a small grocer across the street."

Erin peered at him over the top of her menu. "Maybe later."

Dressed in a white shirt and black pants, their waiter, Sergio, approached to take their orders. Nathan asked for a steak—rib eye, medium, and a side of pasta.

Erin snapped her menu closed and asked for a burger.

The dark-haired Sergio arched a brow. "We don't have burgers."

"It's on the kids' menu." Erin offered her most brilliant smile. "And I want a burger."

Sergio returned her smile, his attempt to cover a sigh, then nodded and left.

Erin slipped a hand over her lips, then dropped it. "Sorry. I didn't mean to embarrass you."

"I'm not embarrassed."

"Oh, right. This isn't a date." She shifted forward and twisted her mouth up. "But it's like an alternaht universe—you, me, sitting hee-ah in a fancy Boston restuh-raunt togetheh. It's just wee-ud."

"That's a great Boston accent, by the way. You're a natural."

"Thanks." A soft laugh escaped her lips as she sat back.

He loved her laugh. She was cute, so cute. So beautiful.

Great sense of humor. The remnants of his past love for her stirred. He had kicked dust over them, but he would need to do more than kick. He needed a big shovel to bury them much deeper if they stirred up so easily.

He couldn't help but chuckle, even in the midst of their private investigative excursion—because he couldn't really call it an investigation. Either way—investigation, excursion—it was quickly turning into a predicament. "We have to get what we need and get out. Dad wasn't supposed to be working on this case that almost got him killed." He rubbed his forehead. "I'm not too proud to admit I made a mistake. I shouldn't have brought you into this."

"Lives are at stake."

What lives, Dad? Well, besides yours.

And Erin's. And if he counted the Seattle incident, if she had been targeted, she could be in double the danger. He stared at the flickering candle in the middle of the table. When he decided to head this way to get a few answers, it seemed straightforward. He wanted to stick to the straight and narrow and be a good, upstanding cop. Never disobey a directive.

This wasn't how it was supposed to be. He could probably kiss that promotion to sergeant goodbye. Nathan wasn't promotion material, as things stood right now. Would Dad be disappointed? Well, if he ever woke up. And would he even care?

"You can't afford to expend energy on regrets." Erin's words pulled him back to the moment. "I'm here. We're here. Move on. Go forward."

"Fine. If you go with me tonight, that means on the flight back to Montana you're telling me about everything that happened in Seattle."

Her lips turned downward. "That kind of seemed out of nowhere."

"It's not out of nowhere. I haven't stopped thinking about it since you got the call from the detective. But as you said, we're here, so we need to focus on what we can find out."

"Agreed." She'd pulled up the image of Dad's crime board on her iPad, then zoomed in to enlarge the image. "We can look at the details." She zoomed out. "And then stand back and take in the big picture. Remember, we're working this backward so we can find the cold case and the connection— the reason your father was shot. Bottom line, we'll use all the information available."

Your reasons had better be good, Dad. They'd better be good.

"What's your take on this, Erin? I mean, you evaluate and assess. I heard what you told the Seattle detective. What do you think about my father's state of mind, given what I told you?"

The restaurant lights were low and the candle flickered, reflecting in her eyes as light danced across her face. "It takes a lot more than a story told secondhand to evaluate, Nathan. Surely you know that." She opened her mouth, hesitating, as if she might say more.

Should he push her? He rubbed his jaw. "While I'm sure that's true, you still have an opinion, and I want to hear it."

She reached across and pressed her hand over his hand, sending a surge through him—but that surge went much deeper than a physical attraction. Nathan struggled to listen to her soft words above his pounding heart.

"I think your father believed himself to be a confident, take-charge problem-solver who was taking action, risking it all to bring about justice. In the face of this risk, he was under tremendous pressure and wanted to maintain control of his environment, his actions, and his emotions. Unfortunately, he couldn't control everything. Like what happened at the river."

Her eyes welled with tears that didn't spill over, and she withdrew her hand as she stared into the flickering candle. "Cops. They protect the rest of us from the ugliest crimes, the evil we don't want to know exists. The monsters that creep into the night and take our children. In protecting us, they aren't allowed to experience the full range of a normal human's response, because that would mean losing control. People hate them for doing their job. Making those arrests. Controlling the crowd. And yes, sometimes using physical force when necessary. Even deadly force. In all of this, they are under-appreciated."

She lifted her gaze to him then, and he couldn't speak, his heartbeat pounding in his throat. All of this she had learned from observing and evaluating criminals?

"I believe your father is a good cop because he's your father, Nathan, and you're a good cop. Good cops get the bad guys. They win the fight and save the victim—" She dropped her gaze to her hands on the table. "But not every battle is won. All you can do is try."

And if this battle was lost, who else would be harmed or worse—murdered?

TWENTY-ONE

Erin dared to lift her gaze to Nathan and wished she hadn't. His eyes were riveted on her.

What was he thinking? That she'd lost her mind? She was overly dramatic?

She'd only meant to encourage him with the truth as she saw it. Her view came from dealing with the ever-growing population of the criminally minded and the psychopaths out there. People had no idea what law enforcement went through to bring these people in, the battles they had to fight under great restrictions, and then the battles they faced again when defense attorneys tried to free the worst sorts of criminals on technicalities.

Clearing her throat, breaking the spell, Erin moved the candle to the side of the table against the wall and placed the tablet in the center between them. Time to get down to business.

He moved to sit next to her instead of across from her. She could have flipped the tablet so he could see, but this made it easier for them to study.

Except for the fact that he was close, and that was a distraction.

They both stared at the tablet—the image of the crime board Erin had taken—in silence. *What are we doing again?* She found it hard to think with him so close, and she couldn't afford anything but a clear mind.

"So much was erased already," Nathan said. "I hope we can figure it out with only the peripheral details."

"As I said, we'll work it in reverse and hope for the best."

"Too bad I can't just walk into the Gifford PD and ask about the case Dad had been removed from."

His cell rang, and he glanced at the screen. The look he shot Erin told her he wasn't happy about the call, and then the way he slinked down in the chair confirmed it.

"Great timing," he said.

"Who is it?"

He eyed his cell. "I should answer and get this over with. I've been expecting this call."

Ah. "Henry."

Nathan nodded and put his cell on speaker but turned down the sound so only they would be able to hear. "Campbell here."

"Nathan! What in the world are you doing in Boston?"

"I wanted to check on Dad's house to make sure everything was okay. It wasn't. I interrupted a burglary in process."

"So I hear. I thought we agreed you would not be investigating your dad's shooting."

He glanced at Erin.

Would Nathan bring her into this now? Or would that make any difference to Henry at all?

Nathan scratched his head. "Technically, I wasn't investigating his shooting. I simply wanted—"

"Save it," Henry said. "We both know you didn't fly out to Boston to *check* on his house. I gave you time off to spend with him and to take it easy after what you've gone through. If you're going to work, you can hightail it right back here and I'll put you on the Rocky Mountain Courage Memorial case."

What? Erin leaned closer as if she could somehow force Henry's explanation out of him this instant.

"I thought we closed that case," Nathan said.

"It was dead, not closed. But it has been revived. Another vandalism occurred last night."

Oh no. Erin lifted her gaze to Nathan.

Erin wanted to ask Henry for the details if Nathan wouldn't, but she doubted he wanted Henry to know she was listening to the call.

"You need to put someone else on that, because I won't be back for a couple of days." Nathan crossed his arms as if Henry could see his resolve.

"Nathan."

"You gave me two weeks off, and you can't change that on me."

"Your actions could interfere with the investigation. I know you don't want this to end in a miscarriage of justice, do you?"

It was then that the waiter showed up with their food. Sergio gingerly placed Nathan's steak in front of him, then set Erin's hamburger in front of her.

Erin nodded and quietly thanked the waiter, who slipped away so he wouldn't disturb the serious conversation. Nathan cringed at Henry's words but waited until the waiter was gone to respond. Erin couldn't believe he still had the cell on speaker, but Nathan apparently wanted her privy to this conversation. A witness, perhaps.

"Of course not."

"Or worse, I might have to suspend you. You're a good detective. You're the son of one of my best friends, so please do not force my hand on this."

Nathan leaned in and spoke in a hushed voice. "Henry, you

gave me some leeway. Remember that? I haven't tampered with anything. I'm not lying or hiding evidence or touching it or messing with it in any way. I've . . . well, I've hired someone to help."

Silence met him on the line.

"Why? Because you don't trust your fellow detectives?" Both hurt and anger blasted across the distance through his cell.

Nathan sagged. "Look, I'm in a precarious position. We need to talk when I get back, and I'll explain everything." Nathan ended the call without another word.

Erin stared at him.

He shrugged and averted his gaze. "There's nothing more I want to hear from him."

Erin keenly felt his apprehension. She also heard his stomach rumble. Poor guy, because he probably wasn't in the mood to eat now.

"Nathan, I'm sorry. Maybe you shouldn't have taken the call, after all."

"Yeah, well, I did."

"Your boss is working off the same lack of information that you are. I suggest we get as much information as we can, and then when you return and face him, you can extend an olive branch in the form of a lead only you could have found, because only you knew what your father had said. If you ask me, he sounded more like a father figure who is worried about you, a man he considers like a son to him."

"Yeah, well, I already have a father, and he's lying in a hospital with a gunshot wound to the head."

TWENTY-TWO

He'd fought so hard to work his way into a promotion for the future, to prove himself to his boss, and yes, to his father. To his family and friends. And for what? For it all to go down the toilet now?

He'd wanted to confide in Henry, and would have, but for that conversation he'd overheard. Nathan needed to confront Henry about that as soon as he returned, but he absolutely was not giving up the lead that had been handed to him today. Someone wanted to talk.

To Nathan.

Not the Gifford PD detective who had shown up at Dad's house—Detective Trap.

On the drive from Dad's house to the hotel, Nathan had told Erin about his conversation with Detective Trap. The detective shared that he'd been assigned to look at his father's past cases to see if the shooting could be some sort of reprisal or payback. He also said he hadn't been by Dad's house before today. Trap's superior had suggested that Dad's shooting was a Montana-style drive-by shooting, aka a hunting accident. Still, Dad's case was Detective Trap's priority. Nobody shoots a cop and gets away with it. The conversation with the detective encouraged Nathan. Still, while the Gifford PD had assured Henry they would look into his past cases with diligence, Sullivan had apparently extracted from Henry an agreement that the Grayback detectives wouldn't dig too deeply. Things weren't adding up for Nathan.

God, help me figure this out.

Erin pressed her hand over his and drew his attention back. He left his hand where it was and tried to savor the warmth and care pouring from her.

"I know you're upset, but let's eat and get out of here. You did the right thing coming here. If we hadn't arrived today, then the intruder could have taken down the entire crime board."

She removed her hand—and he keenly felt the disconnect—and focused on her burger.

He scratched his head, then cut into his steak. Took a bite and tried to savor what would on any other day taste amazing. But right now, it tasted like how he imagined a piece of wood might taste.

He glanced at Erin, who'd taken a bite of her burger but barely chewed. He knew that look. "What are you thinking?"

She finished chewing, then played with a french fry. "What if we're going about this all wrong? Your father warned you. He didn't want anyone to know he was looking into this case. We assume someone took your father out because they didn't want him looking deeper, or they wanted to silence him for what he'd already discovered. But the shooter had to have known that shooting a cop would only ramp up the investigation."

"What are you getting at?"

"Maybe that was the point. The goal. The shooter wanted to uncover the truth, and now no one is going to shut down a search into whatever your father was looking into."

Or they could try to shut it down, cover it up, but they would fail. Nathan chewed on another piece of steak. Finished, he said, "I'm going to have to think on that one."

"It's something to consider, but I agree it seems far-fetched. Someone who wanted the truth to come out probably wouldn't shoot someone in the process. But I want to put all possibilities on the table for consideration." She took another bite of her burger.

"Let's hope our lead at the cemetery will pan out." A subtle pain ignited and shifted to a slow pounding in his head. Nathan glanced at his watch. "We have an hour and a half before the meeting to which you will not be going. I need you to stay behind and see what you can find out from the crime board."

Because she didn't argue, Erin was either ignoring him or hadn't heard him as she finished off her burger. "Okay, then, let's put the time to some good use." She peered at Dad's crime board on her tablet. "We can see names—Jimmy Delaney. Jason Cain. Jamie McPherson. And Cobbs and Byrne. Looks like the first names have been wiped away. The names are written around the edges with arrows to the center, which is now a big fat blank. What kind of detective is your father? Homicide?"

He nodded. "I'm RISS authorized. I can call the Regional Information Sharing System and find out more about these names. But first I want to get all the information so I can make one call. See if any of them already have a criminal record." That was, if Henry didn't remove his interagency access after that conversation they'd just had. "But for tonight, how about we start with the Internet? Just a plain old Google search. Let's find out as much as we can before my clandestine meeting so I won't be blindsided."

"Sure. We can also search your father's name and see what turns up in the newspaper or online articles, especially recent information."

He squeezed his fists. This felt so low-tech. Nathan wished

he could simply ask his dad what he had been working on. He'd asked Detective Trap, who simply replied that Dad's cases had been transferred to other detectives, but none of them had stood out. Dad hadn't wanted Nathan talking about his case or drawing attention to himself because of the danger factor, and that's exactly what he'd done. In fact, Nathan could bring more danger to Dad if he wasn't careful.

What about Mom? What about Erin? Nathan lifted his gaze to peer at her. She studied her iPad. Sergio approached again and poured more water for them. Nathan asked for the check.

Erin nibbled on a few fries that were left. "Everything costs a lot more here. Never thought I'd pay twenty-five dollars for a hamburger on the kids' menu."

"A restaurant like this, you might as well have gone for the steak."

She lifted her tablet. "I'm sending you the crime board image."

His cell dinged with the message. He glanced at the image of the board on his cell, lifted the names, and put them in the search engine. He assumed Erin did the same using her own search parameters.

"I found something." She pointed at the iPad. "This article on Jimmy Delaney came up immediately. See what you think."

He leaned closer and skimmed the article. "So, basically, it says this Jimmy 'the Jackhammer' Delaney was killed in re-taliation. He'd allegedly accidentally ran over a guy who was riding his bike, the youngest son of a mob boss. Delaney was also murdered in front of his house—an action that violates mob rules of respect."

Dread curdled in his gut. "So . . . what? The unknown gun-man now likely has a target on his back too, for breaking the rules of engagement?" Nathan read more details from the article. "Sounds like the police agree. They say he'd be safer in prison because mob gangsters in danger of reprisal are kept separately and with a high level of security. But they don't know who was behind the hit yet."

"That makes sense. The mob has a reputation of brutality when it comes to vengeance," she said.

Just how much had she dealt with mobsters in her capacity as a criminal psychologist?

"Was this the murder Dad was investigating?" He sure hoped not.

"I don't know. Maybe not. There's another name on the whiteboard. Jason Cain. I found an article about a man by that name. I don't know if it's the same man on the whiteboard, but since he was killed in a hit-and-run, that makes his death suspicious." She shook her head. "In his seventies, he worked as a greeter at a big-box store down in South Carolina and was just out walking his dog when he was killed."

Nathan scratched his head. "Okay. Let's keep searching, and then we'll see how they fit together. I have to say, I wish we hadn't veered into mob territory."

"The Irish Mob, to be more specific—especially in South Boston."

"And you know this how?"

"I'm a quick study." She smiled but kept her eyes on her iPad.

He pushed his plate aside and crossed his arms, leaning against the table. "And while some people think the mob died out years ago, it's very much alive and well, though the ranks and numbers have diminished. Basically, the mob isn't like it used to be since the Feds gutted them and so many of their ranks, including the crime bosses, have been imprisoned. But they're like a hydra. Cut off its head and more rise up to take its place. I hear the mob is resurging."

"Sounds like you're a quick study too."

"I read about the WITSEC program—the Witness Security Program run by the US Marshals—and how it all started.

Protecting mob informants and witnesses was the only way to get those in the ranks of organized crime to tell the Feds what they'd seen. The only way to take down the criminals. They had to give the mob witnesses who turned on their own crime family entirely new identities. They could live out the rest of their days in a brand-new life."

"A whole new life established in communities with unaware and innocent people," she said. "A neighbor could be a past mobster, for all someone knows. Could have killed and dismembered someone."

"Now there's a nice image." He tried to push that from his mind.

Her forehead crinkled. "But seriously, if someone was promised a new life in exchange for telling secrets, I can see how that could work. Otherwise, ratting out a mob family would certainly end in death for the snitch and for those closest to him." She hesitated, drawing in a shaky breath. "Which brings me to this next name on your father's crime board—Jamie McPherson. I'm sending you the article now."

Nathan opened it on his cell and skimmed, finding a story similar to Jimmy Delaney's—another mobster killed. "Okay, so Jamie McPherson is in prison, also in quarantine for his own protection from retaliation for killing a Watts family member."

Erin's mouth set in a grim line. "Another member of a crime family."

"What about these other names, Cobbs and Byrne? Nothing is coming up for me when I search."

"Same here. Too many names come up when I type that in. I need more information."

"And looking up more on Jamie McPherson, it looks like he's the mob boss, the head of the McPherson crime family." Nathan was glad he had finished the steak first. "Is there any chance this has nothing to do with Dad's shooting? That we could be completely off here?"

"We could be. But I don't think we are."

"Yeah. Me neither. But I don't like this at all." He wished they had never come to Boston.

She settled back against her seat as if measuring her words. "I worked with a neuropsychiatrist who had evaluated former gangsters. Mobsters who spent years in prison. He wrote a paper on it, so of course I was curious and asked questions. Those criminal minds in particular lacked remorse. They had such a deep loyalty to their 'clan,' that in their minds, murder was the normal way of things because they were helping their group, their people. Their blood ties, family roots. The power structure and established territory are all part of their culture."

"In other words, kind of a brotherhood of psychopaths."

Erin visibly shuddered. "I hadn't thought of it like that."

"Given what you've told me, what are you thinking about how this mob connection is related to my father's shooting?"

"Someone came all the way to Montana to silence him—protect someone in the family—or to expose someone else. I think it could fit, that's all."

Nathan closed his eyes and breathed in a steadying breath and prayed a silent prayer. *Please let this not have one single thing to do with the mob or the cartel or any evil organized crime group.*

He'd wanted to solve a big case and—he would admit—be like his father. But Nathan hadn't left Montana. Unlike his father, he couldn't leave Mom. He guessed living in Montana, being a detective in a small county, had a silver lining, after all. He hadn't had to deal too much with organized crime on this level.

And now he was working the case of his life—of his father's life—against all the rules, and he realized he might not have the stomach for it.

But he would finish it.

Dad, please just wake up. He had the sense that time was running out for his father and for them to find out what they needed before they were shut down completely.

Unfortunately, he didn't like the images of the many forms a "shutdown" could take.

TWENTY-THREE

Erin strolled next to Nathan as they made their way along the brick sidewalk back to their hotel a couple of blocks away. Crossing the street at the corner, they passed a section of clothing boutiques that were now closed. A man whistled for a cab, while a group of women jumped into an Uber car.

Nathan glanced down at her and smiled, and that familiar warmth spread through her. If she didn't already have a history with the man, would she so quickly feel such a strong bond with him? A longing need to press even closer?

They weren't *together* anymore.

Her fault.

But it seemed that her heart hadn't accepted that fact. She tried to listen only to her head—nothing had changed since she broke things off years ago. He'd known that she held back, refusing to open up completely. Well, she still couldn't open up and let him in. Not all the way. Not until she somehow resolved what happened before, found answers and *closure*—for her heart and mind.

Next to her, Nathan tensed.

"What's the matter?" she asked.

"Keep walking and act normal. The hotel is fifteen yards out."

His tone struck fear in her. "We're being followed?"

"Yes. And we could be in danger."

"How are you going to meet the mystery man tonight if we're being followed?"

"We're going to lose the tail, that's how. And I need you to walk right by the hotel. Don't even attempt to go inside."

"So I'm going with you to the meeting, then."

"For now, it sure looks that way." Nathan pulled her into an alley between restaurants.

Grabbing her hand, he ran and she kept pace. He tried a few doors along the redbrick walls. A twentysomething guy exited a door at the same time he pulled off his apron. Nathan pushed past him, dragging Erin inside to rush by commercial-grade refrigerators and storage closets through the kitchen. Food workers shouted and scolded them. Nathan apologized and exited to the front of the house and the dining room where patrons were seated.

He started to weave his way between the tables, then stopped. Erin ran into him.

Nathan turned around and led her down the hall toward the back of the house, through the kitchen door again, and barely sidestepped a waiter exiting with a loaded food tray. Tugging Erin out of the way, he pulled her over to a storage area. He found a door and urged her inside with him. The space wasn't meant for two people to comfortably stand in.

Erin was pressed up against Nathan. The closet smelled like cleaning solution.

"Keep quiet while we wait," he whispered so softly she could barely hear the words.

She pressed her forehead against his chest and felt his pounding heart. They couldn't wait here forever. *She* couldn't wait here so close to Nathan for much longer.

Oh, God, if only I could be with this man. If only I weren't so broken and could be good enough for him.

Why was she thinking such crazy thoughts at a time like this?

But she knew why. Being next to Nathan scrambled her mind.

He palmed the weapon in his holster, slid it out, and held it toward the ceiling, ready to use.

She thought Nathan might hear her crazy-loud thumping heart. The door opened, and Erin almost yelped.

Angry Italian words spewed from one of the waitstaff, then, "This is no place for you to have a tryst."

After apologizing, Nathan tugged Erin behind him again. Her fingers felt like they were welded to his.

She noticed he pressed his palm against the weapon he'd thrust back into his holster. He pulled her out of the restaurant and clung to the shadows under the awnings. "Let's grab a cab."

"What about the rental car?"

"I'll have the cab drive us around the block and then drop us near the parking garage so we can get in and out quickly, and maybe our tail won't have caught on." Nathan peered down at her, his face close, near enough to kiss her.

Oh . . . and she wanted that kiss.

And she didn't want it. At the same time. How could she have such conflicting emotions?

She turned her face away.

"We should at least keep that meeting." She hoped he couldn't hear the strain in her voice.

"We are. I won't give up the lead, but once we're done, we're heading straight for the airport. I can't spend another day here now that someone is following us, and obviously the Gifford PD knows I'm here. Maybe someone in the department was asked to follow us."

"Now that I know more about your father's case, it stands

to reason that his boss asked him to stand down because the FBI is probably also involved somehow."

"Dad never got the chance to tell me, but even if that was the case, if he didn't drop it, then he had a good reason."

His father's reasons had better be good. Erin sensed the danger was closing in on them, and they weren't exactly sure of the source, but the possible players would leave anyone quaking in their shoes. Organized crime. Dirty cops. It was beginning to feel like something out of a mafia film. She shivered.

"I never should have brought you into this."

"Don't push me away. I can help you, Nathan. I *will* help you." Erin wasn't sure why she was committing so much to him, when Mom depended on her more than ever.

Nathan pulled her close enough that she felt his breath fanning her cheeks. His gaze locked with hers, then traveled over her face to her lips. Her heart pounded at the nearness, the attraction spiking through her. Just when she thought he would kiss her, he shifted away and held her against him, then whispered in her ear, "Don't move."

He held her, hugging her tightly while they remained in the shadows. She hadn't seen who had followed them and wasn't sure how Nathan had. Images of gangsters shooting down Jimmy Delaney in front of his house accosted her. Erin held her breath as the seconds ticked by in rhythm with her soaring pulse. Would someone gun them down here on the streets of downtown Boston?

Within a week or so of almost being killed by a boat, she was now once again facing a life-and-death situation, and she didn't much like being in the action. She much preferred thinking about a case long gone cold and solving it after the fact.

Finally, Nathan slowly released her as a group of people exiting a nearby theater walked past. He pulled her with him to join the group. They walked hand in hand like they were a couple. A block away, Nathan hailed a cab and they scrambled in quickly. He instructed the cabbie to drive them around a few blocks, then circle back close to the hotel parking.

Erin watched out the window at the Boston city life going on around them as though everything was perfectly normal. But it was far from it. This had quickly turned into a clandestine adventure, and she couldn't wait for it to end.

The cab traveled another block, then around again and approached the hotel. Erin searched the pedestrians, restaurant awnings, and shop windows. Was their shadow simply waiting for them to return at some point?

"You ready?" Nathan asked. "We're going to make a mad dash into the parking garage to our vehicle."

"Okay. I'm ready."

He paid the cabbie, then they stole into the parking garage. They climbed the stairs to the third floor, where the rental car was parked. Nathan checked the wheel wells and the undercarriage for a GPS tracker . . . or was he also checking for a possible bomb? He didn't say. She held back the rising terror and finally sucked in a deep breath only after they'd exited the parking garage and driven several blocks from the hotel.

"Are we still being followed?"

"I don't think so, but it's hard to know with all the traffic."

She did not like where this search had led them. No wonder Newt had come back to Big Rapids. Maybe he'd come there to get away from the danger, but it had followed him.

Finally, Nathan steered them along neighborhood streets and past a few parks. Up ahead she spotted a cemetery and the sign COOPER HILL BURYING GROUND. The sun would be setting soon, but there was still time before they were completely in the dark—and for that she was grateful. Not that she was superstitious, but she simply didn't relish walking in a dark cemetery with the added bonus of someone potentially following them.

Nathan parked across the street from the big wrought-iron arched gateway into the cemetery. No one was standing out front waiting on them. She glanced at her watch. Three minutes.

"Are you sure we're not going to walk into an ambush of some kind? I would think you'd want to stake out the area first."

"*We're* not. You're staying in the car so I don't have to worry about you. Sit on the driver's side and drive away if there's trouble. Call the police."

She stared at him. *What?*

"Please." Nathan pressed a gun into her hands. "For your protection. You still know how to use this?"

"Wait. Don't you need a gun?"

"I have one."

"Just how many guns did you bring?"

He shrugged. "You know how to use it, right?"

"Of course." She gripped the weapon. Dwayne had taught her how to handle guns.

"Good, then. Watch yourself."

Nathan got out, and Erin took his place on the driver's side. Were they making a mistake? Nathan hiked across the street and then along the sidewalk. He walked under the archway and kept walking until she could no longer see him.

After a few calming breaths, she took pictures with her cell phone. A few of the gravestones had skulls and crossbones, all part of Boston's rich history. She placed the cell on the console, waiting and watching. Hoping she wouldn't have to call the police.

The trees in the cemetery were thick—almost a forest. A soon-to-be dark forest closing in around her. She closed her eyes and slowed her breaths.

Hurry up, Nathan.

Before the nightmares she had chased away every night for far too long stepped out of her dreams and into her reality.

TWENTY-FOUR

uscles tensing, Nathan kept his gun ready but hidden from plain sight as he cautiously treaded the walkway through the cemetery, hoping for the best but preparing for the worst. Their shadow could have followed them and was intending to cause harm.

He struggled to comprehend he was even in this scenario. How had he let things go this far? Had his need to know the truth and find his father's shooter clouded his judgment?

Lord, forgive my stubbornness.

While he continued to pray with his heart, his mind focused on his surroundings. He hoped he wasn't walking into a trap. At least Erin was waiting in the car and could escape and call for help if needed. He'd spotted a couple walking among the gravestones, but they finally exited where he'd entered, leaving the cemetery empty now, as far as he could tell.

He found an old elm tree to lean against, where he waited and watched. He was here at the meeting place a minute early. Why would someone choose this cemetery—or any cemetery, really—to meet, when information could be delivered in so many different ways?

Minutes ticked by and still, no one else was around. Just

him . . . and . . . the night creatures. The sun had set and dusk was falling.

He watched for the man he'd chased two blocks away from Dad's house. Crickets chirped. A bat flitted, chasing after bugs that were drawn by the streetlamps flickering on. Was this the way Dad would have handled it? Nathan hated that he constantly second-guessed himself lately, but this scenario was like nothing he'd ever experienced.

Dad responded to his investigation by showing up in Big Rapids. Nathan might have done better to wait there to see what clues floated to the top. But he'd been impatient and driven insane with the need to know who shot his father—who his father was running from. He was some kind of idiot to come here. This was a mistake. He would find Erin and get out of here. Nathan pushed from the tree and headed back the way he'd come.

Before he stepped from the shadow of the elm tree, he heard soft footfalls along the path. He waited until the source of the sound came into view. A tall, slender woman strolled as if she were walking along the boardwalk by the sea at sunset. He remained in the shadows and wouldn't draw her attention but prepared for anything. Something about her demeanor struck him as odd—then he realized that her wary eyes searched the cemetery as she walked.

"You're at the wrong grave," she said as she walked past the elm.

Nathan stepped from the shadows onto the sidewalk behind her. He remained standing in place as she continued forward.

"Excuse me?" His palms slicked with sweat.

Without a reply, she continued forward and away from him, strolling nonchalantly up the path that weaved between gravestones. He reconsidered moving back against the tree to wait for the man who'd arranged the meeting, but he was done waiting. He and Erin were getting out of here. Whoever had left the message could find another way to contact Nathan if he truly had something important to share. They had the crime board, after all, so their trip here wasn't a complete loss.

The woman moved between the gravestones and onto the grass. A breeze shook the leaves. Dusk made it seem much later beneath the canopy of the old elms. Nathan took one last glance at her before heading back to Erin. The woman stopped at one particular gravestone and lifted a hand to Nathan, waving him over.

What in the world? He didn't have time for conversations with a stranger.

A sound to his left drew him around.

Erin rushed up to him.

"I asked you to stay in the car," he whispered.

"I was getting worried. Sorry. Besides, I didn't see anyone lying in wait for you, so I figured it was safe. But looks like he didn't show." She shivered and hugged herself. Where was the gun he'd given her?

"No one's here, so we're leaving. I was just heading to get you, in fact."

"No one's here except that lady waving us over," she said. "Why don't we see what she wants?"

"I don't want to stay here one moment longer. If we were going to stay, then we'd wait for the man I chased."

"I think we need to talk to her. Maybe the man was just a delivery boy." Erin stared at the woman, who had stopped waving.

"What? You think she's who we came to meet?"

"We won't know until we talk to her." She tugged him across the walkway and down across the grassy knoll to where the woman stood.

"Thanks for coming," she said. "I wasn't sure if you would show up, and then I wasn't sure if you were going to figure out that I left you the message."

Nathan subtly shook his head. "I thought—"

"You thought what? That I would show my face at your father's house? Of course not. That's why I sent a messenger."

"But how did you know I would be there, or even who I am?" Nathan asked the questions but remained fully aware of his surroundings. Even though they spoke in low tones, their voices seemed to echo off the gravestones and trees, reverberating across the cemetery.

"I was expecting your father to return, and when he didn't, I feared the worst." Her voice cracked. "Especially when he never returned my calls. I've been watching the house from a safe distance to see what happened. And then you showed up."

Did she know about the break-in too? Or had she missed the intruder?

Nathan shifted closer. "Can we back up? Who are you, and why are we meeting at a cemetery?"

She crouched next to the closest gravestone. Only then did Nathan realize it was a relatively fresh grave.

"My name is Holly Sandfield. I buried my brother, Ian, here two weeks ago."

"Who *are* you to my father?"

She startled at his question.

Erin pressed her hand against his arm and whispered under her breath, "Be patient. Let her tell her story."

He blew out a breath and nodded. "I'm just trying to find out what's going on."

Holly rose and brushed her hands down her slacks. "I'll answer your question, if you'll answer mine first. Where is Newt? What happened to him? Is he . . . ? Is he—"

"Alive. He's alive, the last I spoke with my mother. He was shot and is still in the hospital. I came out to check on the house." That's all Nathan would say until he knew more. "Now it's your turn."

She stared at the grave. "Your father and my mother, Lena, were in love, though they never married. She died in an accident a few months back. Her grave is over there." She pointed and chewed on her bottom lip. Measuring her words? "Recently he started to think that someone had intentionally killed her to distract him from a case he'd been working. He'd been trying to find out who was behind the hit-and-run that killed her. And now, I think my brother, also a detective, was killed because of something your father told him."

Nathan absorbed the woman's words. Was she telling the truth? If so, he felt blindsided by the news. If only Dad had been able to tell him more.

"He told me that lives are at stake."

"Yes, and now I'm afraid for mine and yours. I asked you to meet me here so you could see and understand the gravity of the situation, and to tell you that you should be careful who you trust. I wasn't sure if you would listen to me, and I had no time to waste convincing you. But here you see the grave"—she pressed her hand against her chest—"maybe you will feel it in your heart. Newt was instructed to back off, so he claimed that he had—at least to his friends and fellow officers and detectives. But, of course, he never stopped. My brother's death, his murder, has not been solved. Someone else is now looking into it, but I can't trust anyone to find the truth. Your father, I trusted. Honestly, I wasn't sure if he'd told you anything, but I suspected he would since he'd gone to Montana."

"And why would *you* trust *me*?"

She smiled. "Your dad talked about you all the time." Her smile flattened. "But you haven't told me much about his current condition. Is he going to be okay?"

"As far as I know, he's still unconscious and has been since after the surgery to remove the bullet in his brain. I'm sorry that no one contacted you. His boss was told about the shooting, and I assumed he would deliver the news to whomever needed to know."

Holly pressed her hand to her mouth, her eyes wide. "I'm so sorry."

"I need to find out what he was investigating. He was adamant that no one know, not even the detective officially working on the case. My sheriff doesn't know. Supposedly Dad's boss will have his department examine Dad's cases—anything that could have led to the shooting. But Dad also mentioned a cold case. What can you tell us?"

"The day Ian was killed, he'd met with Newt. Your father had asked him to look into something for him. I only know suspicions and rumors. That someone is digging deep—but for what, I don't know." She reached into her small handbag and tugged out an envelope, which she handed to Nathan. "And I have this. He gave this to my brother. I don't know what it means, but maybe you'll find it more useful than I did. After our meeting tonight, I'm going to disappear—at least until it's safe."

"How can I reach you?" Nathan asked.

"I'll find *you*."

That prickly feeling crawled over him again. He glanced around and caught a shadowy figure stepping from behind a tree.

A gunshot echoed through the cemetery. Shards of granite exploded from the headstone.

TWENTY-FIVE

et down!" Nathan shouted.

Erin dropped to the ground with Nathan. Holly joined them behind the gravestone.

"Oh no." She gasped for breath. "This is all my fault. I never should have met you here. I never should have met you at all." Her voice cracked with sobs and fear.

Nathan inched forward, still using the headstone for protection. "No time to play the blame game. We need to get out of here."

Erin pulled out her cell and called 911 to report the shooting.

"The police might take too long," Nathan said. "This gravestone doesn't provide much protection. You and Holly get somewhere safe until I can catch up. I'll hold off the shooter."

As if to emphasize his point, Nathan peeked from behind the stone and fired his weapon.

"Come on." Erin grabbed Holly's hand and they ran, darting between gravestones and trees, while Erin kept the cell to her ear. Why did it have to take so long?

Dispatch finally answered and Erin explained their predicament as the two women ran. Nathan continued firing his gun
to provide them cover. How had it come to this?

Holly had taken the lead, dashing through the grass, deeper
into the trees, and off the paved path. As she kept up with
Holly, Erin remained connected to dispatch, though she said
nothing more. She kept the line open so the dispatcher could
hear what was happening. She didn't have time to think or
contemplate the danger as they tried to find a safe place.

More gunshots rang out. This time from the shooter.

When they'd come to the cemetery, it was still relatively light
out, but dusk was deepening along with the shadows. She sent
up a quick prayer, memories of another time and place chasing her. Finally, Erin stopped and pressed her back against a
thick elm. Holly slowed and backtracked to stand next to Erin,
gasping for breath.

"Now what?" Holly's voice shook with fear.

"We'll wait here for a few moments. See if Nathan can
join us."

She spotted the gravestone where they'd been moments
before, but Nathan was gone. At least no one was shooting.

"Ma'am, ma'am, please respond."

Erin lifted the cell. "Listen, please send police. I have to
hide now, so I'm going to hang up. We have to stay alive until
you get here."

She ended the call, then glanced to Holly. "Don't worry,
Holly. Nathan and I will protect you. Nothing will happen to
you."

"How can you be so sure? Remember, I've lost a mother and
a brother. Even my brother being a cop didn't keep them safe."

Erin regretted her words. How could she make that promise? And Nathan could very well lose his father. She'd only
meant to encourage Holly. Her worry for Nathan kicked up
several notches.

Holly grabbed her hand. "Come on. I know where to hide." She pushed from the tree, tugging Erin after her.

Sirens rang out in the distance, but they could be heading to some other emergency. And even if they were headed this way, help was still a good distance away. In situations like this, seconds counted.

Holly dashed forward, and Erin kept close behind while searching the shadows for any sign of Nathan or their attacker. Stopping near an old stone church, Holly crouched near thick vines that grew along the wall.

"What now?" Erin asked. "Are we going to just wait here?"

Holly gestured at the structure. "No, we can hide in the crypt beneath the church."

The woman dashed around the corner, and once again, Erin followed. At the door, Holly jiggled the handle and stepped inside. Erin entered behind her.

Dimly lit sconces gave enough light in the small chapel, but Erin still didn't like this. "I'm surprised this place isn't locked up."

Holly headed to the back, and Erin kept up with her. On her cell, she texted Nathan to let him know where they were going to hide. He was supposed to be right behind them, catching up, something. She didn't think his plan had worked out.

If only help would arrive. Still, Holly's fear of the police was palpable, since she believed that someone within law enforcement couldn't be trusted.

The tall, slender woman started down a set of stairs. Dark stairs. No sconces. "This is the crypt," she said.

Erin ran a finger over the cold stone but remained at the top of the stairs. "How do you know so much about this place?"

"They offer tours certain hours and days of the week." Holly continued down.

"During the week with the lights on."

"No one will find us down there. They won't even look." Holly's voice echoed up the stone staircase, but Erin could barely see her face as she disappeared deeper into the crypt.

This was where Erin had to put her foot down. "Are you kidding? That's because no one wants to go down into a dark crypt, including me. I'm waiting here for Nathan. I can't stay down there. Please, Holly, let's just wait up here."

Holly took a few steps up so the light from the sconces illuminated her face. "If you understood who you were dealing with, you'd come with me."

"Then why don't you tell me who we're dealing with." Erin had the feeling that Holly knew much more, but she was simply too afraid to say.

"A killer." Holly didn't add more.

"I won't leave Nathan behind." She'd made a mistake in coming this far.

Holly's features were drawn. "I can't force you, but I've done all I can. You won't see me again. I have to disappear. Do not mention my name to the police when they arrive."

"Wait, how can I contact you?" She didn't want to lose contact with Holly, but she couldn't keep her here.

"I'll contact you."

Erin shared her cell number with Holly. Would she even remember it? Holly took a step back into the shadows, then disappeared down the stairs. Erin hugged herself. Another door creaked somewhere from deeper in the crypt. Holly obviously knew her way around the cemetery and the church as well as the underground tomb.

Come on, Erin, you're a psychologist. Creepy old crypts, catacombs, whatever, shouldn't scare you.

She recited a few Bible verses in her mind, trusting they would bring the peace she sought.

I will be with you when you pass through the waters, and when you pass through the rivers, they will not overwhelm you. You will not be scorched when you walk through the fire, and the flame will not burn you.

Can I add gunfire and cemeteries to that, Lord?

A sound down the stairwell drew her attention. Rodents probably made their residence down there, a thought that caused a shiver to crawl over her. When she'd insisted on coming to Boston with Nathan, she hadn't imagined such a scenario.

God, why is this happening?

Erin crept toward the front of the church as she considered what to do next. Footfalls pounded along the path outside the church door. Nathan? Because if it wasn't Nathan, then she should have followed Holly, after all. She eyed the back of the church where the dark stairwell led down to the crypt.

The church door burst open, and Nathan rushed in. "Erin!"

Relief whooshed through her. She closed the distance, and he caught her in his arms.

"I was so worried!" Erin soaked in his warmth and strength.

"It's over." He eased back and gripped her arms, looking into her eyes. "I got your text that you were in the church. The police are here now."

"And the shooter?"

"In the wind."

Escaped? So it wasn't truly over, and they were still in danger.

TWENTY-SIX

E rin stood in a room at one of the Boston PD field offices and rubbed her arms. Officer Melanie Brown returned with her coffee. "Here you go."

"Thank you." Erin wrapped her hand around the warm mug and dropped onto the comfy sofa in the small conference room. She glanced at the time on her cell. 12:01 a.m.

"Now can I get you anything else?"

"I'm good." *Totally fine.* Just want to get out of here and go home. Where was Nathan?

Officer Brown slid into the chair across the table and pressed a pen to a paper pad. "So you're a criminal psychologist, is that correct?"

"I write forensic evaluations for the State of Washington." What was she saying? She wasn't currently working in her job. Nor did she feel obligated to offer up her podcast. None of that was relevant.

"Then you should be more than familiar with procedures. I'm going to take your statement now about the events this evening."

She would answer only the questions asked and offer nothing more. However, what was Nathan going to say about why they were at the cemetery if asked? She considered Detective Newt

Campbell, lying unconscious in a hospital bed. She thought of Holly and her palpable fear—both her mother and brother dead, allegedly murdered. Who did Erin trust? How much did she say without the wrong person getting the information? If the murders were related to organized crime, someone within one of the local police departments could be compromised.

"We heard gunshots and took cover. I called 911 as shots continued to be fired, then I went inside the church to hide with another woman."

"Uh-huh. What was her name?"

Do not mention my name to the police when they arrive. "Why would you think I know her name?"

"Do you?"

"She was Nathan's informant, and it's not my place to give her name." She cringed inside at having said that much.

Officer Brown arched a brow as she continued to write. "And why were you at the cemetery?"

"We were meeting his informant."

A knock came at the door and it opened. A man stuck his head in. "Got a Code 23. They want a female officer. You almost done here?"

Brown grimaced and stood but continued writing on her notepad.

"Code 23?" Erin asked.

"Emotionally disturbed person." Brown's dark eyes flicked up from the notepad to Erin. "Maybe you'd like to come along and help?"

Though her words held sarcasm, they also seemed to hold hope. Of course, Erin wasn't licensed in Massachusetts, and she wouldn't even be allowed into this situation. "No, thanks. I'm good."

"Anything else you can tell me about tonight?" Her demeanor sagged.

Erin thought to suggest she find another line of work.

"You have my statement." Erin stood.

"I might need to contact you later if I have more questions."

"You have my contact information." Erin thrust out her hand and, surprisingly, Officer Brown shook it. "You're doing great work here, Officer Brown. I'll pray it goes well with the emotionally disturbed person."

Officer Brown's eyes brightened as she dropped her hand. "I could use all the prayer I can get. Thanks."

This time, her smile seemed genuine, and she lifted her shoulders, appearing bolstered. "You're free to go now. Do you need a ride somewhere?"

"Actually, do you know where I can find my friend?"

"Detective Campbell?" The woman moved to the door. "I'll take you to him."

Erin followed Brown in search of Nathan and found him in the kitchen, of all places, telling jokes and laughing with two police officers. Relief that all was well warred with the smallest surge of outrage. She thought it seemed strange that he would be joking around. Then again, Nathan was probably trying to fit in and possibly learn something of value.

She approached the group, and Nathan's eye caught on her. His smile brightened just for her as he took her hand. He held it as if they often held hands, but she suspected the gesture was more of a protective move.

"We'd better get going now," he said. "Can someone give us a ride to the airport?"

"What about the rental car?" she asked.

"The tires were slashed," Nathan said. "Detective Trap is taking care of it. Impounding it as evidence until the shooting investigation is over."

"I left my—"

"Don't worry. I got your purse."

And the gun he'd given her, she hoped.

"I will," a short, petite brunette said as she dumped the

contents of her mug into the sink. "I'm headed home, so I can give you a ride. I'm Jenny Koenig and work dispatch. I took your call tonight."

"We need to swing by our hotel to collect our things. Are you up for that too?"

Jenny nodded. Nathan led Erin out of the kitchen as he followed Jenny.

"Give my regards to your dad. We're praying for him," Officer Brown tossed over her shoulder as she exited the station.

Newt had worked Boston PD for years before heading to Gifford. Erin wasn't sure what district he'd worked out of, but he'd obviously made many friends. She followed Nathan and Jenny out of the offices to Jenny's minivan.

To Erin, it seemed that Nathan remained tense, though to anyone else, he might have appeared relaxed as he held her hand and they exited the police station. After grabbing their things at the hotel, they headed to the airport. Jenny engaged them in small talk about Boston and her job in dispatch as she steered her minivan into Callahan Tunnel, one of four tunnels beneath Boston Harbor that would take them to Logan International Airport.

Erin was concerned about Holly. When would she hear from the woman again? How would she know if she'd made it to safety?

She couldn't wait to speak to Nathan about all this cloak-and-dagger business. But she'd been relegated to riding in the back seat while Nathan rode up front with Jenny.

Erin's cell buzzed with a text.

I'm okay.

Holly?

Yes.

I was worried.

171

> I didn't want you to worry, so that's why I'm texting. I wanted to make sure you're okay too.

> Yes. We're heading back to Montana tonight.

> Good. I'm ditching this cell phone and disappearing for a while. You have the envelope. I hope you can find justice for my mother, brother, and Newt.

> We'll try, but Holly, please find a way to keep in touch so we can keep you informed.

> I will. Keep safe.

Erin stared at the cell. She couldn't wait to give Nathan the news. One of Holly's words echoed repeatedly in her mind.

Disappearing.

Erin hadn't liked her use of that particular word. Missing persons cold cases had intrigued her for far too long. She prayed Holly wouldn't become one of those statistics. On the other hand, if Holly disappeared by choice because she feared for her life, that could be the only real chance she had of not permanently disappearing at the hands of a violent criminal. God knew she'd read enough transcripts of testimonies and confessions about bodies buried and hidden to make her blood curdle.

Erin hated the evil in this world, and it hurt to think about it too long or hard.

Closing her eyes, she thought back to her Saturday mornings kayaking with Carissa. She'd used that time to refresh herself. To get away from the darkness. Why did she torture herself with it?

God, I need answers.

To a crime that happened long ago.

She considered these thoughts as she stared out the window and Nathan and Jenny jabbered on, sharing cop stories. Nathan really knew how to make friends, and always had. She admired that about him, and it was one of the big differences between them. Erin was more subdued.

"Erin."

"Hmm?" Erin suddenly realized the vehicle had stopped and one of the sliding doors was open. Nathan waited on her. She took his hand and stepped onto the curb.

He leaned into the open passenger-side window to talk to Jenny. "Thanks again for dropping us off."

As soon as they were out of earshot, Erin leaned in. "Holly texted me that she's okay."

He stepped away to look at her, relief in his expression. "What else did she say?"

"Nothing. She just wanted to let me know she was okay. I didn't give the police her name. Did you?"

"Yes." He gently grabbed her shoulders. "They're a good group, Erin. We can trust them as a whole. Of course, Dad left Boston PD three years ago and moved to Gifford. No matter the police force, the issues arise if there's even one untrustworthy person, someone working both sides. So, in that way, we still need to be careful what we say and whom we trust until we have found the person behind his shooting and the deaths in Holly's family."

"Did you tell them why you were here?"

He grimaced. "I answered their questions fully about what happened, only adding that Holly was a friend of Dad's and we met her to look at her brother's grave. Ian worked out of another district, so this crew didn't know him."

"I told them she was your informant and didn't give her name."

"And it's all true. She did inform me. It's okay. Don't worry about it."

As they walked toward the airport entrance, Erin said, "Considering the bloodshed, your father's situation, I hope the truth about who is behind all this comes out soon." The unfortunate truth was that it could still take years.

They entered the airport, and Erin turned to face him. "Was all the joking around in the kitchen an act?"

Nathan scraped a hand through his dark hair. "Look, I was walking a fine line. I tried to keep it light and friendly. Another detective asked me questions about the shooting—an officer-involved shooting, so that's being investigated." He shrugged, worry lines creasing his forehead. "My actions are being looked into. I'm not in my own jurisdiction, so I was a little worried at first. But I think the other officers sensed that, and they were just trying to help me relax. What else could I do?"

"You're right. I didn't mean to question your behavior." She sighed and looked at the ticket counters and kiosks where they could print off their boarding passes. But they were changing their flight, so they would need to head to the ticket counter. "Come on. Let's get our tickets."

"Good idea. I don't want to push my luck and have a run-in with Dad's boss on top of everything else. Let's get out of here."

They started toward the cordoned-off line for the ticket counter. Coming to Boston had been comparable to walking across enemy lines, and even heading home tonight might no longer be safe for them.

"I'm not sure that you shouldn't have made it a point to find his boss and talk it through with him," she said.

Nathan looked at her. "Dad doesn't trust him because he took him off the case. He shut him down."

She blew out a breath. "All these secrets and innuendos. Wouldn't it be best to just lay it all on the table?"

Why don't I listen to my own advice? Erin shut down the voice in her head and focused on Nathan's response instead.

And she didn't like the way he stared at her now. Never in her life had she been put in this awkward position of not knowing where to turn and who to trust. Except Nathan. She knew she could trust him.

A big barrel of a man with thick brown hair, silver at his

temples, lumbered directly toward them. His eyes drilled into them.

Beside her, Nathan stiffened.

The man approached and thrust out his hand. "Nathan Campbell? I'm Chief Jed Hadlow, Gifford PD. You're a hard man to track down."

TWENTY-SEVEN

Tension rolled over his shoulders. Not sergeant. Not lieutenant or captain. But chief. Nathan thrust out his hand to take Chief Hadlow's. Dread filled his gut, sending the bile right up his throat.

The man was dressed in plain clothes, so Nathan asked, "Can I see some ID?"

"Certainly." Hadlow pulled out his credentials.

Nathan eyed them, but he didn't feel better for the knowing. "What are you doing here?"

Chief Hadlow narrowed his eyes. "I could ask you the same thing."

"Since you found us here at the airport, I'm sure you know that we're leaving Boston."

"A moment of your time, please." He gestured to seating over by the windows.

Nathan hesitated, but what choice did he have? The police chief had tracked him down and followed him to the airport. Nathan attempted to calm his racing heart as he slid into the chair catty-corner to the seat Chief Hadlow chose.

Erin sat on the other side of Nathan.

The man edged forward, one elbow against his thigh. "So

you came here to find out who might have shot your father. You went to Newt's home and ran into an intruder. Then I got word that you were in a shootout at a cemetery." Chief Hadlow spoke matter-of-factly.

"That's right," Nathan said.

Erin had suggested laying everything on the table. Nathan agreed it was time to do that, at least here and now. "I overheard my sheriff promising Dad's boss that no one would dig into it."

Nathan stared into the man's intimidating dark-blue eyes. He looked to be in his mid-to-late fifties—same age as Dad. A few wrinkles lined the edges of his eyes, and his brow furrowed. Nathan wasn't the only one whose heart raced. The chief might have the hard edge of years of experience, but this situation clearly had him worried.

Would Erin have the same assessment?

The man leaned back and studied Nathan. "Lieutenant Sullivan was getting reassurance that your detectives would leave the past-cases search to my department. We're walking some tight ropes here. You might have figured that out yourself."

Nathan soaked in those words. "My father doesn't know who he can trust. Neither do I."

"I understand. But I'm the good guy here. Lieutenant Sullivan wanted Newt off the case to protect him, because we believe he was being targeted. Warned away. And now I'm asking you to go home and stay out of it, to protect you."

Nathan wanted to believe him. But . . . "Despite your efforts, Dad was shot anyway."

And I don't know if I'll ever get him back.

"You're in over your head, Campbell. This isn't your jurisdiction or investigation." Hadlow lowered his voice to barely a whisper. "Someone in-house could be working both sides. I'm looking into it, and I want to keep things local."

"I think it's too late for that, considering someone followed Dad to Montana."

Hadlow hung his head, then slowly lifted it. "Any news?"

"Not in the last twelve hours. Someone would have texted me if there was a change. He might never recover."

"And he wouldn't want you in the same danger. I'm afraid you've put yourself into the thick of it by coming here."

"What do you suggest, if I might ask?" Erin slid to the edge of her chair, injecting herself into the conversation.

"Watch your back," Hadlow said. "Go home and stay out of it."

"It would be easier to do that," Erin said, "if you would tell us what we're staying out of. What was the case he was working? What cold case was he investigating? Since we're already in the thick of it, in your words, then help us by telling us at least that much."

Chief Hadlow cautiously glanced around them. The airport wasn't busy at this hour, but a few people were making their way through to catch the middle-of-the-night flights. He inched forward and leaned in. "Someone is cleaning house."

"Or do you mean retaliating?" Erin asked.

Nathan turned and gave her a look. *Please say no more.*

But he recognized the defiance in her eyes. Maybe she was right. The more they got out of this man, the better.

Chief Hadlow said nothing. Instead, he stared at Erin. Trying to intimidate her? "As I said before, I'm on your side. Your team. I'm a good guy here." Then he shifted back to Nathan and sighed. "I want to protect your father. He wouldn't be happy with me if I let you get hurt because of this case. Please leave my state and don't come back unless it's with your father and those responsible for shooting him have been charged."

Chief Hadlow stood, letting Nathan know he was finished. Nathan rose and Erin joined him. Hadlow thrust out his hand and Nathan shook the strong, reassuring grip.

With everything in him, Nathan wanted to believe him.

"Can I ask you one more question?" Nathan crossed his arms.

Hadlow angled his head. "You can ask."

In other words, asking the question didn't mean he would answer. "How many lives are at stake here?"

The man subtly sagged and glanced between Nathan and Erin. "I'm concerned about at least two more."

TWENTY-EIGHT

On the early morning flight from Boston, Erin sat next to the window and Nathan on the aisle. Erin wanted to sleep, but her mind wouldn't stop reliving the events of the last couple of days, even as she was still reeling from the week before when she and Carissa had nearly been killed. She made a mental note to contact Carissa to find out how she was doing. She simply hadn't had a decent moment to contact her friend.

In the meantime, though, she rested her eyes and prayed. And hoped Nathan wouldn't make her tell him about Seattle. Not yet.

God, I don't know what's going on. I thought I was finally getting some kind of stability. I've worked so hard to climb out from under the dark cloud that seemed to hover over me for so long.

Erin took a few slow breaths to calm her heart. She couldn't lose it now in front of Nathan. Her deepest, darkest secrets had kept them apart to begin with. Nathan had confronted her, sensing that she held back a part of herself, and that's when she knew she had to break things off with him. He would never be happy with her inability to tell him the burden she carried—and she'd told him as much.

She'd thought . . . she'd thought that he was going to propose to her, but he held back until he knew everything there was to know about her. And she simply couldn't share that with him, so instead she'd ended their relationship.

Keeping her secret had cost her, and too late she realized that price had been much too high.

But now certainly wasn't the moment to finally come clean.

A relationship had to be founded on truth as well as trust, and Erin wasn't sure she could ever share her true self with him. She'd worked hard to create a new identity for herself. Being Dr. Erin Larson, PhD, went a long way in hiding the scared little girl she remained on the inside. By wearing this disguise, was she living a lie?

She thought she'd wanted to understand what caused men to commit evil acts, to become wicked, but in the end, it didn't start with their minds, but stemmed from the heart first. Even Scripture said, "The heart is deceitful above all things, and desperately sick; who can understand it?"

Could she even know her own heart, her own motivations? Even if she couldn't . . . *I know to trust you, Lord, no matter what. Even in the midst of all the chaos, you're with me.*

Tears welled behind her lids. If only she could *feel* that God was with her, but doubt warred with the truth in her heart.

The flight attendant appeared and offered them both drinks, a welcome distraction from her thoughts. After she took a few sips, she felt relaxed enough to hopefully grab some sleep on the flight to Montana.

Except Nathan had other ideas. He flipped on the overhead light above the empty seat between them and pulled out the three-by-five manila envelope Holly had given them and set it on the pulled-out tray table.

Nathan eyed her, excitement and fear evident in his gaze.

Had their trip to Boston been worth it? It seemed they had only put their lives in more danger. Holly's too, though clearly, she had already been on the edge, given she believed both her mother and brother were murdered.

The flight was nearly empty, and the few other passengers were rows in front or back of them and likely sleeping.

Nathan leaned closer. "You ready?" he asked, keeping his voice low.

She nodded.

Nathan carefully lifted the clasps, then opened the unsealed end. He tipped the envelope and out slid a photograph of a silver-haired man.

He sighed. "Well, I can't say that I'm not disappointed. I had hoped for something more. This tells us all of nothing."

Erin sat up. "Or everything. He could be your father's shooter. We can cross-reference it with the names we pulled from the whiteboard. I don't think you ever called RISS, did you?"

He shook his head. "I will in the morning."

She'd wanted to catch some rest, but they might as well work until they got a few answers. She leaned forward to pull her bag from under the seat in front of her and got her iPad. She compared the names they had retrieved with the images she could find, coming up empty on that front. Who was the man in the picture? By the time her iPad died, her eyes burned, but she tugged out her cell instead.

He pressed his hand over hers. "Don't."

"What? I'm trying to see if I can identify this person."

"We'll find out who he is. Don't worry. You need to rest. I'm going to talk to Trevor West—Henry too—and share what we learned and what Chief Hadlow told me." His gaze drifted past her to the darkness outside the window, then back to her. "I mean, now that people know we're looking, I see no point in hiding what Dad told me."

She nodded. "That makes sense, but it could be more that he was about to tell you what he'd learned and he didn't want you to share *that* with anyone. The intel could be what got him in trouble. I'm just saying to be cautious."

"Or he was afraid of losing more people. Dad was . . . scared. By looking into the case, he believed he had lost a woman he loved and then her son."

Erin nodded again. "I hadn't thought of that, but I should have. I think you could be right."

"For the rest of this flight, let's get some rest." He stuffed the image back into the envelope. "And at some point soon, I want to hear about what happened in Seattle. You're helping me with this, so I owe you big-time. I'll help *you*." He pushed the tray table up and turned off the overhead light. "I would help you anyway, just so you know."

A smile crept onto her lips as she peered out the window into the darkness. She glanced down toward the earth beneath the flying tube. A few lights indicated they were passing over a small town. Finally, her eyelids grew heavy, so she rested her head against the seat and closed her eyes.

A strong, warm hand covered hers on the armrest, gripping it. Nathan's hand on hers brought her comfort. Warmth from his body wrapped around her, and she realized he'd moved into the middle seat to sit right next to her. To hold her hand? She shifted toward him and leaned her head against his shoulder.

He'd somehow known that she needed human touch.

Nathan's touch. He always found a way to be in tune with her needs, it seemed, even before she knew them herself. The scent of him soothed her edgy nerves and stirred something deeper within. She'd denied herself this man before, and at the moment, she questioned that decision so long ago. Nathan offered stability. He was protective. She could trust him because he'd never let her down.

She was the one who had let them both down. Erin no longer wanted to be that person. If anything, she wanted to be the kind of person Nathan could believe in.

God, help me find a way to tell him everything . . .

She drifted to sleep with the image of his warm brown eyes searching her soul.

////////////////////////

At the airport, Erin groggily followed Nathan to his truck in the parking garage. He waited for her to climb in, then shut the door. She stretched while he walked around and got into the driver's seat. One searching glance from him made her feel self-conscious. Was her hair a mess? Did she look as awful as she felt? She wished she didn't care what he thought.

He started his truck and turned the heat on to warm it up in the cool morning hours. She yawned and quickly covered it.

"We have a long drive ahead, so you still have plenty of time to get more rest." He steered from the parking lot.

"I'm good."

"I want you to be awake when we talk about all of this. And I want the truth from you too."

The truth. What was he talking about? Her heart rate kicked up and brought her fully awake. Which truth did he want? She wasn't ready.

She sucked in air. "When have I lied to you?"

"I meant, I want the truth about what happened in Seattle. I don't like that danger seems to be coming at us—at you—from all sides of the country."

She exhaled slowly. "Agreed. I don't know much about Seattle, but we'll talk about it later."

His cell rang, drawing his attention. He glanced at the screen, then at Erin. "It's Mom."

Instead of using Bluetooth, he pressed the cell against his ear. Wanting privacy? "Hi," he said.

Erin couldn't make out the words from the soft voice on the other end but watched his face morph between joy and fear.

"I'm on my way," he said. "We're just steering out of the airport."

He ended the call. "It's Dad . . . he . . . he woke up." Nathan's smile portrayed relief. "He hasn't said anything, but he's awake."

"I'm glad, Nathan. I'm so glad he's finally awake." She wanted to reach across the console and squeeze his arm, connect with him, but held back.

He tucked his cell away.

"Me too. I know you need to get home soon too." He glanced at her.

He didn't want her along? That made sense. Nathan wanted his privacy. "I can take a cab or Uber."

"That would cost you hundreds of dollars at this distance. Besides, if it's all right with you, and you're not too tired, I could use your support."

She heard the need in his voice. He wasn't just saying the words so she wouldn't feel awkward about going along with him. He truly meant them. Was it a good idea for her to let him depend on her? Still, how could she deny encouraging an old friend? "I'm good to go, then. I want to be there for you and see your father too."

For the life of her, she had no idea how she and Nathan had been sucked into a vortex together, even though they'd worked hard and long—a few years, actually—to stay apart.

Why was Providence pulling them together? For what purpose? And she wanted that. She couldn't deny she wanted another chance, but could she trust herself not to destroy them both again?

Oh, Nathan, don't depend on me too deeply, too much. Remember, I have a habit of running.

TWENTY-NINE

Nathan sped out of the Bozeman Yellowstone International Airport toward the hospital. Morning twilight tinted the skies a warm gray. Few cars were on the road at this hour, and the one vehicle that had followed him, well, they could just be heading in the same direction. Still, he'd keep an eye out.

His father was awake. Nathan wanted to focus on that desperately needed good news. But he couldn't shake his thoughts about the conversation with Chief Hadlow.

"How many lives are at stake here?"

"At least two more."

Frustration boiled through Nathan. They had a few names, but he sensed they were far from learning who shot his father. He hoped now that Dad was awake, they could get answers. But even if they didn't get them, Nathan would remain grateful Dad had survived a gunshot to the head.

Erin reached across the console and touched his arm. "This is good news, Nathan. Let's hold on to hope and focus on that right now. We'll figure the rest of it out later."

Warmth surged from her touch all the way to his heart.

"You're right," he said.

"And we can pray for him," she added.

Nathan hadn't stopped praying, and he doubted that she had either. He offered his hand. "Pray, then."

She took it. The sweet words she prayed for his father gave Nathan peace he hadn't had in a few days now—ever since Dad was shot. He squeezed her hand when she finished, and he didn't let go. Neither did she. What did it mean? He didn't *want* to let go. He'd asked her into this because he thought she could help him. Not so they could grow close again. Not so she could hurt him all over again.

Even so, her in this with him felt right. Was he only fooling himself?

The hospital loomed ahead. Releasing her hand, he gripped the wheel and steered through the visitor parking lot. Dad waking up could make all the difference—in all their lives.

He parked and didn't waste time getting out of his truck. By the time he made it around the grill, Erin had already hopped from the vehicle. She wasn't much for waiting on him to open doors. Joining him, she tucked her bag over her shoulder and fluffed her hair, glancing at her reflection in the window of another vehicle. She grimaced but said nothing about her appearance as they headed for the facility entrance. She was a real trouper, having endured so much.

"You look great." He grinned.

"Liar." She flashed an amused glance his way.

"I don't need to lie."

She angled her head at him and looked him up and down, her eyes lingering on his jaw, but she said nothing. Maybe she didn't have the heart to tell him the truth.

"You haven't shaved in a while," she said.

There it was, then. Truth. Now he felt self-conscious and scraped a hand over his scruffy jaw. "Mom and Dad have seen worse."

She cracked a grin. "I'm not saying that you don't look good."

He held the door for her to enter. "Oh, really?"

She walked through, then led him over to stand in front of the elevators.

"You're complimenting me?" He rubbed his jaw again.

She gave him a look that spoke volumes—she thought he looked good, but it was more that longing in her eyes that left him speechless. Better he didn't respond now anyway as others gathered at the elevator. The ride up took too much time, and he wished they'd taken the stairs. On Dad's floor, they got off the elevator and rushed down the hallway.

Nathan couldn't get to Dad's room fast enough. Hope surged that his father would smile at him and give him a hard time about something. Then again, Nathan shouldn't build his expectations, because that would only lead to disappointment. A local police officer stood by the door, and Nathan flashed his credentials, adding, "He's my father."

The officer nodded and stepped aside.

After a light knock at the door as he pushed it open, he entered, treading lightly. Erin hung back in the doorway until he gestured for her to come all the way in. He crept forward toward the bed. Dad's eyes were closed, so Nathan glanced at his mother.

She sat in a chair in the corner, a soft smile playing on her lips. "He's sleeping now."

He was glad he had tamped down his expectations. Nathan had wanted to see his dad's eyes open, to have a conversation with him. But still, Dad was conscious. That was the best news he'd heard in days.

Nathan took in his father's features. His face was still gaunt, but his color had definitely improved. The stress lines in his forehead and around his eyes appeared more relaxed and maybe even peaceful. The tension in Nathan's shoulders eased, though Dad wasn't out of the proverbial woods yet.

He moved to sit on the small sofa against the wall. Erin joined him.

"Has he spoken yet?" Nathan kept his voice down.

"No. He wasn't able to respond to the doctor's questions." Pain clawed his soul. "But he can still get better, right?"

"There's hope, yes. The doctor said it would take time. His brain has been through a major trauma. We don't know how much he will remember or be able to do. He will need therapy."

Years of it.

Nathan swallowed and keenly felt the lump in his throat. "At least he's alive. He survived."

And Nathan would continue to focus on that fact. He squeezed his eyes shut as unwelcome images flooded his mind. Dad falling forward into the water and Nathan discovering the gunshot wound. All the blood.

His pulse raced.

Erin took his hand and squeezed. "Are you okay?"

"I will be." He opened his eyes and looked at his father. He wouldn't think about what happened by the river or dwell in the past and what might have been had Dad stayed in Big Rapids. Stayed with his family. Nathan would focus on the here and now.

And right now, his father could still very well be in danger. That wouldn't change until they captured the shooter, along with everyone involved.

"I'm glad Dad has pulled out of it. And he's going to get better." Nathan held his mother's gaze. "I'm glad he has you here to support him." He stopped there. No point in asking questions about the past.

"I know you wanted more information about what happened," she said. "If he wakes up again, I'll ask him to share what he can tell me and pass it on to you."

Considering the deaths supposedly linked to Dad's investigation, Nathan wasn't entirely sure he wanted Mom asking questions and relaying answers. But they needed to learn the truth.

"You look like you could use some rest," he said. "I'll take you home for some sleep, then bring you back later."

Her lips flattened as she shook her head. "I have a room at the hotel across the street."

"Mom, this could be weeks and months. You can't stay here indefinitely." *The man isn't even your husband!*

She stared at her hands. "I know. But I don't see anyone else here with him. That breaks my heart. And . . . besides . . . a few months ago, your father gave me power of attorney in case something happened."

What? Nathan hadn't known. When she lifted her eyes to Nathan, he saw that she still loved his father. Deeply. And that broke *his* heart.

"I'm glad you and Dad remained friends over the years, after the divorce." The comment escaped unchecked, rising from his own miserable thoughts and questions—including why they had divorced to begin with. Was now really the time to bring that up?

"Mm-hmm."

So that's all he would get on that.

"How was your trip to Boston?" she asked. "Did you learn anything?"

"Like everything in my life right now, I have more questions." His mother didn't need the added burden of knowing all he was dealing with, but she might be able to supply some answers, and it was worth the risk. "What do you know of his life in Boston?"

"We kept on friendly terms for your sake. Your father wanted to know about *your* life."

"He could have called me." *Or come to see me or invited me to see him.*

"And he did. I know there were Christmases he missed with you because he had a girlfriend."

Bingo. "What do you know about her?"

"Nothing."

"Did you know she died in a car accident a few months ago?" It hit Nathan that possibly Dad had transferred the power of attorney to Mom after Lena was killed. Had he suspected something even then?

"Yes. I knew. Why are you asking? What does this have to do with anything?"

"Just wondering. You never told me about her, or that she died."

"Why should I? You struggled after we divorced. I didn't think you'd want to know about her, unless he told you, of course."

"I was a kid then. But I'm a man now. You can tell me stuff."

She shifted in her chair. "I know, baby. But what's the point in talking about things that just bring back the pain? You and your father were so close. I'm sorry things happened the way they did."

He released a laugh. "Yeah, we were close, you're right. He coached me in baseball, until he didn't. I remember that last game. The bases were loaded. The game would be won or lost on the next play. Dad always showed up to the games, but he didn't show up that day, even though he'd promised. I kept looking for him in the stands, and I ended up missing the catch of a lifetime. The other team won. Everyone blamed me for losing our biggest game of the season."

Nathan hadn't thought about that in years. Why was it coming to mind now? In that moment, he realized the incident had impacted him in every way. He constantly feared he would let everyone down. Right now, he worried he would fail as a detective in the most important case of his life—a case that wasn't even his to solve. And yet in a way, it had fallen to him anyway. If he could just save the day and make everything right.

"Oh, honey, I didn't know."

"A friend's dad brought me home. That was the day he walked out on us."

Nathan hung his head, wishing he hadn't relived that memory. He'd lost so much that day. Let his team down and lost their respect. Lost his family.

"Your father took a job offer," Mom said. "A better job in Boston. That had been his dream, to be a big-city detective. I'm sorry, son. I didn't want to move from the place where I grew up—my home—and believed raising you in a small-town environment was better for you. I didn't think he would actually *take* the job and leave us. And when he made that choice, I knew I couldn't live with him. Thinking back to it now, it all seems ridiculous."

Nathan remembered wanting to move with Dad, but he'd been told Dad wouldn't have time for him and couldn't be there for him because of his new job. So their family was ripped apart. For years growing up he fought the belief that his parents didn't love him enough. Weren't willing to sacrifice for him.

"My dream of being a detective has only been following in Dad's footsteps. Trying to fill his shoes." That, and earning the respect of others. Something he'd lost as a kid that day on the baseball field, as nonsensical as that seemed now, years later.

And now he was literally picking up where Dad had left off, still on that journey trying to fill Dad's shoes. An incredulous chuckle escaped. Who did he think he was? Nathan feared he didn't have what it took to solve this case, a case that wasn't officially his—present or past. In the end, he could lose his job and be the department disgrace. Disgrace his dad too. As if he should care.

But the trouble was, Nathan did care. Dad was only human, and he'd expressed his regrets on the river. And Nathan, in some deep part of himself, still wanted his dad in the stands again cheering him on.

He felt Erin watching him. Erin the psychologist. What would she think about all his crazy thoughts?

THIRTY

Nathan wasn't sure he wanted Erin analyzing him and wished he hadn't said so much in front of her. He stood and paced the room.

Erin cleared her throat. "I'm going to get some snacks from the vending machine. You want anything?"

"No, but thank you," Mom said.

"I'm good," Nathan said.

Erin offered him a soft smile and he knew she was intentionally giving them privacy, considering how deeply personal their conversation had turned. She exited the room.

He refocused on the conversation with Mom. Wanting to fill Dad's shoes. None of that mattered anymore. What did he care about being a hero, saving the day, if Dad never recovered, or if the truth about who shot him never came to light?

Everything hinged on finding out who had shot Dad.

He moved to sit next to Mom again. "Did he ever talk to you about a couple of articles that Dwayne gave him years ago?"

Her brow furrowed. "No, I don't think so. Why would he?"

Nathan shrugged. It was worth a shot. "He said Dwayne asked him to look into a cold case. It was before Dad left us. But Dad forgot about it with the divorce and the move."

A knock came at the door.

Henry poked his face in. Dread prickled over Nathan, and he glanced at Mom. "You called him?"

"Of course." Her face twisted with concern. "You didn't want me to?"

Henry strode into the room, hands in his pockets. "I got here as soon as I could. How's he doing?"

Mom shared with Henry what she'd told Nathan. Henry studied Dad, a painful frown carved in his features.

"And did he say anything when he woke up?" Henry asked.

"I was just telling Nathan he didn't speak. He couldn't answer the doctor's questions."

Henry moved closer to the bed. "But could you tell in his eyes that he . . ."

"I think he understood the doctor, he simply couldn't respond," she said. "He has a brain injury, and it will take time for him to fully recover." Mom's tone had grown slightly agitated.

Exhaustion had to be weighing on her, that and maybe she didn't welcome Henry's appearance at this moment, though she'd called him. Was Henry asking as a friend? Or as a sheriff who wanted to know more about who shot Dad? Or was he asking as the man who had assured Dad's boss that no one here would dig into the case? Nathan had gotten Hadlow's explanation, but he didn't like that Henry had agreed so willingly.

Nathan stood. "Henry, a word?" To Mom, he said, "I'll be back in a minute."

Or two or five. Nathan exited the hospital room, trusting Henry to follow. Even the hallway wasn't private enough, so he headed to the end of the corridor where a window overlooked a parking lot, the city of Bozeman, and the mountains in the distance.

Henry thrust his hands into his pockets again and rocked back and forth on his toes.

"Thanks for coming to check on Dad." Nathan crossed his arms to hide his clenched fists.

Henry looked like a sheriff who was about to blow a gasket, as Dad used to say, but instead held his tongue. Maybe Nathan would take a chance on his father's longtime friend, who'd already shared words of wisdom with him.

"You and Dad have known each other and been friends a long time."

"Indeed. That's why I want to learn the truth about who shot him too, son."

Nathan's heart pounded. Should he speak his mind? Or like Dad said, trust no one? He thought he understood better now that Dad wanted to protect others as well. But trust? Henry had earned Nathan's trust a long time ago—until that one overheard phone call.

"I've known you my whole life, Henry. You've been nothing but a good and honorable man. You've always had my back."

"What's this about, Nathan?"

"I overheard you on the phone telling Dad's boss that you promised no one would dig into his case."

Henry's face twisted up. "What exactly are you trying to say to me?"

"I think you know."

"You're reading into this something that isn't there. I'm not participating in a cover-up, if that's what you're suggesting. I hear you, son—the fact that you're bringing it up now tells me you want to believe that I'm on your side."

"But why promise him no one is going to dig into my father's shooting? Explain that to me."

Leaning in, Henry pressed his hand on Nathan's shoulder. "Calm down. I assured him no one would dig into the case your father was working or had been working before he'd been relieved of it."

"Sheriff—"

"Let me finish. Sullivan had called to share that they would be looking into your father's old cases from their end and requested we leave that part of the investigation to them." Henry threw up his hands. "They know the details and have the access, so I had no issue with that. But he called early this morning and told me what happened last night. He shared that you had been targeted. You and Erin both."

His brows had forged together as anger twisted with relief in his features. "I'm glad you weren't hurt. But what were you thinking dragging Erin out there and almost getting the both of you killed?" Henry leveled his gaze on Nathan. "As your father's friend, as your friend, Nathan, I don't want to have to tell him that I let something happen to you. So why don't you share with me what you know, what you've learned."

Nathan dropped his arms and rested his hands on his hips as he stared out the window. "The last thing my father said to me was that the only person he trusted was me. That no one can know what he was going to tell me. I even asked him if he'd told you."

Clearly stunned, Henry widened his eyes and his head inched back as if he'd been slapped.

Nathan hated that he'd hurt the man, and pain pinged around inside. "After what I learned in Boston, I think it has more to do with the fact that everyone who knows the truth is now dead. Dad needed at least one person to know. That was me."

Had Dad thought that Nathan wouldn't do anything with the information? That maybe he was just a country detective and could be trusted not to act on what he'd been told?

Henry's eyes softened—he'd taken the metaphorical rope Nathan had thrown him. "And that just confirms what Sullivan told me. Your life is at risk. Erin's too. All the more reason to tell me what you know."

Nathan hung his head.

"It's just me here," Henry said.

"You and Trevor. Don't forget you assigned him to work this."

"Yes, but this is personal to me," Henry said.

"A murder case he was investigating reminded him of a newspaper article about a cold case Dwayne had wanted him to look into years ago, but he'd forgotten about it. Dad's boss told him to drop it, and according to Dad, had suggested there wasn't a connection. Chief Hadlow's story was a little different. He came by the airport to speak with us before we left—but Hadlow said Dad was told to drop it for his own protection because he had been targeted. My understanding is that Dad's murder investigation was reassigned. Dad took time off to look into things on his own."

"You mean like you're doing." Henry's head bobbed in a silent chuckle, only it wasn't funny. "Like father, like son."

Yeah. Nathan had heard that enough.

"Chief Hadlow mentioned there was someone on the inside, someone in his department working both sides, and that he wanted to keep it all local and was only trying to protect Dad. If we can learn what specific murder case Dad was working and the connection he'd found to the cold case he mentioned, then we'll know more."

The tension in Nathan's shoulders eased a bit. Sharing the burden with Henry had to be the right thing to do. He realized that now. Like Erin had said early on, he needed more information before he could know if talking to Henry, against Dad's wishes, was the right thing.

"Thanks for trusting me, Nathan. I guess you know you're officially on desk duty while the Boston shooting is being investigated. Shouldn't take more than a couple of days. Do you need a loaner pistol in the meantime?"

Nathan chuckled. "I didn't take my department-issued weapon to Boston. I still have that at home. And I have the second gun that I took to Boston. It remained in the rental car during the shooting, so I brought that back with me."

"Good. Keep protection with you at all times," Henry said. "You've learned a lot more than we could have sticking around town. I'm sure Trevor will appreciate your efforts. Anything else you want to share that we can look into?"

Nathan would send the crime board images to Trevor, and he would let Trevor call in the names to RISS. But there was one thing he could hand over to Henry right now.

Nathan pulled the envelope Holly gave him out of his pocket and handed it over to Henry. "I want to know who this man is."

THIRTY-ONE

Feeling better than he had in a couple of days—mentally, that was—Nathan steered them back to the county seat of Big Rapids. He was ready to take a shower and wipe all the grime from last night away, and he knew Erin was eager to return home to check on her mother. Next to him, Erin slept in her seat.

He took the turn off the main highway onto the two-lane road that would cut across the counties. The curvy mountain road would give him the views he'd missed on their excursion back East. When he crossed the Grayback County line, he breathed a sigh of relief.

Almost home.

Except two of the most important people in his life who made Grayback home were back at the hospital in Bozeman, and truly he had no reason to be relieved—not until they were well on the other side of solving the investigation. It felt right and good to have Henry in the mix with him now, and he expected to hear from Detective Trevor West soon.

Erin shifted in her seat, pulling his thoughts to the present. She mumbled something about the fact that she could sleep while with him. That let him know she was comfortable with him—and that he had earned her trust. That part he enjoyed, but not the fact that she talked in her sleep or even had a few bad dreams. That disturbed him. He feared telling her would make her feel awkward and less comfortable with him, so he said nothing. He was glad she'd dozed off so she wouldn't ask him questions as he processed his troubling thoughts.

Like who was the insider Hadlow had mentioned? Chief Hadlow himself? Lieutenant Sullivan? Was Hadlow or Sullivan protecting Dad or the person playing both sides—someone working for organized crime—in their pockets, as the saying went? Whatever the situation, Nathan would make sure Trevor West was aware of this and let him dig around in Boston this time. Nathan would stick close to home . . . protecting Erin.

He still didn't have the full story about what happened in Seattle.

At the next turn, Nathan stopped at a small gas station on the corner. He'd need to fill up before heading down this road. While getting gas, he felt the familiar, subtle rumble of a small earthquake. Nathan finished and opened the door of his truck.

Erin stirred and yawned. She glanced at him.

Before climbing back in, he smiled. "You want coffee?"

She stretched. Did she have any idea how beautiful she was?

"Yes, and to use the little girls' room."

While she used the bathroom, he grabbed them both coffee and then met her back at the truck.

In the cab, he buckled, turned on the ignition, adjusted the temperature, and then finally took a sip of the coffee—it was still much too hot to drink. Unfazed by the heat, she sipped on her own, then leaned back.

"We still have forty-five minutes on the road, so feel free to go back to sleep," he said.

Her head against the seat, she turned to him. "I could drive and you could sleep."

"I'm good, actually. I'm accustomed to pulling all-nighters."

And he couldn't sleep with the tumultuous thoughts warring in his mind.

"Oh, really? Grayback County keeps you that busy?"

He steered onto the road. "You'd be surprised."

"I *would*, actually." She laughed softly. But her tone turned serious with her next words. "Do you think it was worth it, Nathan?"

"Was *what* worth it?"

"Our trip to Boston. It could have gotten you into big trouble, and now it seems like we might be targeted."

"Yes, I think it was worth it. Dad was already targeted, and we have much more information than we would otherwise have." He glanced her way, then quickly focused back on the road. Her eyes were bright and her cheeks a soft rosy color. She was definitely awake. "Can I ask you a question?"

"Of course." She took another sip of coffee.

"Did you believe Chief Hadlow when he said he was one of the good guys?"

"Yes."

"Why? How can you know?"

"I can't actually know, but I believe he is. Logically—psychologically, that is—if we look at his actions, then he was telling the truth. He didn't have to seek us out and warn us about the danger."

"That makes sense. But what about your feelings? Let's say you remove those actions, do you have any gut feelings about him?"

"I think that I believe him. Why do you ask? Are you wondering why your dad asked you not to tell anyone?"

"Yes. I feel like I'm missing something." Hadlow had thought convincing Nathan that he was a "good guy" was important. Nathan wanted to believe him. He wanted to believe Henry too.

"Let's look at the context of the entire conversation you had with your father. After what we learned in Boston—a woman he loved and her son, another detective, murdered, so he believed—it seems to me that he was afraid of putting more people in danger. He was with you at the fishing hole, a place he deemed safe. He needed to confide in someone. Maybe it wasn't a matter of trusting, as much as it was a matter of protecting."

He scratched his scruffy jaw. "I think you're right. I said as much to Henry."

The truck hit a pothole and bounced. Nathan almost lost his coffee.

"Wow, I don't think I've ever been on this road." Erin peered out her window. "It's . . . beautiful, and a little terrifying." The road overlooked a massive drop of several hundred feet and offered a view of the mountains and foothills for miles. A gentle mist rose from the valleys, weaving in and out of thousands of acres of evergreens. "It's breathtaking."

"And bumpy. Sorry."

"It's the scenic drive," she said. "Thank you for that."

"I've been here once or twice. And it's scenic. But unfortunately, we have some trouble." He slowed the vehicle at the sight ahead, then stopped.

A rockslide.

"Well, that's just great," he said.

Giant boulders blocked their way. The couple of cars he'd passed heading in the opposite direction must have turned around.

"So no chance we can wait for someone to remove the rockslide?"

"It'll take hours for them to get here, and once they're here with the necessary equipment, even longer to remove the rocks and secure the area." Nathan maneuvered the truck and turned around.

A logging truck rumbled above them on a road carved out of the hill of mostly stumps and meadow grasses. The truck would be exiting onto the road at the intersection just ahead. Nathan thought to speed up, especially since the truck was hauling pretty fast. The last thing he wanted was to follow one of these trucks all the way.

Erin seemed completely relaxed despite this wrinkle in their plans.

Coming toward them on the road was another vehicle. Nathan would warn them about the rockslide if he could. Except the vehicle stopped in the middle of the road on the other side of the intersection where the logging truck would turn. Had they spotted the rockslide down the road? Good.

Wait a minute. He'd seen this vehicle before when he thought someone might have been following them from the airport, but he'd dismissed it. Nathan slowly continued forward but slammed on the brakes when a man got out of the car.

"What's he doing?" Erin asked. She shifted taller in her seat.

The man lifted a gun and aimed at the logging truck speeding down the hill. Disbelief edging over him, Nathan reached for his own gun, but before he could act . . .

Pop, pop, pop, pop.

The shooter had taken out the truck driver, and now the logging truck barreled forward at full speed. The trailer leaned precariously, then rolled all the way over, taking the cab of the truck with it and dumping its load of logs.

The lumber rolled and bounced, thundering down the hill directly toward Nathan and Erin.

THIRTY-TWO

et us out of here, Nathan." She grabbed the handgrip on the door.

"I'm working on it." He put the truck in reverse.

The tires spun out, burning rubber and throwing pebbles, before getting traction. Nathan could only back away from the oncoming rush of deadly logs. He couldn't drive them forward and out of harm's way because the same man who took out the logging truck driver was now aiming his weapon at them.

"Get down!" Nathan shouted.

She ducked, as did he, though he maintained his grip on the steering wheel and his foot on the accelerator. Bullets pelted the windshield and the grill.

Erin gripped her cell and tried to call 911. The call wouldn't go through because she couldn't get a signal. The truck lurched, moving backward now. Speeding away from the bullets but not outrunning them. Ducking in the seat, she glanced through the passenger-side window to peek at the hill above. Logs continued to bounce and roll and would soon be upon them.

"Faster. You have to go faster!" She squeezed her eyes shut. "I don't think we're going to make it."

The truck bumped and wobbled.

"He took out the tires." Nathan sounded both angry and determined.

Her protector. If anyone could get them out of this, it was Nathan.

She didn't want to imagine the reasons why the shooter wanted to slow them down—what with logs bouncing down the hill above. *Just bounce right over top of us, please.*

"Are we going to make it?" Erin hated the fear and desperation resounding in her voice.

"I'm giving it all I got," Nathan said, "but you might want to pray."

She'd never stopped praying, but she would pray out loud. "Lord, please help us. Save us!"

Nathan opened his door and leaned out.

"What are you doing?"

"I need to see where I'm going. I don't want to send us off the road to our deaths either."

Now *there* was a great image—that gorgeous view of miles and miles of mountains and the drop that could kill them. Erin trembled as time seemed to drag on forever, and she looked up at the hill that appeared to ripple above them. The toppling timber had spread out across the hill and would roll over and crush them in mere seconds.

Were they about to die? She squeezed her eyes shut once again, her heart pounding in rhythm with the thunderous danger cascading toward them. Any moment now . . .

Tears surged. Her heart palpitated.

A powerful force rammed into the truck, spinning it. Erin was flung forward, but her seat belt kept her in place, though she dropped her cell phone. Her stomach lurched as fear invaded.

Nathan never released his grip on the steering wheel and shifted gears, accelerating forward this time. Had they come to the end of the road where it stopped with the rockslide?

He leaned toward her and peered out her window as well as the front windshield as if he could dodge the oncoming logs, the man with the gun momentarily forgotten.

Filling her vision, a log rushed directly for them but crashed into the truck bed and hung there, lifting the front end. It dropped down again, and Nathan accelerated, but the log dragged behind them. With the deflated tires, the addition of the log slowed the truck to a crawl, then to a complete stop. The tires spun but barely moved them.

"Get out! Get out and run."

Erin hesitated for a few seconds, then shoved her door open and practically fell out. She righted herself and, watching for logs, ran back toward the rockslide. She dashed away from the crushing logs, second-guessing her decision to leave the truck, which had offered at least a modicum of protection.

After a look over her shoulder, she realized that Nathan hadn't followed her. A log had toppled and jammed against the driver's side of the truck.

"Nathan!" she shouted.

Pulse thundering in her ears, she wanted to rush forward to save him. But what could she do? She couldn't remove the cause of the jam. Maybe he could crawl out on the passenger side.

Erin knew the danger from the logs would pass soon enough, but what she didn't know was if it would take Nathan from her. "Nathan!"

Once the logs stopped, a shooter remained—watching and waiting.

Should she race back to the truck? She glanced beyond the vehicle to the shooter and the cacophony he'd caused. He smiled—a sick, twisted grin. Behind him, other vehicles were turning around because of the onslaught of logs and the rockslide—the road was obviously closed. Did any of the drivers understand a shooter had caused the overturned logging truck?

She hoped someone had called for help. Erin covered her mouth and watched the last log bounce on the road and almost hit the truck but miss it on its way down the mountain. As for the logging truck, the cab lay on its side up the hill. Was the driver dead or simply injured?

All these thoughts raced through her mind at the same moment.

Across the way, the shooter was still smiling. Terror gripping her, Erin darted behind a boulder. She pressed her back against the smooth, cold surface and gulped for air.

A killer was after them.

Targeting them.

Had he been the one to shoot Nathan's father? Had he shot at them in Boston last night? They could have been on the same flight with him!

Carefully, she peered around the boulder. She would commit his face to memory, as much as she could make out from this distance. What was taking Nathan so long? She watched the truck and the shooter.

The passenger-side door popped open again. Nathan slid out onto the ground, holding a gun in his hand and her bag over his shoulder. He crawled toward the back end of the truck and used the log resting in the bed as cover.

"Over here!" she called.

He dashed forward and crouched next to her behind the rock. She wrapped her arms around him, good and tight. No words would come. No words were needed.

Nathan was safe. He was here.

Danger seemed to chase them at every turn. How many near-death experiences would she have in this lifetime? They were starting to stack up while she was with Nathan. She eased away and looked him in the face. Dust and mud covered his scruffy features. She smiled and chuckled as tears rolled over her lips.

Without thinking, she pressed her lips against his, her hands cupping his face. In that one simple kiss, she sensed all the passion he held back, and all the longing for him she could no longer ignore. But this wasn't the time . . . She stepped back.

He looked a little stunned, his eyes wide, then appeared to shake it off. "We're not out of danger yet."

"But you're here now."

"Yes." He chambered a round and tossed her the cell she'd left behind in the truck.

She caught it. "Thanks."

"Call the police."

"I tried already and couldn't get a signal."

"Keep trying."

"We need to take a picture of the shooter. Maybe he's the one who shot your father. Maybe he shot at us in Boston too."

Nathan peered around the rock, then his shoulders went slack. "He's gone. The car is gone. Other cars have stopped and people are getting out of them. If we're fortunate, someone took a picture of him and the license plate."

"But he only shot at the truck or at us when no one else was around. They could have thought he was waiting to help."

He sighed and put his gun away and offered his hand, which she took.

"I need to go check on the truck driver."

Erin took in the disaster zone and the toppled logging truck. "Looks like a few others are already up there."

He nodded. "I feel somewhat responsible for what happened to him."

Nathan's father brought serious danger back to Montana with him when he returned. Erin almost wished she hadn't agreed to help. She had so much on her plate already, but now that she was in this with Nathan, she couldn't turn her back on him.

He looked her up and down. "Are you hurt anywhere?"

"No, I'm okay. That was close, Nathan. So . . . close." Her voice shook.

"Come here." He reached for her, but she stepped back.

"Please go check on the truck driver."

"Will you be okay?"

She gave a subtle nod. "I'll keep trying to call for help, though I hope someone else has already gotten through."

Nathan left her and started hiking up the hill.

How much more will we have to go through before this is over?

And if there was a next time, would they both survive?

THIRTY-THREE

The thunderous sound of logs bouncing down the mountain still echoed in her head, even though yesterday was behind her. Other than that, Mom's house was quiet this morning as Erin sat at her desk in the makeshift office and stared at her computer. If there had been any doubt before that she and Nathan had been targeted, the logs tumbling down the hill and the shooter standing in the road with his sick smile removed it. She and Nathan had given their statements about the logging truck incident after an already exhausting night that included practically fleeing from Boston.

Mom was already struggling, and Erin had brought danger into their lives. And in the middle of yesterday's chaos, she'd missed the Seattle detective's call. She'd left a voice mail in response, though, explaining that she would need to reschedule the conversation. She felt bruised inside and out.

At least Nathan had seen to security so she didn't have to be concerned. He'd made sure a deputy was on duty twenty-four seven to watch Mom's house. If Erin went somewhere, the deputy would go too.

As for Mom, she'd started back at her volunteer job today, so Erin had seen her off this morning to work at the Main Street Thrift Shop. Already Mom's spirits seemed lifted. Erin hadn't shared with her the full nature of the events in Boston or their drive home from Bozeman. Keeping that to herself was for the best. The extra security was a simple measure provided because Nathan's father had been targeted, she'd told Mom, who hadn't asked for further explanation.

Erin needed to take a few steps back from Nathan's covert investigation—though it sounded like he would be working with the sheriff and detective, after all. Time would tell if that was a mistake. As for her part, she couldn't look at the crime board again until she cleared her mind.

In the meantime, she could focus on completing her podcast, especially since she was growing an unintended audience—Carissa, Nathan, and now Detective Munson from Seattle, who let her know he was anxiously awaiting the next episode. Closing her eyes, she tried to quiet her thoughts and think about what came next. Except her mind still churned too much information, and every small sound, every noise, set her on edge. She understood that she could be suffering from PTSD after a week's worth of terrors.

Erin rubbed her eyes. This wasn't normal. This wasn't real life—or at least any life she'd ever known.

Lord, what is going on? Please, please just give me peace. Help me to rest in you, despite everything that's happened.

And her continual heart's cry resounded . . . *I need answers.*

Blowing out a breath, she focused on creating episode 4. She had to get the story out for her own peace of mind, and for the old fans and new ones who were waiting for the next episode. No matter what else happened, she needed to consistently build her fan base—growing it could help solve crimes. Maybe she could even build this into a sustainable income instead of going back to work writing forensic evaluations.

She read through the script she'd written for the next episode. After opening up the software, she put on her headphones and took a deep breath.

Welcome to Missing Children: Deadly Rabbit Trails, Episode 4

Erin recapped the previous podcast, then moved on to the new material.

With her mother's permission, Erica shared her story with the police. She and Missy had gone outside after playing in her bedroom and discovered her rabbit—Mr. Bojangles—was missing. They searched the yard for him, then decided he must have somehow found a way through the chain-link fence and escaped into the woods. Erica and Missy loved Mr. Bojangles and were worried a predator would get him. Though they had each been instructed not to go off into the woods alone, or at least without permission, they didn't want to waste time asking for it.

They ran around the front to go through the gate, then made their way into the darkening woods. Erica had snagged a carrot from the refrigerator to coax Mr. Bojangles close enough so that she could grab him. Before long, though, she and Missy had gotten lost, and the woods were dark. Erica was scared.

The police report said she told them what happened through tears. Officer Farley hated pressuring the child, but she didn't want to waste time. Any information Erica shared could help save Missy. Erica continued with her story, stating that a man emerged from the darkness, from behind a tree. Erica and Missy both backed away from him, instinctively knowing he was a bad man. Erica told police, "He scared us when he looked at us and smiled." Erica then sobbed into her hands. Her mother, Mrs. Weeks, insisted the police had enough information, but they countered that they must hear the entire story in order to help find Missy. Erica continued and explained how the man lunged for Missy, but they escaped and ran as fast as they could. Erica held Missy's hand and wouldn't let go. "I wouldn't let the man take Missy," she said.

According to the report, Erica then sobbed, barely able to get the rest out. "I was wrong," she said. Erica stumbled and fell, and the man

grabbed Missy, then disappeared into the darkness. Erica scrambled to
her feet and called out to her friend. But Missy and the man were gone.

The last few days weighed heavy on Erin, but she powered
through even as her voice shook.

Your assignment is to think back to that night when the bridge
collapsed and a little girl was abducted. Taken in the night. Talk to
friends and family. If you remember anything out of the ordinary, no
matter how small, or if you think you saw Missy Gardner, please call
the Wisconsin FBI field office or your local police.

Erin gave those numbers, added the appropriate advertisements, then ended the podcast. She didn't want to revisit this
episode, so she published the recording. Then she blew out
a breath and hung her head, truly spent for the day—maybe
even the week—but she still had more left to do today. At least
she'd finally gotten most of the podcast out to help find Missy
Gardner, and her efforts had utterly drained her.

She needed to pull herself together for Mom, who would
return in a few hours. And Nathan, who would stop by this
afternoon. He had questions for her about Seattle and wanted
to know the truth, but after yesterday's events on the highway,
maybe he had forgotten. In the meantime, she needed to
shower and change out of her T-shirt and sweats.

After getting ready, she took one last look in the mirror and
dabbed on concealer to hide the dark circles under her eyes.

Her cell rang, startling her. She glanced at the number.

Detective Munson. She didn't have the emotional stamina
to speak to him at the moment, but if she didn't get this over
with, he would just keep calling.

Erin headed down the hall to her office as she answered
the cell. "Yes."

"Dr. Larson. This is—"

"Hello, Detective. I know I missed our agreed-upon time yesterday. I was in an accident." She eased into the chair at her desk.

"I'm sorry to hear that. Are you okay?"

No. "Yes. I'm alive." She waited for a breath, then asked, "Have you learned anything more?"

"I'm afraid so. We found the man who was driving the boat." She sat up at that news. "And?"

He cleared his throat. "Unfortunately, we found him floating in Puget Sound. Dead. Dr. Larson, I'm concerned about your safety. I've spoken again with Miss Edwards. She is going to stay with some friends in California for a week."

Oh, thank goodness. Carissa should be safe then. Erin steadied her voice. "I'm glad to hear that. And I'm here in Montana with family, so we should both be safe while you solve this. I have a good friend here who is a detective. He's protecting me. In fact, there's a deputy watching the house where I'm staying right now." For a completely different reason.

"Good. Can I have your detective friend's name and number so I can call him?"

Erin didn't want to add more to Nathan's plate, but she offered the requested information.

"There's more to this, but I need to talk to you in person," Munson said. "I'd like to drive out to see you."

Wow. "Okay, then. I'll meet you here in town. I'll text the place if you can give me the time."

"Thanks for your cooperation. I'll meet you in the morning at the location you designate."

"Let's say nine o'clock at Thelma's Café." On the outskirts of town. Mom would be at the thrift store by then.

Detective Munson agreed and ended the call.

Erin stared at her cell. What terrible timing. She didn't believe she could offer the detective answers, but she was glad she was here instead of in Seattle. She would need to tell Nathan everything.

Everything. Including the dark secret she hadn't been able to share before. But could she truly do it? Was she finally ready? *God, help me tell him . . .*

And if she did, what then? Did she think her opening up to him would magically bring them together again? That he would even want her?

She touched her lips. Their kiss—so simple and gentle and yet so much more—told her yes.

Still, her hands shook at the idea of revealing what she'd kept hidden for so long.

Erin left the office to go to the kitchen. She grabbed a tall glass of water and guzzled it, then headed to the bathroom for two ibuprofen and downed them.

Was she even in any condition to care for her mother, who seemed to be doing much better than Erin at the moment? Once back at her desk, she sent an email to Carissa to check on her. Then decided she needed to review Newt's crime board. If nothing else, it was a distraction. She pulled up the image on her iPad, then sent it to her laptop. Erin put her iPad away in its case, but her hand still trembled and it slipped from her fingers and clattered on the desk before landing facedown on the rug.

Dropping to the floor, she reached under the desk. She felt the smooth case of her iPad and grabbed it, hoping she hadn't cracked the screen, then lifted her head. Her face was eye level with the computer. She must have accidentally toggled the screen because she was back on the podcast page.

Someone had already responded, and the comment gave her pause.

You forgot to mention the pink hat that your friend wore that night.

THIRTY-FOUR

Since Erin had read the comment, her legs had continued to tremble. Her hands shook too. She had to get her composure before she headed over to Main Street Thrift Shop to see Mom. Though maybe accosting her at work wasn't the best idea, Erin had to talk to someone. Mom hadn't answered Erin's calls or texts, but she could be busy. She loved her volunteer work and giving back to the community. Erin hated to shatter both their worlds.

She grabbed her purse and headed out the front door, rushing right into Nathan. Surprised to see him, though she shouldn't have been since he'd planned to stop by, Erin yelped and took a step back.

"Whoa, whoa." He gently gripped her arms. "Erin, what's wrong?"

She couldn't breathe and gulped for air. "I need to get to Mom."

"I don't think you're in any condition to drive. I'll drive you, but is your mother okay? What's going on?"

Erin shook her head. Maybe she wasn't in any condition to talk to her mother either. She stepped back into the house, and Nathan followed her. He urged her to the kitchen table and pulled out a chair for her to sit.

"I'll get you something to drink," he said.

Erin stared at her shaking hands. Fisted and refisted them.

She had lost control. What good was being a psychologist if she couldn't maintain control?

The Seattle detective's call tangled up with the eerie comment on her podcast. Once again, she struggled for breath.

Nathan glanced at her, concern carved into his features. He set a mug of hot water with a tea bag in front of her. "It's green tea. That's all I could find. Calm down and tell me what's got you so upset."

She tried dragging in air to calm her frazzled nerves and shook her head when the words wouldn't come.

Nathan gently took her fingers and rubbed them. "You're having a panic attack. This is just the culmination of the last few hours. I never should have told you anything. That's all on me. Relax, Erin. You don't need to be involved in my investigation anymore."

"No. You don't understand."

Nathan bolted from the chair and started looking through cabinets and drawers. "Found it." He pulled out a small paper sack and handed it over. "This will help you breathe."

Just like old times.

Erin had had a few panic attacks years ago, and Nathan remembered what she needed.

She breathed into the sack so the mixture of gases, oxygen and carbon dioxide, would balance out. Then she dropped the sack. Finally, she could talk. "This isn't about your investigation. I'm not going to be able to calm down until I talk to my mother. I can't get her on her cell."

"I'll call the thrift store and have someone locate her and bring her here. Please tell me what's going on. What happened?"

Nathan's cell rang, but he ignored it.

"That could be the detective calling you."

"What detective?"

"Munson from Seattle." Erin rubbed her arms and shared with Nathan what the detective had said.

Nathan studied her but said nothing as the furrow in his brow deepened. He scraped a hand down his face and leaned back. "I can see why you're so upset."

No, he couldn't because she hadn't told him everything.

"So you have no idea what happened back there? What it's about or why someone would have tried to harm you?"

"It could have been about Carissa and had nothing at all to do with me. Except . . ."

He leaned forward again and placed his hands on the table as though he would reach across and take hers, but he didn't. "Except what, Erin?"

"My nightmare, what I've been running from for years . . . I think it's found me." This part would hurt Nathan more than anything.

"I can't help you unless you're willing to tell me." Hurt flickered in his eyes.

And that was the crux of it. She'd finally decided to tell him. But in her own time and in her own way. Now that had been taken from her. She hadn't trusted him enough to open up back then. And she was hurting him all over again today. He'd known all along that she'd kept something from him, and that secret had cost their relationship.

Oh, Nathan. She would give anything to deserve a man like him.

Tears rolled down her cheeks. She hated that her tears revealed how vulnerable and exposed she truly was when she'd worked so hard to be strong and cover up how broken she still felt inside.

Erin swiped at the tears, staring at the knots of wood in the oak table. "I focus on cold cases because I have one specific case that I have longed to resolve." She risked a glance at him.

Compassion and understanding poured from his gaze, replacing the hurt. His eyes shimmered with concern. She needed to feel his touch and reached for his hand, which he quickly offered. He was risking so much by being here. Risking the pain again. She knew because the hurt ignited inside her all over again.

She cleared her throat and lifted her gaze to him. "You listened to my podcast?"

"I finished your latest episode, yes. Today I got an email that it was available. So before coming over here, I listened."

She held his gaze, willing him to understand, then said, "It's what I couldn't tell you before."

He took a few breaths, then his face morphed and twisted. "That's . . . you? That's *your* story? *You're* Erica Weeks?"

She hung her head. Couldn't look at him. She had to get to the point. "Someone posted a comment on today's episode."

His grip tightened. "What did it say?"

Erin lifted her face again and held his gaze. "The comment asked about the pink hat."

Nathan frowned. "Pink hat?"

"I didn't include information about the hat in the podcast. The only person who would know about that . . ." Her throat grew tight, and she couldn't finish.

"Is the person who took your friend."

"Missy was wearing a pink hat that night."

"You're sure nobody else knew? Not even her mother? Other friends?"

"Nobody knew. And I never mentioned the pink hat to anyone. Looking back now, maybe mentioning that would have helped find her, but I was just a kid."

Nathan pushed from the table. "It sounds like the abductor found you, then, but why bother?"

She stared at her unsteady hands, though she felt calmer now. Nathan's grip and the way he listened helped soothe her. "After all these years, I don't know."

Nathan pulled out his cell. "Looks like that call was from the Seattle detective, just like you said. I'll call him back, but right now, we need to get a forensics guy on the comment and see what they can find out."

Erin nodded.

Nathan made the call and then finally spoke to someone about getting a computer forensics tech involved. Erin doubted that would yield anything to help them.

He ended the call, then studied her. "You're the criminal psychologist here. Maybe you can come up with why someone would stalk or troll you years later. That's why you went to great lengths to keep your identity anonymous."

She nodded. "I don't understand how anyone could know that it's me, Erica, telling the story. Maybe I'm overreacting. It could be the abductor, yes, but maybe he doesn't know I'm Erica and he's simply commenting on a fact that I didn't share on the podcast."

"I still don't like this." Nathan had crossed his arms, clearly as disturbed as she was.

Closing her eyes, Erin shuddered. "I might not be overreacting." But how could she know, considering she was traumatized?

"Explain."

"From a psychological perspective, I'm not sure the abductor would comment unless he hoped to get a reaction because he knew it was me, Erica Weeks, sharing the story." And he certainly got a reaction. "I just don't get how he could know it's me."

Nathan stared at her. "Something you said. The way you said it. He might have commented to get a reaction to find out if it was you. I'm more worried that if it is the abductor, that he can find out your new identity."

Erin rubbed her arms. She didn't need one more thing to worry about.

"Erin . . ."

She hadn't realized Nathan was talking to her again. "I'm sorry. What?"

"Someone with know-how could dig through the many layers and find your true identity, couldn't they?"

"Yes."

Erin was much too close to look at this logically or to ferret out the criminal mind behind it—though hadn't that been the whole reason she'd become a psychologist and focused on the evil?

She'd wanted to learn why. Why had someone taken Missy?

Compassion flooded his gaze, and he pressed his hand over hers. "I don't know what or who is at play here, but I do know that I don't want to see you get hurt. Just know that I'm here for you. We'll go through this together."

This time.

She saw encouragement in his eyes, and more understanding than she deserved. In return she gave him a subtle nod, hoping he, too, understood her silent message—they would make it through this together.

"I think I understand now why Mom whisked me away so fast and changed my name. She understood what I couldn't back then. She told me people would look at me funny. The news would chase me. The best way for me to get over it and move on was to relocate and change my name, our names. Our lives and identities. But now I wonder if she was just worried that the abductor would come after me because I was the only one who had seen him."

And now he's found me.

THIRTY-FIVE

N athan felt like a bomb had dropped on him. Why hadn't Erin shared her story, her past, with him before?

Then again, he understood. Her mother had moved them. Changed their names. Started a new life. And influenced Erin to hide everything she'd lived through. Push it all down deep. That's why she'd had to see a therapist for so many years. Maybe her panic attacks and the necessary therapy had more to do with hiding information and keeping secrets than the actual trauma. He was no psychologist. Who was he to attempt to psychoanalyze Erin?

Still, Nathan wanted answers. He *needed* answers.

"After all these years, why did you suddenly choose to talk about what happened before? Why did you create that podcast *now*?" He tried to hide the hurt he felt. Yes, he was hurt that she hadn't trusted him enough to tell him everything, but he hurt *for* her also. He understood her even better now.

This was the deep, dark story of her past that she kept inside. The reason she feared the dark and the woods. Had the panic attacks. The reason for her nightmares. The drive and motivation behind her career choice and the end to their relationship.

Nathan wished she would have trusted him enough to tell him before. He would have been there for her, but in the end, maybe she'd known that opening up to Nathan wouldn't have been enough to make a difference—the kind of difference she needed in her life. "I'm sorry, Erin." He'd pushed too hard. He was asking too much. She owed him no explanation. He ached for her in the deepest way because he still *cared* deeply for her. And sitting here in this moment of truth and vulnerability, he could at least be honest with himself . . .

He still loved her.

Erin. She was in danger, and he would protect her with his life. She pressed her face into her hands and rubbed her eyes.

"Oh, honey," he whispered, wishing he could do so much more for her. Take the pain away.

"I thought . . . I thought if I became a psychologist, focusing on criminals, that nobody would ever see how broken I am on the inside. No one would look past my doctorate title. And I thought picking through those evil minds, I could find answers. Why do people commit such heinous acts?"

Nathan nodded, simply listening. She was telling him everything now, sharing her heart like she never had before. He'd seen her deep struggles but hadn't known the cause. Until now. "Go on."

"Even so, I couldn't find the answer. So I turned to podcasting about cold cases. I wanted to dig into the past. To learn how to find the answers—*why* people went missing. *Who* were the people who dared to take someone, and then what did they do with them? Deep down I wanted to solve cold cases. Find answers."

Erin finally dropped her hands. So many emotions swam in her gaze as she looked at him. "And there was no cold case I wanted to solve more than the one I played a role in. I couldn't move forward until I'd finished this podcast. At least speaking the words, getting them out there for more people to hear.

Or so I thought that somehow, some way, that would help me. That it would help bring closure. And if not, I at least wanted to know what happened to her. And in all of that, I hoped and prayed for answers." She opened her palms. "In the end, maybe I'll never know. In that case, I might always be broken."

He eased his hand forward to take her palm. He couldn't speak to her brokenness, but God help him, he wanted nothing more than to encourage her. She was kind and generous, sharper than anyone he knew. The most beautiful woman he'd ever met. But on the inside, she believed herself to be broken.

How did he fix that? Only God could fix her, if she was indeed broken. He knew that God drew especially near to broken souls.

"Erin . . ." Her name was barely a whisper on his lips.

"My efforts have backfired on me in the worst possible way."

"Maybe not. Maybe now we can finally catch this man *because* of your podcast." So, there was hope in all of this. He should have recognized that immediately. "It's the silver lining, Erin. Don't you see?"

Her blue-green eyes searched his face, as if she were finding her way out of a fog. His smile was for her, and she smiled in return, tears welling then spilling.

She swiped at them. "Do you really think so?"

His insides twisted just seeing the hope his words had brought her—*God, please let it be so.*

"I think this could be a breakthrough for you." For *us?* "The big question is what to do next. How to keep you safe."

"You're already doing that. There's a deputy outside, re-member? And . . . you're here." Her eyes warmed, and the corners of her lips remained tilted upward.

All good signs. *Thank you, Lord.*

Nathan had wanted to solve a big case, but right now, it felt like he had too many investigations, especially since they involved people near and dear to his heart.

People he loved.

He took in Erin's face, the hope swimming in her gaze, and wanted to pull her into his arms and love her fully. And he would, given the chance.

But danger lurked around them.

The man might have caught on to the podcast but still did not know Erin's current identity or where she lived. Nathan wouldn't take any chances, though. "Please tell me you did not respond to him. He might simply want to confirm what he suspects is true."

She shook her head. "I'm too shaken up. Now I wish I had, but then again, I had no idea what to say in response."

"Good. We'll wait to hear what the computer forensics tech has to say. Someone is supposed to call me back about the comment on your website."

"I don't think someone would comment if they thought it could be tracked."

"It's a start. We need to look into this, regardless."

"Thank you, Nathan. I'm . . . We're supposed to be trying to find your father's shooter. I don't want to take you away from that."

"I'm glad I handed over the picture to Henry. Part of me feels like I betrayed my father's trust, but things have gotten out of hand. Now others are looking into the shooter. While I keep a hand on the pulse of that investigation, I can focus on helping you with this. Between this and Seattle, you could be in imminent danger, so we need to get answers as quickly as possible. But when I got here, you were rushing out the door to get to your mother. What do you want to do now?"

"I wish she were home with me here and I could tell her what's happened."

"I'm not sure that you should stay here until we know the man from the past hasn't figured out who you are and where you live." He called Henry and put the cell to his ear.

She pressed her hand over his. "No. I don't want anyone else to know about this for now. Not yet. Help me keep it quiet. Before I tell anyone else, I need to tell Mom. Please."

Nathan took a deep breath to corral his frustration. What was it with people and their secret lives lately? Dad not wanting him to share had put him in the worst kind of position. Now Erin wanted to continue to hold her past close. He ended the call without leaving a voice mail. "All right. But seems to me that the more people on this, the better."

He would also like to hear what Erin's mother had to say about the past, but then again, Celia might pack up their lives and disappear.

Nathan would prefer he didn't lose Erin again. He would do whatever it took to keep her safe, and though it would break him all over again, if that meant she had to run and hide again, then he would wish her all the best.

THIRTY-SIX

itting in the passenger seat of Nathan's replacement vehicle the next morning, Erin stared out the window as he drove them to Thelma's to meet Detective Munson. Erin still hadn't told Mom about that podcast comment. Her mother was in a sensitive place, and Erin thought the past blowing back into their lives at this juncture would unsettle her far too much. She thought of the attic—something had already sent her mother over the edge. What was it? With their lives potentially targeted, Erin had more pressing matters to worry about.

But she and Mom should be safe for the time being. With the deputy sitting outside the house in his car and, of course, their neighbor Delmar also watching the house, that should be enough security for now.

Erin absently shook her head—she didn't understand why Mom trusted that guy. He gave Erin the creeps. A shudder crept over her, and she rubbed her arms.

"You okay?" Nathan asked. He'd been unusually quiet this morning too.

"I'm fine." She yawned and stretched. "I'm looking forward to another cup of coffee at the diner." Though not necessarily meeting with the Seattle detective and learning what more he had to share. The shadows were creeping into her life from all directions.

"I've already had too many. I'm not sure there's enough caffeine to keep up with what's ahead." He cringed as if in pain, though he tried to hide it.

Wishing he'd kept those words to himself? She let her gaze linger on Nathan—handsome and the most devoted, loyal person she'd ever met. Her long-kept secret was out. He knew about what happened before. He knew her true identity—just how broken she'd always been inside. None of it changed the way he looked at her.

Being with him now made her heart stir in a thousand new ways. At the possibilities and the what-ifs. But only if they made it through this.

Not if . . . but when.

She couldn't accept any other outcome, even though evil wouldn't let her forget and dark storm clouds were building up and moving in.

Except in the middle of this storm, Nathan was the silver lining.

And that gave her a measure of hope.

As they passed the high school on the way to the diner, she pulled her attention back to the moment. "Can I ask you— what do you think of our neighbor Delmar?"

Nathan shrugged. "He's a biology teacher and basketball coach." Nathan slid his gaze over to her, along with a teasing grin. "What's not to like?"

"Don't you think he's kind of strange?"

"He's a proverbial pillar of the community."

Erin rolled her eyes. "That tells me exactly nothing. I don't know. Maybe I don't like him because I think he likes Mom as more than, well, a neighbor."

Nathan chuckled. "And that bothers you? Relax, Erin. Your

mom is getting better. She has a network of friends around her, including Nadine." He leaned over. "I'll tell you a secret Jack told me not to tell you, but I feel kind of bad."

She stiffened. "What is it?"

"Nadine is bringing a puppy for your mother."

"A what? Um . . . no. Just no. We can't have a puppy. Mom is back to work. I mean, sure, it's a volunteer job, but I'm working at home now, and who do you think will be training it?"

"Well, let me clarify. It's older. A stray, but it's house-trained."

Erin rubbed her forehead. "Why didn't she ask me first?"

Nathan shot her a look. "Really?"

"Okay, okay. I am acting like I'm the adult and Mom's a child. Still . . . a puppy?"

"Scratch the word *puppy*. Katie is a young English mastiff and boxer mix. You're going to love her."

"You *met* her?"

"About a month ago when I had dinner with Jack and Terra at Nadine's."

Right before Erin had come back to Montana for a good, long, indefinite stay. Despite the stress of her circumstances, the slower pace of this small town in the mountains and her friends and family brought Erin a measure of peace. Part of her wondered why she'd fled to begin with.

Nathan reached across and grabbed her hand and squeezed, as if he'd known she needed the reassurance. He steered into the parking lot at Thelma's and found a spot near the main entrance. "This is as good a meeting place as any, but I don't like talking out in the open like this."

"Where did you want to meet? Under a bridge?" She snorted. "We're not doing this at the house. I wouldn't want Mom to suddenly come home for some reason, or Delmar to report to her."

"You think he spies for her?"

"Most definitely. He wants to earn points any way he can."

She crossed her arms and slid her gaze to Nathan, who stared at her with an incredulous look.

He shook his head in mock disdain. "Listen, before the detective gets here, I wanted to say this. Let's focus on Seattle and then later, we need to talk to Henry about the comment on your podcast. It's too dangerous to hold that close, Erin."

Nathan was pushing aside his own personal concerns about his father . . . for her. The least she could do was be open and honest with him. She hung her head. "I know. I'm scared, Nathan."

She braved a look into his dark eyes and let him see as deeply as he was willing to look just how scared she was now. How scared she'd always been. How she'd tried to run from the fear that one day that night would find her again.

A car pulled in next to him, and a man got out. He eyed them both.

"That's him," Erin said.

"You know this how?"

"I met him. He talked to me before I left to come home." She blew out a breath.

Erin got out, and they walked around the vehicle to shake hands with Detective Munson. Nathan gestured toward the diner, where they entered and found a booth in a back corner facing the doors. When the waitress approached, she set cups out for them. "Coffee?"

"Please," Nathan said.

She poured from a carafe into all three cups, then set a small bowl of creamer and sugars on the table along with three menus.

"I'll give you a minute." She started to leave.

"No need," Munson said. "I'm starving."

"Okay, hon, what'll it be?" She pulled out her pen and pad.

"I'll have your biggest breakfast plate, whatever that is," Munson said.

"Just keep the coffee coming." Erin wasn't hungry.

"An omelet and a side of bacon." Nathan hadn't even looked at the menu.

How could these guys eat at a time like this? The waitress finally left them. Erin wished she'd chosen a place where they could have this conversation without food or interruption.

"What have you got," Nathan said, "that you thought it was important enough to drive all the way out here? It's what, a ten-, twelve-hour drive?"

Munson rubbed his jawline. "I could use the change of scenery, plus I can talk on my phone on the way and listen to reports. So I can get some work done while I enjoy the drive." He clasped his hands on the table, and his eyes zeroed in on Erin. "As I mentioned on our call, I had more to talk to you about." He opened up a small portfolio and slid out a couple of photographs. "Recognize this guy?"

She frowned. "Maybe. I . . . He had sunglasses on. It all happened so fast. Did you ask Carissa?"

"I did, but I wanted to hear your response. I wanted to see your reaction."

Erin should have called Carissa. She would have if she hadn't been buried with so much happening. "I think it's him. Yes. But I can't be one hundred percent sure. Who is he anyway?"

Detective Munson arched a brow.

"I'm waiting, Detective. You didn't just drive out here to show me a picture of a dead man."

"A dead man who tried to kill you."

"Or my friend. So who is he?"

"He's on the FBI wanted list. A hired gun."

Erin fought to breathe.

"Wait," Nathan said. "Someone actually *hired* this man to kill?"

"Yes. We're looking into the who and maybe that will tell us the why, unless Dr. Larson or Miss Edwards knows something they aren't telling us."

"So someone hired this assassin, and now he is also dead. What are your theories?" Nathan asked.

The waitress delivered their plates, and Erin thought she would scream while she waited.

Finally, the detective unfolded his napkin in his lap. "This is what I love about diners. The food is fast but not too fast."

"If you take one bite before you share your theory, I'm going to walk out of here," she said.

He almost smiled. "You see, you're lying to me. You won't walk out. I could see you dumping coffee over my head, but you're not walking out."

"Why all the drama, man?" Nathan sounded irritated.

"No drama. Just waiting for privacy." He put the portfolio back on the table. Shifted through and found another photograph, which he laid in front of them.

Erin gasped and shared a wide-eyed look with Nathan.

"I see you know this man."

She pressed her hand against the image. "Yes, but where did you get this picture? How is this related?"

"You first." He sipped on his coffee.

She glanced at Nathan, and he nodded. Erin didn't much like Munson's games. "Two days ago, someone tried to kill us. He took out a logging truck driver. The driver's in critical condition but not dead. This man stood in the road and shot at us."

"So the boating incident is about *you*, then, and not your friend. This man was seen at the docks near the time of the boat owner's murder. Evidence is circumstantial, but we're working on bringing charges—that is, if we can find him."

"So you don't have a name yet?"

"A couple of aliases have popped up. We're still digging."

Nathan shifted away from the table. "Aliases. Murderers. Hired assassins. If the man driving the boat was hired to kill, and he was also killed, who do you think was behind it? This guy?" Nathan pressed his finger on the photo.

"Possibly. I'll be honest, I'm no expert in the world of hired assassins. Was it a competition? An argument between them that ended badly? Or had the assassin in the boat botched the operation and was then taken out? I don't know." Detective Munson's gaze shifted to Erin, and regret surged in his eyes as if he wished he wasn't having the conversation in front of her.

But he had, and there was no going back. A lump grew in her throat. She dropped her hands to her lap and squeezed her fists. "How . . . How could it be about me?"

Munson leaned back. "I've been looking into the stats on public broadcasters, radio hosts being stalked—that kind of thing. Podcasting falls into that category. Hiring assassins is next level stuff, though."

At Erin's surprised look, he continued.

"You never answered my question about why you keep it a secret. Anonymous."

"Because as you brought up, no one would know it's me." At least that had been her hope. But after the comment left on the podcast website, she wasn't so sure.

The detective watched his tapping fingers on the table. He was thinking about something. Building up to something. "What if . . . What if someone listened to your podcast? Maybe it's a particular cold case you've featured in the past or are currently featuring. Maybe you're digging into things, questioning things, and he wants to keep you silent. So he sent someone to silence you."

She sank back against the hard booth. "Podcasters aren't targeted in this way. You're reaching." And maybe that was because she was the only podcaster who'd lived through a crime to talk about it. Maybe the abductor had always known who she was and where she was. She rubbed her arms at the thought.

She'd spent most of her childhood, and many years in therapy, trying to learn how to deal with what happened that night. Regardless, Erin's way of handling it was to keep secret from the world around her that she was Erica Weeks. Now the secret she'd kept so close, held so tightly, about that horrific night was bursting out from every direction. Now was the time to open up, but her throat grew tighter, and the words wouldn't come.

Nathan pressed his hand over hers and squeezed, his silent message loud and clear.

Tell him.

THIRTY-SEVEN

ll right, if she wouldn't share, then Nathan would have to. "I think you're onto something. Erin has had an incident involving the podcast." Nathan angled toward her. "Do you want to tell him? Or should I?"

Nathan hated seeing that look of betrayal in her eyes. She'd shared something personal with him. She'd trusted him. Still, he would not let harm come to her.

"I get it," he whispered to her. Then he glanced at the detective. "It's hard for her to talk about, but it could be related."

The podcast about what happened that night confirmed how desperately she needed to talk about it. He wasn't entirely sure what had held her back all these years. The trauma? Her mother pressuring her? Whatever the reason, he wished she'd told him everything long ago, or at least told him about the recent attempt on her life.

"I know," she said finally. "I haven't talked about this to anyone since that time. My mother whisked us away. Changed our lives. Forced us to forget and never speak of it again."

"That could be why you needed the podcast," Nathan said.

Her eyes flashed at him.

Okay, so maybe she didn't need him stating the obvious.

Detective Munson had started in on his breakfast, slowly chewing while he waited patiently for Erin to share her morbid past.

She stared into her coffee cup. "I'm a psychologist, and yet it's so hard to see the truth. To admit it." Erin blew out a breath. "I'm going to need more coffee."

Her disturbed features hardened with determination.

"My latest podcast is about a child abducted in the woods."

While Erin told her story, Nathan watched Detective Munson, who listened intently. He'd mentioned working on the drive to Big Rapids. Had Munson gotten all the way through the "Deadly Rabbit Trail" season of *Missing Children*, including the last episode?

Last night, Nathan listened to all the episodes again, to make sure he hadn't missed any details. The investigations were quickly shifting. Nathan, as well as everyone else in his department, had gone with the assumption that the man who had followed them on the mountain road and very nearly taken them out had everything to do with Dad's shooting.

A BOLO had been put out on the man.

But what Munson shared today revealed that he was connected to the Seattle incident instead. Could Erin's past have somehow truly caught up to her? Regardless, Nathan would be on the lookout for threats from both Boston and Seattle.

Tears shimmered in her eyes, but none of them spilled as she finished her sordid tale and topped it with a pink hat.

Munson leaned back and stared at the ceiling in thought. "Why the pink hat? What's the significance?"

She shook her head. "It wasn't public knowledge."

"Maybe someone else could have known about it. The missing girl's mother. We'll question her, see if she left you the comment."

Erin rubbed her arms. "I don't see her as someone who

would comment on a blog post, at least like that, leaving me a cryptic message without signing it. Something."

Erin had told Nathan that Missy's mother hadn't known she'd worn the hat.

"Are you sure you're not overreacting to the message?" Munson asked.

"I don't think we are." Nathan answered for her. Still, Munson had caught on to something, and Nathan was missing it because he was too close to it. "What are you thinking?"

"Let's say—and of course, I'm speaking hypothetically here—this person listened to the podcast and realized you are speaking of a crime he committed. And let's say *he's* the one who commented. Why would he focus on the pink hat? It seems like such a small detail for even *him* to remember or care about."

What is the man getting at? "It's the one detail that she left out of the podcast," Nathan said.

"Think back to that time, Erin." Munson pushed his plate aside and pressed his palms flat on the table, leaning forward.

Erin, instead of Dr. Larson, this time.

Nathan watched her. "You don't have to do this."

Munson shot him a look. "Two people are dead. Her life has been threatened."

True. Nathan hated seeing her go through this, though. "She's been over this a thousand times, and all the information is in her podcast."

"No. No, it's not." Erin glanced between Nathan and Munson. "I see it now. I see that I left out the pink hat, but I left out more than that. Yes, Missy wore the pink hat that night. But she wore it instead of me. I wore it everywhere, but that night, Missy and I traded. I wore her blue sweater, and she wore my pink hat."

Nathan stilled at those words and shared a look with the detective.

Pain ignited in her gaze. "Don't you see? It was *my* hat."

THIRTY-EIGHT

Erin rode with Nathan as he drove them back to town.

Darkness pressed down on her. That night she'd been running from for so long and had only imagined she'd put to rest had finally caught up to her.

The memory played over and over in her messed-up mind. *Mom shook her. "Why didn't you listen? . . . I told you not to do this."*

Nathan hit a pothole, and it jarred her out of the past. After Detective Munson's revelation that what happened in Seattle was about her, after all, Erin would insist her mother come with her to a safe house. Or rather, safer than her own home. With the danger factors increasing—almost daily—Erin and her mother could both be in real trouble.

Her temples throbbed, and her heart rate inched up.

A neighbor and a deputy weren't enough.

Her mind went right back to that day Mom packed their things into the trunk of the car and left their small neighborhood in Wisconsin behind. Erin hadn't known they would never come back. She hadn't paid attention to how her mother had handled all that went into disappearing. She'd been too young.

God, I don't want to vanish again.

Nathan gave her a paper sack. Confused, she stared at it. Oh. "Am I?"

"Just breathe."

She took the sack and breathed into it. Her breathing slowed. She hadn't realized she'd been gasping. This time she wouldn't run and hide. There was no need. Erin was an adult, and she would be the one to protect Mom from the strangers who had inexplicably arisen out of the night long ago.

Her cell buzzed, dragging her thoughts back to the moment. "It's Terra, returning my call," she said to Nathan, then answered. "Hey, thanks for calling me back."

"You sounded upset in your voice mail. Erin, what's going on?" Terra asked.

Erin eyed Nathan.

He nodded vehemently and glared at her. Pointed at her and mouthed, "You do it or I do it."

"I have a situation. Nathan thinks Mom and I need to stay somewhere."

"I . . . see. I'm glad you're finally coming to that conclusion. You can use the ranch. Gramps won't mind at all. He's on a big cruise anyway and won't be back for another four days."

Gramps, Terra's deceased mother's father who raised her, had always been so good to both Erin and Alex when they would hang out at the ranch. Terra was fortunate to have known her grandparents.

"You haven't even heard what's going on. I mean, the new stuff."

"More than what's already happened?"

"Yes, and once you hear that, you might not agree."

"Doesn't matter. You know I'm here for you. The ranch is like a fortress now since Gramps installed a state-of-the-art security system to replace the last failed one. What about protection?"

"I'm sure Nathan will take care of that. Right now, I need someplace besides my own home, and I think the ranch will do. Now if I can just talk Mom into it."

"You think that'll be a problem?"

"I hope not." She pinched the bridge of her nose. Though Erin hadn't been able to convince Mom to move to Seattle, this wasn't a permanent setup. "Terra, I can't thank you enough."

"It's *me*, Erin. You don't need to thank me. Oh, and I forgot to mention, Alex is here. I called to tell him about the memorial vandalism, and he said he would try to take some time off and head this way. The next thing I knew, he was here. Maybe on the other side of this we can all hang out again for a bit."

Alex? Erin's heart warmed at the thought. "I'd love to see him. We don't see him often enough. But right now . . . I just can't think straight." Especially with Nathan next to her, listening intently as he drove. Nathan got along with everyone, but he'd been kind of jealous of Alex when she and Nathan dated before. And then Alex got angry with Nathan. Alex didn't understand that Erin was the one to break things off. And Nathan didn't understand that Alex really was like a brother to her, albeit a mysterious, hard-to-reach brother.

"Are you coming right away?" Terra's question pulled her thoughts back.

She glanced Nathan's way as she spoke. "After I pack a few things and Mom gets home from the thrift shop. Will that be a problem?"

"Of course not. I need to wrap things up here and stop by the house. I have no clue what shape it's in."

"Oh, please don't go to any trouble for me."

"I'm not going to trouble for you. I'm doing this for Owen." Terra laughed. "He would appreciate the heads-up."

Erin wasn't sure why she hadn't thought about Terra's brother, Owen, living there on the ranch.

"Will he be put out that two women will be staying there at his home?"

"It's a big place. Besides, he's heading out of town on a trip with Dad."

"I'm glad to hear they're spending time together." Terra and Owen's father had come back into their lives only a few months ago.

"My point is that he won't even be there for a few days," Terra said. "But even if he was home, he's busy with his equestrian therapy classes. I'll stay there too as an extra precaution. In fact, you can count on me to bring dinner tonight. What are you up for, fried chicken?"

"Sure. That sounds good. I'll talk to you soon." Though Erin couldn't imagine she would have an appetite.

"Let me know when you're headed that way." Terra ended the call.

Erin stared at her phone. "I hope the detective is wrong. I hope the boating accident was just that and has nothing at all to do with me or my podcast." She blew out a breath. "Don't even say it. I know that two dead people means it wasn't an accident. I know someone tried to kill me. And I know you were caught in the cross fire."

He stared at her a few moments with that soul-searching gaze of his. Could he read her deepest thoughts? Her dreams and desires? Her fears? "Like you were caught in the cross fire in Boston." The light changed, and he turned onto Main Street. "And Erin, there's nothing wrong with holding out hope. Like right now, I'm holding out hope that the text I just received from Jack while you were talking to Terra is something big, or nothing at all."

His words elicited a small laugh from her. "What are you talking about?"

"According to Jack, he lifted a package that was meant for me."

"Can you give me the details?"

"It was a cryptic message, so no."

"Are we going to meet him now?"

"No. Jack can wait. I'm going with you to your house, and I'll help you pack up—"

"Stop right there. Just drop me off, and you go see Jack. There's a deputy watching the house. I'll be perfectly safe. Not to mention, it's broad daylight. And Delmar is always watching, remember? Besides, I can pack faster without you there to distract me."

"I wouldn't distract you, I promise."

Erin had already said too much and chewed on her lip.

"Wait, you don't mean to say that my mere presence distracts you, do you?" He grinned her way, tossing a quick flash of his amused gaze along with it.

But even in that glimpse, she'd seen the hope there—a forbidden hope. Yes, Nathan was the silver lining, but Detective Munson's news had set her back. She sensed her own fragile hope slipping away. Why was it so fleeting? So difficult to hang on to?

No . . .

The fear and uncertainty closed in around her, and Erin wasn't so sure she wouldn't just hurt Nathan all over again. After all, she was still that scared, broken little girl inside, and now the past was rushing forward to catch up to her. She could imagine the tree limbs reaching for her, grabbing her and pulling her into the darkness.

"Earth to Erin," he said.

Heart pounding in her throat, she was grateful Nathan got her attention again. "I'll pack Mom's bag too, and we'll be ready to go. I can drive to the—"

"I can either take you there or follow you, but we'll go together."

"Then what are you going to do?"

"I might just hang out there at the ranch, watching out for you."

"We could do more research on your father's crime board and see if we can find answers. Terra will be there, and maybe Jack can join us. Alex too." She wanted to add, "Just like old times," but that was pushing it.

"I'd rather focus on this man who is trying to kill you and the link to what happened in your past. That's the bigger threat here."

Could the man who took Missy that night have truly found Erin? Could she finally get answers?

Was Missy . . . Was she even still alive? Erin couldn't imagine that she was, but if she'd survived, Erin hoped and prayed that Missy had found a new life somewhere safe and sound— and far from the nightmares that had chased Erin most of her life.

He pulled into the driveway and waved at the deputy sitting in his vehicle. Before Erin got out, he grabbed her hand. "Don't go anywhere. Just stay right here at the house. I won't be long. Promise me."

"Okay. I promise."

Delmar stepped off his porch and waved.

Nathan laughed. "I'm glad you have friends who can help keep you safe."

Great. "What about you, Nathan? You need to stay safe too. You're in as much danger as I am."

"Maybe, but my fellow deputies and detectives have my back."

She could see in his smile that he'd made the right decision sharing everything, despite his father's warning. That had to be so hard, considering he coveted his father's approval. She'd always known that, even before he'd recognized it himself.

"Still, you're in danger. Your dad was shot. They know you've been looking into his cases. You're a target."

"Tonight, then, we'll talk about our concurrent investigations."

"I'll see you in a while." She opened the door and headed toward the porch. When she turned around to wave, she realized Nathan had followed her.

What was he doing? Her breath hitched.

Oh, Nathan . . .

Now that he knew everything about the night Missy was taken, she realized it shouldn't have been difficult to open up. Except she'd worked so hard to change her identity, change who she was both on the outside and the inside, but her effort hadn't made much difference. In the end, it all came crashing back anyway.

She couldn't be sure she wouldn't leave him again, so how could she ask Nathan to take that risk with her?

Okay. Just. Stop. Thinking. No decisions should ever be made during a time of crisis.

At the door, Erin stared at the welcome mat.

Lord, I don't even know who I am anymore. Erica Weeks or Dr. Erin Larson?

THIRTY-NINE

Nathan lifted her chin and gazed into those blue-green eyes that sparked with so much passion and life. He hated to even think that she'd hidden away so much pain and grief. So much darkness.

More than anything, Nathan wanted to keep her safe and protect her. And to that end, he longed to share how deeply committed he was to her, but he wasn't sure how to make her understand. Or if she would even want that from him. If she would close herself off again and run away. Pausing here in front of this door like they'd done so many times before, for a brief moment he could almost imagine them back years ago, standing in the very spot with the same welcome mat—okay, a different one, because that was then and this was now. Still, how had their lives circled back around to this moment?

All he could think was that he had never stopped loving her. He'd kept that love deep in his heart. Protecting her at every turn had knocked the walls down, and the love came surging back.

Despite the hurt she'd caused him.

But he couldn't dwell in the past and instead focused on the woman standing in front of him. The emotion pouring from her could almost make him believe she'd never stopped caring either. Now that he understood why she'd walked away before . . .

"Erin, I—"

He tilted his head down toward her and pressed his lips against hers, surprising and, hopefully, wooing her. Nathan's heart jumped, then clanged around behind his rib cage. Panic and fear rose up, along with the myriad sensations that swept him away. He'd taken a big risk, but she needed to know how he felt.

He gently pressed his hand to the back of her head and pulled her closer, deepening the kiss that stirred all his senses, all his heart. He ignored the warning signals in his head that she could break his heart all over again. She was the one to step away, and she slowly opened her eyes. He took in her lips, still raw from their kiss. He swallowed against the tightness in his throat.

"Stay safe, Nathan."

Deputy Blaine hiked up the driveway. "Been watching the house all day. But I can clear it for you if you'd like."

Nathan nodded. He wasn't sure he trusted himself to focus, and maybe Blaine had seen the kiss. Nathan appreciated him stepping up to the task. If Nathan wanted to stay on top of Dad's investigation and now Erin's, and keep them both safe, he couldn't afford the distraction Erin was quickly becoming, but he would have to find a way.

Erin let Blaine in, and Nathan followed and helped him clear the house—as an extra precaution.

Deputy Blaine headed back outside. "I'll be switching out with someone in about an hour. Not sure who's coming yet."

Nathan acknowledged Blaine as he crossed the yard, then turned back to Erin.

"Go on, Nathan. Go see Jack. I'll be fine." She smiled and gave him a small wave, shutting the door.

Focus, man.

This wasn't the best time to fall in love. He needed all his wits about him. Back in the vehicle, he texted Jack to let him know he was on his way, then steered from the house. Jack had requested that Nathan meet him at his aunt Nadine's house, which oddly enough signaled the seriousness of whatever he'd found. Nathan took that to mean Jack didn't want to talk in public or at the sheriff's offices. Once Nathan was finally standing outside Nadine's home, Jack opened the front door before Nathan's fist connected to knock.

"Come in." Jack moved out of the way so Nathan could enter.

Nathan stepped into the small foyer, taking in the familiar living room with floral sofas and taupe carpet. The house was unusually quiet since no dogs were barking. "Is your aunt home?"

"She's at the beauty salon getting her silver covered." Jack gestured for Nathan to follow him into the kitchen, where he poured orange juice into a glass. "You want some?"

"No, thank you. What's this about, Jack?"

"Have a seat."

"I'd prefer to stand. I'm in a hurry, actually. Erin and her mom are staying at Stone Wolf Ranch tonight. The detective in Seattle thinks someone tried to kill her, and his theories include that it's related to her podcast. In fact, he flashed a picture of the same man who shot at us. I had thought that incident was related to my father's shooting and our trip to Boston."

Jack's brows creased as he drank the juice. He set the glass on the table. "I'll have to listen to her podcast. I only recently learned she had one."

"That makes two of us. So why am I meeting you here?"

Jack lifted the tan envelope that was resting on the table, then dropped it. Only then did Nathan zero in on the address. "It's my mail from work. Someone sent it to me there."

"Because that's a secure place. Nobody's going to mess with your mail there. Except in this case. It was on Henry's desk."

Nathan shrugged. "He was going to bring it to me."

"If that were the case, he would have taken all the mail addressed to you. He just took this one package."

Nathan fought to understand the implications. "You saw him take it?"

"No. I was looking for him and stuck my head into his office to pass a message on. He dropped the envelope, then answered a call. I stepped in to write a note for him on a slip of paper, and I noticed it was addressed to you."

Nathan took that seat, after all. He rubbed his hand over his mouth and chin and stared at the envelope. "How'd *you* get it?"

"Henry rushed out and left his door hanging open. I took in some papers, then came back out with the envelope too."

"Why would you do that?" Nathan stared at Jack.

"I've got your back, Nathan. You know that."

"Sure, but this could be stepping over a line, even for you." Especially for Jack, a former FBI special agent.

Jack grinned, but the serious situation reflected in his eyes. "I'm trying to be a good friend to Henry and prevent him from opening mail meant for someone else."

"And now here we are." Nathan scraped his hand over his jaw. "You want to see what's inside too, don't you?"

"Dude, you can take it or leave it." Jack rinsed the glass out in the sink, then stuck it in the top rack of the dishwasher.

Nathan looked closer. "It was mailed from Boston." From Dad? Nathan's chest tightened. He looked at the date. "It was mailed the week before Dad got here. Why would Dad mail—"

"Open it already, Nathan. That will give you answers."

"That's why Henry wanted it. He knew it was from Dad and could help."

"Whatever the reason, I figured you'd want to see it as soon as possible. You can turn it over to Trevor if it's important."

Nathan wasn't going to wait for Trevor or Henry. He opened the envelope and gently pulled out copies of two newspaper articles and slowly exhaled. "The articles about the cold case that Dad had been looking into."

He took a picture of the articles with his cell and sent them to Erin and Trevor, and then he read through them. These articles would certainly fit in the middle of Dad's crime board filled with the names of members of organized crime. With this new piece shifting into place, dread filled him.

FORTY

rin finished packing a few items, then moved to Mom's room.

Lord, please help me convince her that we need to stay somewhere safe.

Maybe she and Nathan were overreacting, but there was nothing wrong with being cautious. And right now, the idea of spending a day or more at the ranch surrounded by her closest friends and Mom sounded right. And yes, it would be like old times, especially with Alex there. Except now Terra and Jack were officially engaged—their wedding fast approaching—and well, Erin and Nathan had been apart, had gone their separate ways for several years now.

But that kiss . . .

She pressed her fingers against her lips, thinking back to the moment when he leaned in and gently kissed her, then caught her up and kissed her with fire and passion. She could tell even then that he'd held back, but it was enough to know that he still—what? Loved her? No, no, no. She couldn't be thinking about that during these uncertain times.

A familiar flutter thrummed inside—and she hadn't felt that in much too long. How was it possible that Nathan could still stir her after so long? Maybe it had everything to do with the fact that Erin had never truly let go of him. Emotionally, she'd held him at arm's length. While mentally, she'd wished him well and for him to simply move on and forward with someone else. But in the deepest part of her heart, she'd never let him go.

Maybe another time. Another place. Another set of circumstances. Like a normal life. Erin had accepted she would probably never have one, and this last week had confirmed those deep-seated fears.

She rubbed her tired eyes and forced her thoughts back to finishing packing for Mom. She zipped up the small duffel, then plopped on the bed and listened to the clock ticking in the hallway.

Mom should be home any minute. Erin had no idea how this disruption would affect her stability. Then again, Mom had always been the strongest person Erin had ever known.

Her cell buzzed.

Nathan texted he was going to send her some images. He had gotten the articles about the cold case his father had been looking into when he was shot. She sat up and looked at the images coming through, skimming the articles.

They were about a missing woman.

Right up her alley. She was glad Nathan had sent them to her and was keeping her in the loop. She moved to her office and downloaded the pictures to her iPad, then enlarged and printed them so she could get a better look. She could center them in the image of Newt Campbell's crime board and see if they fit.

Newt said he'd been investigating a murder and something about it—she didn't know what—had reminded him of this cold case Dwayne had asked him to look into. Why had her stepfather been so concerned about a missing woman, and who was she?

She stared at the printed images and skimmed the articles. Dread crept up her chest.

Erin rushed to the hallway, pulled down the attic steps, and scrambled up into the attic. Heart racing, Erin stared at the boxes of junk.

She moved to the last box she'd searched through where most of the old photographs were tucked away. The other newspaper clippings. Nothing stood out to her. There was nothing about a missing woman, or even a picture of the missing woman.

Wait a minute.

Erin peered more closely at the picture in the article. Then, digging through the box, she found an old photograph that she'd seen when she was up here before.

The missing woman in the article . . .

Shock rolled through Erin. She couldn't believe her eyes. She *recognized* the missing woman.

FORTY-ONE

The articles in his pocket, Nathan steered back toward town—Nadine lived outside the city limits—and headed straight for the sheriff's department. He called Deputy Blaine so he wouldn't "distract" Erin from packing. He smiled at the idea that he could distract her, but those thoughts quickly faded when Blaine answered.

The deputy was just handing off security duty to Atkins. Nathan was glad a fresh deputy would be there for the short time Erin remained at the house, and then they would adjust the security detail as needed at Stone Wolf Ranch since they wanted to keep her whereabouts known to only a few.

In the meantime, Nathan wanted to catch Trevor to ask about the picture Nathan had handed over to Henry. He also wanted to ask Henry why he'd taken the envelope meant for Nathan. Still, he had no clear reason to distrust Henry. Nathan still had a half hour before Erin's mom would be home, and he would be there to help Erin persuade Celia they had to leave.

Inside the county offices, Nathan hiked up the short stairs to the landing and Carol buzzed him through. "Hello, Nathan. Any news on your dad?"

"He's doing better every day." Though not nearly as well as he should be doing.

At Henry's door, Nathan saw that the sheriff wasn't in his office. He looked around the office cubicles—a recent addition—and spotted the back of Trevor's head. Nathan made a beeline over to Trevor and knocked lightly on the side of the cubicle.

The detective had been looking at his phone—answering a text?—and glanced up at Nathan. He smiled and put away his cell, then stood and thrust out his hand. "Just the man I wanted to see."

"Oh?" Nathan said.

"I got the images you sent and was about to call you." He grabbed a chair from an empty desk and set it near the small space in his cubicle. "Have a seat so we can talk."

Nathan was eager to hear what Trevor had learned. The man opened a manila folder on his desk and pulled out the picture Nathan had passed on to Henry.

"Who is he?" Nathan asked.

"Jason Cain. Now that he's deceased, the information was easier to obtain."

Nathan shook his head. "I don't understand."

"I have contacts from my previous position with the US Marshals and was able to learn that Mr. Cain had been in the WITSEC program."

"You're saying he was a witness who gave state's evidence to convict . . . who?"

"I'm still working on all those details."

"You saw the image of my father's crime board?"

Trevor nodded. "You did good work in Boston. Thanks for grabbing the intel, Nathan."

Nathan nodded. "Mr. Cain was connected to the organized crime characters on that crime board, then."

"I'm still working on how they're connected."

"The articles I sent over should help." He pulled the

envelope from his pocket, then tugged out the hard copies, unfolded them, and set them on Trevor's desk. Dad had gone to some trouble to mail these to Nathan, so he hoped he wasn't making a mistake by sharing them.

Trevor lifted one of the articles and glanced at it, his gaze shifting back to Nathan. "Have you learned why your father didn't want anyone to know about this?"

Nathan shrugged. "I have a theory, nothing more. I hope I didn't make a mistake, but I see no way forward without help from the department that has had my back for years."

"Care to share that theory?"

"He told me that lives are at stake. Back East, Erin and I learned that Dad's girlfriend was killed in an unresolved hit-and-run. He suspected she was murdered to distract him from a case he was working, and then just a few weeks ago after he met with her son, another detective, to talk about finding answers, her son was shot and killed. His name was Ian Sand-field. His sister, Holly, gave us the photograph of Jason Cain."

Trevor pursed his lips, then said, "So you believe your father feared that someone was taking out anyone who might know of the case, but he had to tell someone and he trusted you? He told you at a fishing hole where he thought no one would know or see, so you would be safe."

"His last words to me were 'in case something happens to me.' Then he was shot. I don't know what more he would have said."

Trevor nodded, then slowly flipped through the file and revealed another set of photos. Part of a steel canister and some muddied bits of wire.

Nathan's gut clenched. "What am I looking at?"

"Evidence. The state is only beginning to assess the cause of the dam failure. But someone found these parts under the rub-ble near the failed buttress. Evidence techs are on the scene."

"So it was bombed?"

"It looks like it. I know it was a traumatic experience to survive the flood. Did you hear anything that sounded like a bomb going off?"

He thought back to that moment. The shock of seeing the dam break. "I heard and felt something, yes, but I thought the sound was the dam collapsing. It all happened so fast."

Trevor leaned back in his chair and concentrated, reading the articles, and Nathan absorbed this new information. He would need to head to Erin's soon. But for the first time since this started, he sensed they were getting somewhere.

Trevor dropped the article back on his desk and scraped his hand around his jaw. "So the big question is, the missing woman whom the article identifies as the daughter of this mob boss, how does she fit in with a murdered WITSEC witness and several members connected to the Irish mob? Someone wants to find her? Or someone doesn't want her found?"

"I'd say there are several big questions. I think we're on the same page."

"Good. And I get the feeling that someone is cleaning house. Getting rid of loose ends. In the meantime, I have another photograph for you."

He pulled another photograph out of the folder.

"Someone was out taking nature photos. Caught this guy sticking a rifle back in his vehicle. The photographer would have deleted the image, he said, but heard about the shooting and that we were asking for information."

Nathan's chest tightened. The image confused him. "I can't be sure, because his face is somewhat hidden, but I think I've seen this man before. And if it's the man I'm thinking it is, it doesn't make sense. Do we know who he is?"

"Not yet." A call came through for Trevor. "I need to take this. Can you wait?"

Nathan glanced at his watch. "No, I need to go. I'll check back with you later. Keep me updated on what you learn."

"Will do," Trevor said.

Henry hadn't returned, so Nathan left the county offices. He needed to head to Erin's. Just as he climbed into his vehicle, his cell rang. Mom. His heart rate kicked up. Did she have news about Dad?

"Hey," he answered.

"Hey, honey, just letting you know that your father is sitting up and eating on his own today. His words are garbled and he's frustrated, but this is progress. He's alert and aware, just not communicating all that well."

Nathan hung his head—grateful on the one hand, grief-stricken on the other.

Lord, please help Dad get back to his old self. Please help us find who shot him. I'm doing all I can here, so help me.

"Oh, and I meant to tell you, honey. Hold on . . ." A shuffling noise, then, "I'm out in the hallway while the nurses attend to him. You asked about the articles."

"Yes, did Dad . . . Was he able to . . ." What was he asking? Dad couldn't tell them anything about the articles. He couldn't communicate.

"I remembered something. You asked about some articles that Dwayne wanted him to investigate."

"Mom, I have the articles now. I know what they're about."

"Oh, okay."

Guilt flooded him that he'd been a little short with her. She was only trying to help. "But go on, what were you going to tell me? Anything you remember could help."

"Since sitting here with your father, I've had a lot of time to think back and wonder why we divorced. Memories I've put out of my mind are coming back. It's like everything around the time he left—vivid memories, unfortunately—is coming back. Dwayne had just married Celia. He hadn't known her all that long, and she'd just moved to town. Your father warned him about that—"

"Mom. Enough on Erin's mom."

"You're right." She sighed. "Except Dwayne found those articles in *Celia's* things. He asked your father to look into the articles."

Nathan frowned. "Why would he do that?"

"Come on, he married someone he didn't know all that well. He loved her, but then maybe he started having doubts. He became suspicious."

Nathan rubbed his forehead. Erin's mom had kept those articles.

And *that's* why Dad had called Celia. It hadn't been just a friendly call. He'd had questions about the articles, or maybe even answers. Then she tried to commit suicide—though she claimed she hadn't.

And Dad was shot.

And right now, given the image that Trevor showed him of the man in the woods, it looked like the same man who shot at Dad also shot at them in the logging truck incident and was also seen in Seattle.

How could it all be related?

Looks like they're cleaning house.

FORTY-TWO

The forest was black as midnight and she crumpled to her knees, hiding behind a tree. She tried not to sob as fear clawed her.

She screamed when something furry rubbed against her. But then she realized it was Mr. Bojangles. She lifted the rabbit into her arms and buried her face in his fur.

Erica wanted to pray, but the words got choked up in her throat and even her heart. She had to find her way back home. She had to tell someone that a bad man had taken Missy. A flashlight grew brighter, bouncing all over the woods.

Oh no. He'd come back for her. She released Mr. Bojangles. At least one of them could escape this night.

The flashlight fell to the ground and rolled. Feet pounded against the ground.

He was coming for her.

She pressed against the tree and screamed, ready to claw and fight.

Arms gripped her. A familiar vanilla scent wrapped around her and chased away the fear. Erica's mother pulled her into a tight hug and spoke soothing words, but Erica couldn't be calmed. She told her mother what had happened. That Missy had been taken.

Her mother's face twisted in anger and fear until Erica didn't even recognize her. The same hands that had comforted Erica now shook her.

"Why didn't you listen? Look what you've done! I told you not to do this. I told you never to come out into the woods, especially at night."

"I'm sorry, Momma. I'm sorry. I should have listened. It's all my fault that Missy was taken."

Or was it?

Mom had changed their names. Moved them far away. And now Erin was learning there could be much more to that story.

A noise drew her attention. Mom was home.

Her limbs trembled. Erin hoped she was wrong, but her mother looked a lot like the missing woman in the article. And if she was that woman, then Erin didn't know her mother at all because . . . because Mom couldn't be that person who'd gone missing. She couldn't be the missing daughter of a mob boss!

Nausea ripped through her insides.

While Erin wanted to demand answers, she was in no way ready to talk to Mom. She paced the attic, wiped her face. How could she talk to her mother when she herself was in turmoil? Plus, questioning Mom could send her over the edge again.

God, I need your help like never before. I'm completely out of my depth here. I don't know who my mother is. I don't know who I am.

Help!

She needed to persuade Mom to go to the ranch, and now . . . this. She closed the boxes and calmed her panic. Her breaths.

She could do this. *I have to do this.* After persuading Mom to come with her to the ranch, where they would be safe, she could ask her about her past and the articles Dwayne had found—clearly he'd wanted to know more about the woman he'd married. But Erin had to wait. If she brought it up now, Mom could be inconsolable.

Palms sweating, she climbed down from the attic. "Mom?"

A door slammed in Mom's room. Erin closed the attic and once again calmed her fear and panic.

Even though I walk through the valley of the shadow of death, I will fear no evil . . .

Erin mentally recited the verse to herself over and over to help with the panic, and in this case, she had every reason to feel terrified. No way would she be able to keep the questions firing in her head to herself.

Erin opened the closed door and entered her mother's bedroom just as Mom backed out of the closet holding a shotgun.

Erin's heart pounded. Her worst fears had come to consume them both.

"Mom! What are you doing?" Erin had to de-escalate the crisis enough to call the police. She remained calm even as tears welled in her eyes. At this moment, she didn't care about the past. She only cared about saving her mother. Keeping her alive. "Just put the gun down, please, I beg you." Erin slowly reached for the weapon.

"Get down!" Mom shouted, her expression fierce, determined. "Get out of the way."

Erin stood in her path in the doorway as Mom tried to push past.

"Mom, please, you're not yourself. Please hand me the gun before you kill someone."

"That's the idea." Mom barreled past Erin into the hallway. "Now get back into my room."

Mom's strength surprised Erin, and she wasn't sure she could physically hold her mother down or wrestle the weapon from her. She called 911 as Mom stood in the hall and aimed the gun at the front door. Erin had no time to wait for the call to connect.

Instead, she had to take matters into her own hands and dropped the cell in her pocket, then rushed forward. "Give that to me—"

Before Erin could reach her, Mom fired the shotgun and blew a wide hole through the front door. Erin screamed and covered her mouth, but she couldn't stop the screaming as disbelief gripped her. Mom cocked the firearm again and aimed.

"No, you don't!" Erin lunged for the shotgun, and it blasted a hole in the ceiling.

Mom looked at her—as lucid as she'd ever been. "They're here. They're after us. We have to get out of here."

"Who's here? Who are you talking about?" Was her mother suffering a psychotic break? Paranoia? Erin wouldn't consider the other mob-related possibilities. Not yet.

Her mother gripped her arm, eliciting pain with the action. "Let's go."

She dragged Erin to the back of the house as if they would escape that way.

"I'm not going anywhere. Please, just put the shotgun down."

Bullets—return fire—sprayed through the front of the house and continued, unrelenting.

"We have to leave. Please, just trust me. Just listen to me," Mom said.

"It's the deputy," Erin said. "You shot at the deputy sent here to protect us, and now he's shooting back. We have to give up the shotgun and walk out there with our hands up."

"No." Mom peered out the back door, then hesitated. She pressed her back against the wall, holding the shotgun like she intended to use it yet again. This was Montana, after all, and Dwayne had taken Mom hunting and taught her how to use all manner of guns, but the sight of her holding the shotgun like she practiced with it every day scared Erin.

Erin pulled the cell from her pocket to call 911 again. This time for emergency medical services too, in case the deputy was hurt and couldn't call for backup himself. He hadn't announced his presence or tried to enter the home, though he'd returned fire.

A lot of gunfire.

Her stomach clenched and twisted inside. She wasn't going to get out of this on her own or talk Mom down.

Cell to her ear, she waited for the call to connect. "What is going on, Mom?"

Sweat beaded on Mom's temple. She was definitely having some sort of hallucination. Erin's knees shook. Now wasn't the time for her to collapse. Mom was depending on her.

Her mother's eyes narrowed, and she shook her head. Erin had never seen her mother like this, and it scared her more than anything she'd experienced, including the last several days.

"That's it." Mom panted the words. "We're taking the secret passageway."

Her mother pushed from the wall, still holding the weapon like she was prepared to shoot now and ask questions later. "Stick close to the walls. Stick close to me."

Grief twisted with fear in Erin's chest. This could not be happening.

"The secret passageway?" Erin couldn't stop the tears as she followed her mother's instructions. "Mom? You're being delusional. There's no secret passageway."

Erin finally spoke with the emergency dispatcher and explained about the shooting. She tried to sound coherent, then she ended the call. She didn't need to stay on the line. She needed to focus on Mom. Erin's mother led her into her bedroom and stopped at the closet. She hadn't closed the door after retrieving the shotgun, so it remained open.

Mom grabbed more ammo from a shoebox and reloaded her shotgun, then handed it to Erin. "Watch the door. Watch our backs. Shoot anyone who enters the house."

Erin took the shotgun, but now stared at it.

Mom then dropped to her knees and tossed out boxes. Erin stepped out of the way, stunned as she watched her mother in the middle of a psychotic break. And yes, she watched the door too. But no one was coming for them except the police. In that case, Erin should put the shotgun down. But she couldn't move.

Watching her mother like this filled her with excruciating pain. *Haven't we been through enough, Lord?*

"Mom, you're delusional!"

"No, *you're* delusional," Mom said. "You've been pretending you don't know what's going on for years."

Clearing the boxes revealed a wood door at the bottom of the closet. Erin couldn't believe her eyes. Shock rolled through her. Mom was right . . . Erin was in denial. She had yet to process the newspaper articles she'd read with Mom's picture—the missing woman had been presumed murdered by a gangster.

But no—she was very much alive.

Mom pulled the door open. "It's small, but we can both fit."

"In the crawl space?" No thank you.

Mom snorted a scoffing laugh. "What good would that do us now that we've been found? We needed an escape in case this day arrived."

"This day?"

"Delmar dug the tunnel for me. It took him years to dig it, and he has kept it a secret this whole time." She glanced at Erin. "That's why we're close. We're friends. I keep him close. You understand?"

She swallowed. "No, Mom. I don't understand any of this." Deny. Deny. Deny like so many of those criminal minds she'd picked.

Denial didn't change the facts.

A sound—someone kicking in the front door—startled her.

Mom yanked the shotgun out of Erin's hands. "Get in. Go down there, and I'll follow." Mom turned her back to Erin and held the shotgun, ready to fire to protect them. "You need to hurry," she whispered.

"Mom, it's the cops. It's help. I called for help." *Please, God, let it be the cops.*

"You're wrong. They're here for us." Mom glanced back at Erin and stared, her eyes clear. Everything about her seemed coherent except her words and actions. But she hadn't hallucinated this opening in the floor.

A man appeared in the doorway and exchanged gunfire with Mom. Erin ducked and climbed down the ladder into the tunnel. Mom followed her, shut the door, and left them in darkness. Then she switched on a flashlight.

"More of them will follow." She locked the tunnel doorway. "This will only deter them so long."

Mom hopped to the ground of the small tunnel and picked up a duffel bag next to the ladder, lifting it over her shoulder. The bag had been sitting there, waiting for this day.

"Let's go."

But Erin couldn't move. Her legs wouldn't cooperate. "Tell me what this is about."

Mom pressed her hands against Erin's cheeks like she was a little girl. "Don't you understand what's happening? They found me. Oh, my baby, my darling, I never meant for this to happen."

"*Who* found you?" The article was a blur in Erin's mind. She didn't want to accept the truth.

"We can talk while we keep moving." Mom made her way down the tunnel, and Erin had no choice but to follow.

She forced her legs to move and put one foot in front of the other. "*Who* are you?"

"I'm your mother, Erin."

"But I mean, who are you beyond that? You're the missing woman in the articles that Dwayne wanted Newt to look into, aren't you?"

"My father, your grandfather, was put in prison for a long time. He was the leader of a crime organization. The night before he was arrested, he killed someone and knew they would want retribution. They would want me. He told me to disappear. I had no choice if I wanted to live."

"Are you in WITSEC?" If so, then why weren't the US Marshals whisking them away to a new life?

Mom paused and turned back to look at Erin. "No. There was no time to negotiate with federal agencies. I had to leave, so I disappeared and started a new life in Wisconsin. Got married and had a child. I lived a happy and good life, and then your father died. You were only three and too young to remember him, but I stayed and we had a good life—that is, until Missy was taken. I knew we had to disappear again because someone had found us. They tried to take you to lure me in and get their retribution."

"So the man who took Missy made a mistake. He meant to take me."

"Yes. They found us. They wanted you, baby. To take you from me and hold you hostage. I'm not sure what they had planned. But they took the wrong child."

"Because that night, Missy wore my pink hat." They thought Missy was Erica . . . Erin. She thought she'd been part of only one tragic cold case—but now she at least had the answer to why Missy had been taken.

God, I need answers. Unfortunately, the answer to her question brought no peace.

"Yes." Mom's voice croaked with tears, but she swiped them away, then turned and started making her way through the tunnel again. Erin looked around her and thought about Delmar, spending years of his life to dig this tunnel—an escape—for her mother.

Mom continued, "And Dwayne took us in." Mom paused again, glancing back to offer Erin a weak smile. "We had a good life here in Big Rapids, didn't we? Sure, you moved to Seattle, but you were doing well. Everything was good, and I had hoped we were lost forever. Lost and forgotten." Her smile faltered. "Until now."

She continued through the tunnel. Erin followed, struggling to wrap her mind around any of this, and held on to a small hope that maybe it was all a dream, or maybe she was the one hallucinating and none of this was happening. That would be better than if this were reality, wouldn't it?

Mom leaned against the dirt wall to catch her breath. Erin choked back tears as they came to the end of the tunnel.

"The trick will be to get out of here before they start looking," she said. "Once they find the tunnel, they can catch up to us."

A strange numbness clung to Erin, and she nodded as if she were watching from outside her body. "Where does this come out?"

"An abandoned water shaft that we'll follow to a deserted train tunnel."

"And then what, Mom?" Realization slowly dawned as Mom whispered the next words.

"Then we disappear again."

FORTY-THREE

Mom's words echoed in Erin's mind and ricocheted through her heart.

Erin didn't want to disappear.

What about her friends and family? Well, they didn't have family—and now Erin understood why—but she couldn't accept that leaving behind her friends, and yes, leaving Nathan all over again, was the answer. Now in the face of such a violent departure, she was dangerously close to becoming a missing person. And eventually a cold case.

While Erin had gotten completely lost in her thoughts, Mom had climbed up a short ladder.

She stared down at her. "Snap out of it. We have to move."

Her mother shifted into a militant person right before her eyes. She was strong and had her act together. Erin struggled to reconcile this new mother with the woman who recently had tried to commit suicide. All of this she considered as she followed Mom into yet another tunnel—an old, out-of-use water or steam shaft.

Erin took in the dank passageway. It resembled what Delmar had dug for their escape, except it was much wider. "I can't believe you persuaded Delmar to do all this work—years' worth of work—for you. It seems so far-fetched."

"It got us out of the house. That was the point."

Wait . . . "This is why you didn't want to move to Seattle with me, isn't it?"

"It took a while to plan and then to dig the tunnel. As for persuading Delmar, I paid him a significant portion of my savings and retirement. I paid him to keep quiet, and now I hold over him the fact that he dug an illegal tunnel, if needed. He's become a dear friend." Mom shrugged. "But I guess I learned something from growing up in an organized crime family—like father, like daughter. I covered all the bases."

Erin couldn't stop shaking her head in disbelief.

I'm walking in a tunnel to escape the mob. My mother is the daughter of an imprisoned mob boss.

"There wasn't an easier escape plan than digging an underground passage?"

An incredulous huff escaped her mother. "Once they find you, there's no escaping the house. So a tunnel it is."

"But wouldn't those after you know that too? Think of that?"

"Sure, but they don't know where it ends up. They will have trouble breaking through that door, or at least it will deter them." Mom paused next to a small pack. She leaned over and pulled out a device.

A detonator?

"And now I'm going to blow up the tunnel."

"Wait!"

But Mom pressed the button.

Who are you, and what have you done with my mother?

Erin held her breath, expecting to hear or feel the explosion. She felt a shudder and heard the collapse, but only because she had been intently listening. "I barely heard anything."

"It was small. Just enough to bring down some dirt and rock.

Block their way. Now we have to get moving so we can connect with the train tunnel."

The scale of her mother's escape operation was hard for Erin to grasp. "You have truly been planning this for years."

"I've been hoping I wouldn't be forced to use it. It has been a couple of years since Delmar completed the tunnel, and I had almost put the need for an escape out of my mind. Until recently."

"Why do you say recently? What happened to remind you about your past and the possible need to disappear again? Was it because Nathan's father called you? Is that what set you off?" To try to commit suicide? Except that attempt didn't match the efforts and preparation of her escape plan.

Erin sloshed through a few puddles, peering at the walls again. Rainwater or groundwater leaking into the tunnel?

"What? No. Why would a phone call from him set me off? Your podcast reminded me that we might never truly escape."

My podcast. Erin sagged under the weight. Had her podcast truly been the catalyst for the killing? Or had it been Newt? He'd started his investigation long before Erin had published "Deadly Rabbit Trails." Still, it could be, as Detective Munson had mentioned, that her podcast had caught the ears of the wrong person.

Either way, everything that had happened in the past two weeks was all part of the same morbid story about a crime family, brothers and sisters who were tied together by blood or organized crime. It was their strange psychopathic sense of loyalty that compelled them to exact revenge—killing in the most brutal ways—no matter time or distance.

"Mom, why have you never told me any of this? It's a shock to me. Did you ever imagine how this would affect me when I learned about it?"

Mom turned and gently gripped her arms. "Of course!

Everything I've done has been to protect you. I never wanted you to know." Mom ran her hand down Erin's hair and cheek.

And suddenly Erin was a child again.

Mom released her, turned, and stumbled forward. Defeated, discouraged, and yet determined to make it through. Erin had had her mother all wrong for far too long. Mom carried a burden that no one should ever have to carry. "Tell me about him. Your father, my grandfather. Tell me about your life."

"I try hard not to remember, but if you want to know, I promise to tell you. But not yet. Not until we're safe again."

Safe again. Could Erin truly disappear again and leave behind the life she created? Leave behind her career . . . Nathan?

Oh, Nathan.

She at least wanted a chance to explain. To say goodbye. She'd been a fool to walk out on him before without a true explanation for the brokenness she carried inside. But now she knew the reasons for all of it, and she wanted that chance with him more than ever. She'd feared she would hurt him again. But facing the real possibility of running—vanishing— now she knew if given another chance with him, she absolutely wouldn't walk away this time.

Lord, I don't want to do this. Why is this happening? I'm so confused . . . I don't want to leave. And I thought, I thought maybe I would have another chance with Nathan, even though I'm scared to take it. I thought you were giving us a second chance.

"Here's our way out of the water tunnel." Mom climbed up a rickety ladder.

Erin followed her and at the top of the ladder crawled through an opening, then scrambled to her feet to stand. The tunnel was dark, but Mom shined a dim flashlight around. Erin spotted the tracks. Breathed in relatively fresh air compared to the water tunnel.

"This way." Mom's voice had softened to almost a whisper.

Erin kept her voice equally quiet as she spoke, pressing her mother for more information. "You've planned the escape, yes, but do you have a long-term plan? I mean a real plan for disappearing?"

"Yes."

Nausea roiled in Erin's stomach. "What if we don't disappear? What would happen?"

"They won't stop until they have one or both of us. We could be tortured and then killed."

"Maybe we can survive. I don't want to leave."

Mom turned again. "Pull yourself together. I don't know what will happen. But right now, we have to get somewhere safe. Whether or not you agree to disappear with me again, that's up to you."

"Okay, fine." She had time to think about this. To figure it out. Mom was right. Just get somewhere safe. She still had her cell phone and pulled it out. She could text Nathan.

Mom whirled around and swiped it from her hands.

"Hey!" Erin lunged for her cell.

Her mother threw it on the ground and stomped on it. "I don't know how they found us, but we can't take chances. Oh, wait, I do know. The same podcast that got me thinking about my past must have tipped someone off."

"It was anonymous."

"In general. Anyone who wanted to know could find out who you were and keep digging all the way down to your original birth certificate. Then start looking at my identity closely."

Unfortunately, that was true. Erin hadn't imagined someone with such nefarious intentions would take the time to dig so deep. And now it all made sense. She understood how Seattle was connected to Boston, and now Montana. Someone connected to her mother's past had tracked her down. Newt Campbell must have found the truth as well, and someone tried to kill him before he warned Erin and her mother.

Still . . . "That's the part I don't understand. How could

they have known just from listening to the podcast? I went out of my way to sound disconnected, only sharing what anyone could find in the public record."

"I suspect the person who was hired to abduct you has never stopped searching for you. You said something that gave you away, or at least caused suspicion. We slipped away into the night days after Missy was abducted. After all the questions from the local law officials and FBI were answered but before the contingency of law dispersed. We had protection at least for a short time."

"If we disappeared, then we would have been a cold case too, Mom. The FBI—"

"The FBI had what they needed from you, and I made it clear you were traumatized. They knew we were moving. The house was only a rental, and I settled all my affairs quickly, leaving behind misleading breadcrumbs to throw the abductor off our trail." Mom whirled around. "None of that matters now that we've been found again."

"If this is my fault, I'm so sorry."

"There's no point in playing the blame game."

"You said your father killed someone. Who did he kill that would warrant them to go through this much trouble to find you?"

Mom sighed heavily as they approached one end of the tunnel, where the tracks led out into the open. Light from a dusky night spilled in, so Mom turned off her flashlight. She didn't leave the tunnel but instead remained in the shadows and sat on old, cracked concrete steps. "Let's take a break before the next phase of our escape." She glanced at her watch.

Erin sat next to her.

"A rival family's son." Mom turned to look Erin in the eyes. "The night I left, I knew I would never see my father again."

Absorbing everything, understanding, would take Erin time—and maybe some distance from the situation. Her heart still pounded, and adrenaline coursed through her. For too many days now she had felt on edge, and she might have reached her limit. Anxiety gripped her.

"What's the next phase of the plan? Just wait here? It's getting dark."

"Exactly."

So Mom was waiting for nightfall. They sat in silence until the tunnel was well and truly dark, but Erin could still see the moonlit night at each end of the tunnel carved through the mountain.

Something bumped against Erin's leg and she yelped.

"It's only a rat," Mom said.

Only a rat?

Erin quickly stood. When she lifted her gaze, a sound drew her attention to the closest end of the tunnel.

Three figures stepped into view.

"Uh . . . Mom?"

Her mother rose slowly. "Erin, get behind me," she whispered.

Terror coursed through her at the familiar sound of a round being chambered next to her. Mom had a gun ready and waiting. Just in case.

"Is there another gun in that bag for me?" she whispered.

The three men continued forward.

"Take one more step, and I'm going to shoot," Mom said, but with much less bravado than earlier. What had changed?

"Run, Erin," Mom whispered.

"I'm not leaving without you."

"Who said I wasn't coming too? Run!"

Erin turned and ran toward the other end of the tunnel, their only escape. Mom shot at the men. More gunfire echoed against the stone walls. Would she feel the pain of a bullet in her back at any moment? Or be killed instantly? She thought to glance back at her mother but heard her breaths at her heels.

"Keep going. Head for the woods," Mom said between gasps.

Gunshots erupted right behind her.

Erin gulped for air as she pushed her limbs harder and faster, attempting not to stumble on the uneven ground running parallel to the tracks. Erin longed for that flashlight. They'd left the duffel bag behind.

She dashed out into the open. Someone grabbed her in a stranglehold, choking her.

He grunted, then released her. Erin turned. Mom stood over him with the butt of her weapon raised.

"Run to the woods, Erin!" Mom gestured up the east embankment.

Erin started forward, careful not to get her feet tangled in the railroad ties. She scrambled up the ridge. Mom was right behind her. At the top, the trees instantly grew thick.

Mom stayed on Erin's heels as she continued running through the trees and up an incline. Branches and underbrush grew thicker in places, slapping her arms and legs and even her face.

When she couldn't run anymore, she stopped to lean against a tree trunk and catch her breath. Erin had avoided the dark woods for so long, but here she was again running for her life, only this time her mother was in the nightmare with her. Suddenly she couldn't breathe. She pressed her back against the trunk, the bark cutting through her clothes. Erin cupped her hands over her mouth while Mom searched the area around them, guarding them with her gun.

Had they lost the men?

Her mother was in the shadows, so she couldn't see her face but somehow felt the tension rolling between them. Erin held back sobs.

"You have to have faith, Erin. God is going to see us through this. He's going to make a way." Mom grabbed her hand and tugged her forward. "They're coming. And right now, the way for us is through the woods."

Moonlight dappled the ground, lighting their way. How long could they hide? They continued hiking east and away from town. Mom stumbled, and Erin caught a glimpse of her mother's wince in the moonlight.

"Mom! You're hurt."

"Just my ankle. But it's going to slow us down. You keep going. Just hide and get away." Mom handed her the weapon. "I'll draw them away."

"No." Missy's face came to mind—that night of terror. Both of them running hand in hand. Erin didn't leave Missy then, but her friend was snatched from her just the same. "I'm not leaving you behind."

The men shouted. Flashlight beams signaled their approach.

"There's no time to argue. Let's go."

Mom almost fell to her knees. Erin grabbed her and shouldered her. "I'll help you. Now where are we going? Where can we hide?"

"I know a place. It's just a couple of miles. If we can just—"

"You're right, it's the perfect hiding place. I agree." A man stepped in front of them and shined a flashlight at them as he held a gun to Mom's face. His wicked grin seemed familiar and sickening. He tugged something from his pocket, then flipped his wrist to reveal a pink hat, which he placed on Erin's head. "I've waited a long time to finally get my hands on Collin Byrne's granddaughter—Erica Weeks. *And* his daughter"—his seedy eyes shifted to Mom—"Cara Byrne."

FORTY-FOUR

Breathless, Nathan rushed up to the crime scene tape surrounding Erin's home. He'd had to park several houses down since law enforcement had the entire neighborhood blocked off. Emergency lights still flashed, though sirens had been shut off. Darkness had fallen, leaving street and porch lights to illuminate the crime scene.

While he'd been jawing with Trevor, Erin and her mother had been attacked, coming under gunfire. He didn't have the full story yet and wasn't sure he was brave enough to hear it. Each breath he took felt like a knife to his heart.

He stared at the bullet hole–laden front of the house. A leaden ball of shock crushed him.

Oh, Lord. What happened here?

Terra and Jack both stood on the other side of the crime scene tape but kept their distance from the house, their features grim. Nathan ducked under the tape. Before he made it far, Officer Flannery with the local Big Rapids PD thrust a clipboard at him. "Gotta keep on top of the scene, Campbell."

Nathan quickly signed it and made a beeline for Jack and Terra. Neither of them said anything as he approached, because there were no words. He got that. Instead, they shared looks of shock and grief. From here, he got a much better look at the destruction, and gulped for air.

How could Erin have survived? Nathan couldn't form words to even ask the question. His limbs quaked with fear. He had to find her. Wanting to see the inside of the house, Nathan rushed forward, but Jack stood in his path and gripped his arms.

"Get ahold of yourself, man," Jack said.

"Where is she?" Nathan demanded.

His detective counterpart and friend tightened his hold. "She's not in the house. I've already walked through once and will go back in after the bodies are removed."

"Bodies?" Nathan braced himself for the rest.

"Yes. Two unidentified men were found inside the house. The gunmen, I presume. We learned some of what happened from Celia's neighbor Delmar Wilson. By the way, Deputy Atkins, who had just relieved Deputy Blaine, is in critical condition in the hospital. He's fortunate to be alive."

A team of evidence techs arrived along with Emmett Hildebrand, the county coroner. Each donned the required sterile attire before entering. Nathan watched as if in a daze. Jack tugged both Nathan and Terra over to the side, farther away from the house.

"And what exactly did you learn?" Grief swelled in his gut as he stared at the hole blown through the front door. "What happened here? Where are they?"

Jack leaned closer. "The neighbors heard gunfire. Saw some men descend on the house."

"What about Celia? Had she come home yet? Do we know if she's missing too?"

"Mr. Wilson next door said Celia had come home. He saw the men approaching, and it all happened fast. He called 911. He also claims Erin and Celia didn't leave with the men when they left. Apparently, there were five in total. Two are dead and three left."

"Then where are the women? What if the men took them and Delmar somehow missed that?"

"I don't have the answer. I just know we have to find them." Jack stared at the house.

"Oh, Nathan." Terra's eyes welled with tears—the professional façade slipping away—as she stepped forward and wrapped her arms around Nathan. Jack squeezed his shoulder.

He held Terra and closed his eyes, sending up a silent prayer begging for Erin's safety.

Terra stepped away and swiped at her tears. "We're going to find her, Nathan. Don't worry."

Nathan struggled to comprehend Terra's reaction. She and Jack were as close to Erin, closer even, than Nathan, yet they seemed to be reassuring *him*. But then again, Terra and Jack probably recognized that Nathan still loved Erin. He was coming to that realization much too late or, rather, finally admitting the truth to himself. He had no control over his heart, and none of it mattered at this moment. He had to find Erin, no matter his feelings for her.

Terra's eyes brightened as she glanced beyond Nathan. She rushed over to the yellow tape, where she met up with Alex Knight. He ducked under the tape and signed in. Terra dragged him over to join their huddle. Nathan had overheard Erin's conversation with Terra earlier today that Alex had come back to town.

Hands in his pockets, Alex lifted his chin in acknowledgment. "Nathan."

Nathan easily recognized the anger that burned in the man's gaze. Supposedly Alex had been like an older brother to both Terra and Erin. And wasn't he some sort of special agent? Jack was former FBI. Maybe with their added efforts, they could pull out all the stops and find Erin.

"What can I do to help?" Alex asked.

"We have to find Erin and her mother." And Nathan was

just about done standing here. "Even if what Wilson said is true, and the men after them—let's just call them what they are, mob gangsters—left without the women, they're still out there somewhere searching for them."

Just like they had been for years. Much longer than either Erin or Nathan had realized until today.

Terra, Jack, and Alex all eyed him in surprise. Nathan shared what he knew so far, though he was still putting all the pieces together. Their faces grew increasingly grim as they listened.

"We'll find them, Nathan," Terra said, sounding as if she was encouraging herself as much as him.

"County deputies and local police officers are searching," Jack said. "Henry has called in the state too. He's requested a triangulation of both Celia and Erin's cells, but nothing yet."

"Then what are we doing here?" Alex asked. "Any idea where they would hide?"

Terra shook her head. "We should just spread out and search different regions of the town and the county. Keep in contact. I tried calling her cell but have heard nothing. She might have gotten rid of it if she thought it could lead anyone to her. If they were trying to escape, why didn't they just come directly to the county offices or the police department? I don't understand."

Henry stepped out of the house. "Detective Tanner, I need you in here."

At that same moment, Trevor West stepped under the tape, signed the crime scene log, and headed for the house. It would seem Nathan hadn't officially been invited to this party, but he was good with that.

Jack stiffened, and his shoulder lifted as if he would argue with Henry. Nathan nudged him. "Go. Learn more for us so we can search for her."

Because that's exactly what I'm going to do. Erin needed him out there looking for her. Then again, considering what he already knew, she and Celia could be long gone. They had disappeared before.

Nathan took a few moments to look at the house, silently praying for Erin's safety. Maybe if he got into the house, he would see something that would let him know where they had gone. But it was probably better that Nathan be left to his own devices rather than get wrangled into one side of the investigation. To that end, he was only wasting time standing here. He'd learned enough.

"I'm heading out now." He nodded to Terra and Alex and started across the yard.

"Wait," Terra said.

The pair caught up to him and ducked under the tape after him.

"We're searching too, Nathan," she said. "We'll find her. Keep us updated. Together we can do this. I'm texting you and Alex so you'll have each other's numbers. We can communicate anything we find."

He headed down the sidewalk alone toward his vehicle. Alex and Terra had parked in the opposite direction. Inside his vehicle, he called Erin's cell. Terra said she'd tried to call, but Nathan had to try again too. The call went to voice mail. If she was in control of the situation, she would have texted or called him. At least he hoped she would have. Jack had mentioned there was a 911 call.

Darkness and fear clawed at him, trying to bring him down.

"Lives are at stake."

I think I understand now, Dad.

The cold case Dad had been looking into was about Celia's past, and Dad had learned enough that he was terrified of it catching up to her—and *those around her.* Dad had already lost someone he loved because he was close to making the connection.

While Nathan didn't know all the connections yet, he now

understood why Dad had told him and no one else. Nathan still cared deeply about Erin.

Dad was terrified of what could happen in Big Rapids. He was terrified of what *had* happened, and of those who would get hurt and possibly killed, including Nathan.

That terror raced through Nathan's blood now. He called Mom and informed her in no uncertain terms to remain at the hospital where she would be safe and protected and to pay close attention to every person who entered Dad's room. He wished Dad could communicate and tell him more.

A few neighbors stood outside to watch, gathering in groups and talking. Some to police officers who were canvassing the neighborhood asking questions. He steered from the curb and slowly made his way around the block to the other side of the roadblock and parked against the curb for a few moments. If Celia and Erin weren't taken, someone here had to have seen them leave on their own.

Nathan spotted one neighbor who normally was outside watering or weeding or popping in to say hello. Delmar Wilson peeked out his window, the mini blinds barely moving, but enough that Nathan caught the movement. Erin had shared that she'd always thought he was creepy, for no good reason, she'd admitted.

Nathan didn't know where to search first, but he would have a word with Mr. Wilson to start. Nathan got out of his vehicle and moseyed over to the neighbor's house and knocked on the door.

Wilson didn't answer. Nathan knew he was inside. Was he avoiding the police for a reason now?

Nathan knocked again. "Mr. Wilson, we need your help. Please talk to us. We're looking for Erin and Celia. You care about them, don't you?"

Nothing. Nathan tried the knob, but the man had locked his door. Nathan rubbed his chin. He would prefer to simply break down the door instead of play games. But he reined in his frustration and hurried back to his vehicle, where he waited for a few moments.

Where would Erin go? *Come on, think like her. Think like her mom.*

He considered everything that had happened.

Dad called about the case and then Celia tried to kill herself. Nathan was leaning toward Dad's call being the catalyst for her attempt. Or was that completely wrong? Celia claimed she'd woken up in the hospital and couldn't remember anything. And she denied she had tried to kill herself. Was she telling the truth? Had someone tried to kill her and stage it as a suicide?

Wilson's garage door slowly opened, and a small red sedan backed out. He was trying to get away rather than answer more questions. Why? Nathan followed the car, remaining far enough back so Wilson wouldn't see him.

Anxiety twisted inside—was he wasting time?

The man steered around town as if he were trying to lose someone. Nathan hung back even more. He contacted Jack and left a voice mail about what was going on, then did the same with Trevor, Terra, and Alex.

Celia's neighbor was acting suspiciously. Or maybe Nathan was looking for answers where there were none. Nathan's gut told him that Delmar Wilson knew more than he had told the police.

FORTY-FIVE

Wilson parked behind a warehouse at the edge of town. Nathan hung back and watched him with binoculars. Wilson pulled a big backpack out of the trunk of his car, donned it, then climbed down an embankment to old railroad tracks. He disappeared into the abandoned train tunnel.

Nathan sped forward and parked next to the red sedan. He hopped out and slid down the embankment, following Wilson, letting moonlight guide the way. Pulling his weapon out, he crept slowly toward the tunnel entrance. A flashlight beam shone around in the tunnel.

Wilson could be keeping the women against their will. Or protecting them. Nathan didn't know. His heart jackhammered as he quietly entered the tunnel, hoping his eyes would quickly adjust to the darkness barely illuminated by Wilson's flashlight. Nathan kept close to the walls so he wouldn't be so easy to spot at the tunnel entrance. He was almost walking into this situation blindly.

"Celia," Wilson called out. "Where are they?" he mumbled quietly, though his voice echoed in the tunnel. "I don't understand. She said to meet her here if . . ."

Wilson stood near the wall, his face awash with confusion, frown lines carved deeper by the shadows.

"Police." Nathan flicked on his own flashlight and lifted his firearm as he slowly crept forward. "Slowly place your hands on your head."

Wilson's eyes widened, and he dropped his flashlight. "No, wait."

"I said, place your hands on your head."

The man dropped to his knees. Nathan hadn't asked him to do that. Wilson's face twisted up—grief? Regret?

Nathan approached, trying to suppress his anger. "Where are they?" He ground out the question.

"What?" Wilson opened his eyes and glared up at Nathan. "You think I know?"

"What are you doing here, then? You came here for them. You called out Celia's name."

"But she's not here, is she?"

"You know something, Mr. Wilson. Something you didn't tell the police. I want to hear the whole story and now. They're in danger, and I have to find them."

"Don't you think I know that?" Wilson climbed back to his feet. "Can you stop pointing that thing at me? I'm not a criminal."

"Fine. Slowly remove your backpack and toss it to the side. Then put your hands against the wall. I need to make sure you don't have a weapon." Nathan didn't think he had anything to fear from Wilson, but he couldn't afford to take that chance, especially considering Wilson's strange actions.

He frisked the man, patting down his outer clothing with one hand, then stepped back and lowered his gun, though he kept it warm and ready in his hand.

"Look, man." Wilson stepped over a railroad tie. "I . . . I'm just the neighbor. I was *helping* them."

"Why didn't you tell the police that when they asked you?"

"They asked me what I saw, and I told them. I answered their questions."

In other words, the police hadn't asked him the right questions.

"And I didn't open the door when you knocked because I was pretending I wasn't home. I couldn't wait any longer. I had to leave."

"You're withholding information that could help find Erin and Celia. So tell me everything, and make it quick."

"Okay, okay. Celia shared a secret with me that she hadn't shared with anyone and commissioned me to dig a tunnel that led away from her home in case she needed to escape. All I had to do was dig to the steam tunnel that runs under the town, and from there, she would make her way here."

"Escape from whom?"

"Some bad people after her. She said she'd been running from them most of her life and had to prepare for the day they would catch up to her."

This confirmed what Nathan had pieced together, though he didn't know the exact connections. Celia was the woman in the article, the crime boss's daughter who had disappeared. And Erin—had she known any of this? If she didn't know before, she definitely knew now.

"And that escape plan included you meeting her here?"

He nodded. "She texted me that they had found her and told me to meet her like we'd planned. But I'm here and . . . well . . . she isn't." He scraped his hands through his hair.

Nathan had the feeling the guy was in love with Celia. At the very least, he cared deeply for her. "After meeting here, was the plan that you would drive her somewhere? Escape with her?"

"That wasn't *her* plan, but it was mine. I was going to take her far from here. She hadn't told me where. I had planned to disappear with her, though."

Could Celia have figured that out and simply lured him

here so he wouldn't follow her? Nathan paced the old train tunnel. He noticed a duffel. "What's that?"

"Her bag, I assume."

"I'm going to search your backpack and make sure you don't have a weapon. Then I'll look inside the duffel to see if it'll give us any clues."

Wilson shrugged. "I'm good with that, man. I just want them to be safe. I don't have to find her, but if she's in trouble, I want to help if I can."

Good enough. Using his flashlight, he gave Wilson's backpack a quick look to make sure he wouldn't get any surprises from the man, like a knife to the back, then tossed it to him. Wilson hefted it onto his back.

Nathan checked inside the duffel to confirm there wasn't a bomb, then he carried it outside and back up to his vehicle. At his vehicle, he plopped the duffel in the back and got a better look inside. Clothing and toiletries. Everything one might need for a few days away from home. But what was the bigger plan? Where had she intended to end up?

Nathan tossed it all back in and growled. He looked up to the sky—at the stars. *Lord, where are they?*

"I think they're just gone," Wilson said in a breathy exhale. "They got out of here. Didn't wait for me and left. They're miles away by now."

"As long as they're safe, that's all that matters, Mr. Wilson."

Not again, Lord. I've lost her again.

His cell rang. His heart jumped. Erin! But it was his mother. Nathan couldn't talk to her now.

"Just call me Delmar. What now?" Delmar asked.

Nathan considered his next move. "You need to come back with me to talk to the police."

Delmar's shoulders sagged. "Am I under arrest?"

"No. But you want to help us find them, don't you?"

"I want them to be safe."

Nathan understood where the man was coming from. "Agreed. But we also need to make sure they haven't been abducted—or worse."

He and Delmar climbed into Nathan's vehicle. "I'll take you downtown so you can tell your story—the full story. Someone will bring you back to your car, okay?"

"Fine." Delmar stared into the woods swallowed up by darkness, shaking his head and mumbling to himself. "I should have known this would happen. She was under so much pressure, she couldn't keep it all bottled up. The signs were there all along."

"What are you talking about?"

"I don't think I meant anything to her."

"Listen, since the bag was in the tunnel, that means Celia made it to the tunnel like she planned, but she left without it. We have to assume she and Erin were taken. Let's get her back, and you can ask her how she feels. Or tell her how you feel. Get it out in the open."

And take your own advice, dude.

His cell buzzed again, and he glanced at it to make sure it wasn't from Erin. Pain ignited in his chest at the thought that she hadn't contacted him. Did he mean so little to her? Now he truly sounded like Delmar. But he *knew* that he meant something to Erin. He knew it in his heart of hearts. And that was another big reason why he knew that Erin and Celia hadn't escaped and were not well on their way to safety. He knew they were in danger.

Erin wouldn't have abandoned her friends so easily without at least telling them goodbye.

The text was from his mother. *Your father is trying to communicate. Repeating one word. "Rare."*

Nathan scraped his hand down his face. He didn't know what that meant. He should be there now with his father, but Dad would want him to find Erin if he could. He would reply to his mother on the other side of this. Nathan steered back toward town and thought back to something Delmar had said earlier. Something about those words gnawed at the back of his mind. *Think, Nathan.* What was it?

"*She was under so much pressure.*"

Erin had said similar words to Nathan when they were hiking to the dam.

"*When someone is under tremendous pressure, they often give something away . . . Think back and try to remember everything he said.*"

Nathan's mind was caught up in those thoughts as he sped through town to hand Delmar over to be further questioned. He thought back to his conversation with Dad by the river and tried to remember every word Dad had said.

Almost everything had carried weight. Dad had called Celia. He was working on a cold case. Dwayne had given him the articles. Lives were at stake. It was all there, just loosely connected. But what else had he talked about?

Think, Nathan, think.

Headlights flashed at him and a car honked.

"Watch out!" Delmar shouted.

Heart pounding, Nathan gripped the steering wheel and swerved back into his own lane, then pulled over to the side of the road and stopped the car. He needed to think.

"What are you doing?" Delmar asked.

"*I thought we could fish here today before everything's ruined.*"

Dad's statement had struck Nathan as odd, even within the context as Dad explained. The dam had suddenly collapsed—possibly bombed?—so that statement fell in line with everything else that had happened, but there was something else he'd referred to.

He turned to Delmar.

"What do you know about the new copper mine?"

FORTY-SIX

rin sat on the cold, hard earth next to her mother, their wrists and ankles bound with plastic ties. She'd learned the man's name was Finn McPherson—he'd taken Missy when he'd meant to grab Erin.

But now he finally had his hands on her, and she struggled to remove his ghoulish face from her mind. Fortunately, she'd lost the child's hat he'd forced onto her head. He'd kept it all these years to remind him of his mistake and that he could never stop searching for Erica.

Erin fought to gain clarity over the turbulence that had taken hold of her very soul.

Calm, deep breaths, Erin. Hyperventilate now and she could pass out.

Erin and Mom had been prodded down yet another long tunnel in the new copper mine. The flashlight beam shone over their faces as a henchman dragged someone away—to be questioned? Recognition slammed into Erin as the woman locked eyes with her—fear brimming in her gaze. Holly was gagged and bound, though her ankles were free so she could walk.

That had been what seemed like hours ago.

She couldn't understand what Holly was doing here in

Montana to begin with. Unless . . . Had the woman traveled to Bozeman to check on Newt? Or was she trying to somehow reach Erin or Nathan to deliver another clandestine message? Whatever the reason, the henchmen had found her and brought her to the copper mine instead of killing her outright, but where had they taken her? Or was she already dead?

Erin thought she would lose her mind. Her back ached from the cramped position against the rocky wall, and her limbs had gone numb. Initially, their mouths had been gagged, but she and Mom were able to remove their gags since their hands were tied in front. Erin had tried to work her way out of the plastic ties with her teeth, but it was no use.

Cold started to seep right through her jeans.

But the worst part was that she couldn't see her hands in front of her face as she lifted her bound wrists. She'd wanted answers, yes, but more than that she'd wanted to make sense out of her life. Build a stable existence in which she could escape the past that had continued to haunt her.

Now she understood why she could never truly forget about what happened—because her past, that evil, had been hunting her all along. Deep inside, she must have sensed it.

And her desperate need for answers or, rather, closure had led them back to her, to Mom, who was in some ways a stranger to Erin. But now everything that had happened made sense, and it started long before Erin was even born.

Erin pushed down the anger over the fact that her mother had hidden so much from her. She'd only been trying to protect Erin and forge a new life. Erin couldn't blame her for that.

But now look at the two of them. The future did not look good.

Mom coughed next to her, and worry spiked through Erin. She leaned closer, feeling her mother's movements, her rocking shoulders, and the warmth from her body. Erin should scoot closer, but she waited for the coughing to subside.

"Are you okay?" she whispered.

"Yes. Just biding my time."

Whatever you say. "While we're biding our time, I have a few questions. Jimmy Delaney. Jason Cain. Jamie McPherson. Somebody Cobbs. These names were on Newt's crime board, and we believe the articles about the crime boss's missing daughter—you—were at the center. I want to hear your story, Mom."

Mom had gone silent. In fact, was she holding her breath?

"Mom?"

"Okay, you want to hear my story? I'll tell you. I was born Cara Collette Byrne. I never knew my mother because she died in childbirth. I had nannies and caretakers. My father protected me from the darker side of his business, but as I got older, I saw things. I knew crimes were being committed. He always told me he wanted something different, something better for me, as though he had regrets."

Interesting. Erin hadn't thought a crime boss could have any other mindset, but then again, they scored lower on the psychopathy evaluations than non-mob criminals. Because, well, they actually cared about their family.

"Go on. What happened that sent you running?"

"I already told you some of it. My father killed a man. He claimed it was in self-defense. I don't know why Ryan McPherson had come after him, or why my father was even alone without his usual protection. But Ryan was Finn's brother, and Jamie McPherson's son. Jamie was the head of the McPherson crime family."

"And your father feared they would come for you."

"Oh, he knew they would. He told me to disappear for good and never contact him. Start a new life with a new identity. My father sent me away with the tools to make that happen. I landed in Wisconsin as Celia Jones. Married your father, Tim Weeks, and had you."

Erin thought she could hear the smile in her mother's voice. The love. And a few tears.

"You know the rest. Your father died, and, well, Missy was taken and we had to move."

"How did you know they had found you? And it wasn't just a random abduction?"

"Because I knew they were always searching. Then when the bridge went out, I had my confirmation."

"Why would *that* confirm it for you?"

"The McPherson family employed an assassin. A henchman who was an explosives expert—Ricky 'Flashpoint' Flannagan. The bridge was blown the night Missy was taken, giving the abductor ample time to escape with her before the police could arrive."

Had her mother just shivered?

"Why didn't you tell me that what happened when Missy was taken was tied to your past? All this time I thought it was my mistake. That she was taken because of me!"

"I wanted to be someone else. I couldn't do that if you knew the truth about me. I had to make a clean break. I . . . That's why I volunteer at the thrift shop. To become someone other than the daughter of a mob boss. I have to give back and help others. I love their motto, 'By our work we are known.' So I'd hoped to be known by my good works, my fruit, not my family history. Not the sins of my father. What good would telling you have done? What could the truth of the past do except destroy you? I wanted to protect you. Don't you understand?"

"But we're here, Mom. All because I didn't know the truth long ago." Erin would press her mother for answers while she still had the chance. She had no idea if either of them would make it out of this alive.

"It's not your fault, Erin. I think they've been closing in. Newt Campbell even could have led them here. But it doesn't matter how they found us now."

Erin tried to absorb all her mother had shared. None of it really mattered to her except the one morbid fact—Finn McPherson took the wrong girl. *Oh, Missy.* Erin shoved back the tears. "Do you think there's a chance Missy's still alive out there somewhere?"

"I don't know. All you can do is pray and give it to God. Cast your cares on him."

How did her mother do that, exactly, in the middle of this battle? "I'm glad you're in a good state of mind at the moment."

"I've told you repeatedly that I didn't try to commit suicide. Don't you see? They found us and tried to kill me and make it look like a suicide. I would have died had Nadine not found me. They wanted to kill me, but something must have changed or I would already be dead."

Of course! The henchmen had been sent to kill both Erin and Mom on the same day.

"I'm sorry I didn't trust what you told me," Erin said. "It seems incredible that we've survived this long."

The boating accident and Mom's suicide—both meant to appear like something other than murder. The shooting that should have killed Newt and then the dam . . .

The dam. "You mentioned to Nathan that someone might have intentionally caused the dam to fail."

"I had hoped that if the dam had been bombed, Nathan would tell me and then I could be concerned that we'd been found. I was hoping he would tell me I was wrong, and he would just think I was a crazy old lady to even ask. I was still piecing it all together. Maybe even in denial at first."

"If the dam was blown, why do it? Newt was taken out with a gunshot." He should have died.

"I've been thinking about that," Mom said. "If Ricky was sent to take him out and make it look like an accident, the old dam breaking was his strategy. Maybe Newt had gone there several times, and Ricky was waiting for the moment he would return. I think the explosion didn't happen like it was supposed to, so he shot Newt instead."

"Then, the next day when Nathan and I were there, the bomb finally went off?"

"Or he planted the bomb to take out Nathan, reasoning a detective's son—also a detective—would return, and he wanted to make that look like an accident. Ricky probably thought Newt had told Nathan what he'd learned, so he needed to be taken out too. Now . . . it's time to get out of here."

"What? Just how are we going to escape? You don't have a shotgun to blast your way out of this." Mom had been stripped of her weapons when they were captured in the middle of their grand escape.

"Give me some space."

Erin scooted over and leaned away. She felt movement followed by a *snap*. Mom groaned. Cold replaced the warmth emanating from Mom's body. She must have moved.

"*What* are you doing?"

Erin was yanked to her feet.

"We need to be gone by the time they get back," Mom said.

"How did you get out of the ties?" Erin asked.

"An old trick I learned years ago. Now hold still. I need to find the locking mechanism, then slip my nail under it."

Mom slid the ties off Erin's wrists.

"I'm free." Erin almost fell over, forgetting her ankles were still tied.

Mom held her steady. "Let me get your ankles too."

"Thanks," Erin said. "You've had practice at this, have you?"

"Not really. Just planning ahead in case this day arrived."

"So that's what you've been doing with your time." Erin hoped her mother heard the smile she'd injected into the words, because she certainly couldn't see Erin's face. "I'm sorry, I was only—"

"No regrets, Erin. No time to be sorry. We have to leave before they get back."

"I'm not sure I could find my way out of here. I've never been here before today."

"I have. They opened it up for one day to show people it wasn't going to hurt the environment. The only issue is my ankle will slow us down."

"I'll help you. Which way, then, Mom?"

"We keep walking into the mine. They're digging a two-mile-long, truck-sized shaft. It's angled, so we have to be careful not to trip."

Erin envisioned falling and then rolling into the depths of the earth surrounded by darkness.

"You can't be serious. We are not going to walk deeper into this mine in the dark. What are you thinking?"

"There's equipment down there. The cabs of those rigs are almost bulletproof. We could potentially drive it out of here. But if you'd rather we walk toward the hired guns standing outside the mine, then let's go. Be warned. If they catch us trying to escape, they'll either kill us or truss us up so there's no chance of escape. Do you understand?" Mom's angry, determined tone was meant to strike fear.

Erin had heard that tone before—that night in the woods when Missy was taken.

A flashlight shone in the distance and illuminated the wide tunnel. Erin never wanted to see another tunnel in her life after today.

"Let's go." Mom grabbed Erin's hand, and together they made their way deeper into the mine.

She wished they could run, but Mom's ankle wouldn't let them. Erin had hurt her ankle and foot as well days before, but the pain was barely perceptible now. Her pulse pounded in her throat. Roared in her ears. What if the flashlight stopped and they could no longer see where they were going?

The idea that they should head deeper into the earth, deeper into darkness, warred with her better judgment. But the options were few—men with guns or a dark, treacherous mining shaft.

"Hey!" an angry voice shouted from behind them.

Gunfire spattered from an automatic weapon. Mom yelped as she plummeted forward. Erin tried to prevent her mother from tumbling, but her efforts weren't enough and they both hit the ground hard.

"Come on, Mom." Erin tried to help her mother get up.

Mom groaned and grabbed her shoulder, crimson seeping between her fingers.

"Mom!"

"Go, you have to get out of here. I'll stall them."

"Forget it. I'm not leaving you."

Erin applauded her mother's effort to try to find a way to escape. Her mother was a survivor and because of her, Erin had survived too. She wouldn't give up now.

She tried again to assist Mom to her feet. "Come on. We can make it to the equipment just like you planned. We can do this."

"Go without me. Leave before it's too late. Please, you don't understand . . ." Tears choked Mom's voice, surprising Erin. So much bravado moments ago had quickly bled out of her with the seeping wound.

"That I could die today? Mom, I'm not afraid of death." She pressed her hands against Mom's wound and glared at the approaching men.

She couldn't make out much behind that light. "You shot her! She's bleeding and needs medical attention."

"The chopper's on the way." The man's voice was gruff. "Get her up, and we'll meet it outside. We need to be out of here in five."

Another man entered, waving his flashlight around the tunnel as if taking it in for the first time. "What are you doing here?" He growled the question. "Why are you in the mine? It stinks and it's dark. Gives me the creeps."

"That's the point. Nobody's going to look for them here. The town is crawling with cops. The whole county and probably the state by now. We get out of here at night. They'll think the helicopter is part of the search."

"We need to keep a low profile, and this operation has already put us on the radar"—he glared at the other two men— "thanks to you guys."

The first man reached down and helped Erin lift Mom to her feet.

"Keep pressure on the wound, Mom."

Without the flashlight beaming in her face, she got a better look at the new man who'd complained about the mine. Shock and anger rocked through her.

He grinned at her as if appreciating that she recognized he was the man who'd tried to kill them with rolling logs. According to Detective Munson, he'd been involved with the accident in Seattle as well. Had he also been the one to shoot Newt?

"Lucky for you, my instructions have changed. The boss wants you back in Boston to make a big splash. A big point." He grabbed Erin's arm and tore her away from her mother. To the other man, he said, "Carry her. We need to get out of here, and if they aren't alive by the time we get back to Boston, then we might join them."

Mom spit at him. "Ricky Flannagan, you can just kill me now."

Ricky . . . the explosives expert who took out the bridge the night Missy was taken, and likely the dam here in Big Rapids.

"Mom, please . . ." Erin was holding out hope they would be saved.

Mom's accent seemed to shift as she spoke to Ricky. "You were just a kid back then."

Back when? When Grandpa Byrne killed someone's son?

"He was family."

"Not by blood," Mom said.

Erin understood that mob loyalty ran deep and was *thicker* than blood.

"It's been years," Mom continued. "*Years.* Why hold a grudge for so long?"

Erin was surprised to hear her mother practically begging for their lives. She probably understood far better than Erin the terror that awaited them.

Still, Erin had seen inside criminal minds.

Evil wouldn't let her forget.

"If it was up to me, you'd already be dead," Finn said. "But my father wants to make an example of you two, but not before we get the hidden money."

"Money?" Erin looked at her mother. "What money?"

FORTY-SEVEN

N athan ran through the woods, then slowed at the edge of the tree line on his approach to the copper mine. He'd communicated with Jack, Terra, and Alex, as well as Trevor. But there was no time to waste. If there was any chance of getting Erin and Celia away from these deadly men while they were at the copper mine—*if* they were at the mine—then that time was now.

Delmar kept pace with him. The science teacher had visited the mine before and discussed all the advantages and disadvantages of it with his students, and he'd given Nathan more information than he needed to go along with the more crucial fact—the mine wasn't far from the abandoned train tunnel where Celia had left her duffel.

Piles of excavated dirt edged the perimeter where heavy equipment had been left.

Multiple flashlights shone near the entrance of the mine, which was just a big gaping hole in the earth, and several vehicles were parked nearby. Were they mine workers? If so, he would think the floodlights would be shining bright for their safety. His gut told him this group was up to no good. Nathan wasn't able to get a handle on how many were there. Some were outside the entrance of the mine, but there could be others inside. He peered through binoculars, trying to find out more, and if, in fact, these were the same men who could have taken the women.

"No way." His gut clenched.

"What it is?" Delmar asked. "Let me see?"

"Just a guy I ran into while in Boston." Ginger Man was here too. That meant Erin and Celia were probably here.

"What are we going to do?"

"You're going to do nothing. You shouldn't even be here. As for me, I'm waiting until I see them bring the women out of the mine"—*God, please let these mobster goons bring them out alive and well*—"and then, I'm doing something." He just wasn't sure what yet. Any action he took could be risky. Erin and Celia could end up becoming hostages or getting shot and killed. He prayed they were not already dead.

"I can help."

"By staying here. You've already helped a lot." In fact, Nathan had more questions. "Why do you suppose they came to the mine?"

"I thought we already decided it was close enough. A good place to hide until they could make their escape."

It just seemed like too many men sent to grab two women, but what did he know about the mob? From the looks of the house and the tunnel—Delmar had shared about digging it—Celia was a force to be reckoned with.

"Tell me more about mines. Copper mines. I don't know—*this* mine."

"What else do you want to know?"

"I'm trying to figure this out. I'm missing something. Humor me and just keep talking as if you're in class, only keep it to a whisper."

"Okay, well, copper is used in all kinds of things, and we're even looking to copper as an alternative to rare earth minerals, especially in wind turbines and electric vehicles. But rare earth can occur as a byproduct of copper."

"And how much money is generated from such an endeavor?"

"Money?" Delmar huffed. "Billions. Hundreds of billions."

Nathan fell back on his haunches. Rare earth? His mother had said Dad kept repeating the word *rare*. Was there a connection between the copper mine and Celia or the mafia? Who were the investors?

Whop-whop-whop.

A helicopter's approach drew his attention upward. Was it SWAT? One of the county helicopters responding to his call for help?

A commotion near the entrance of the mine pulled his gaze back down. The men shuffled three women between them. Erin, Celia—who appeared to be injured—and . . . Holly Sandfield? Nathan's pulse skyrocketed.

So the helicopter was their transportation out of the mine and escape from the grip of authorities.

Nathan couldn't wait on help to arrive. He couldn't wait on backup. He took in the heavy equipment—three times the size of his county SUV—parked along the perimeter. Could he somehow use that as a distraction? One was an excavator with a long arm.

He could use it to keep the helicopter from landing. Then he could delay their planned getaway until help arrived.

"Stay here." He handed the binoculars over to Delmar and got to his feet.

"Wait! Where are you going?"

Nathan didn't have time to explain a plan he wasn't even sure would work. But, somehow, he had to save the day. The helicopter drew closer but still hovered above the mine, lights flashing down as the pilot searched for the right place to land. Nathan could see the spot easily enough, and if he could start that excavator, he could prevent the bird from landing.

He raced between the trees, jumping over logs and scrambling around the bottom of a dirt pile to climb up the ladder on the back side of the Hitachi excavator. He chose this over the dump truck because of the arm. Plus, Dad's cousin, Ned, had taught Nathan how to use one back when he was clearing property. That, and he'd learned to drive a combine during harvest. All part of living in the country.

The cab rested at the top behind protective glass. If that door was locked, no way would Nathan break through it. Unless he could shoot a hole in it, but even that might not work since it had a ballistic rating to protect it from flying debris. Even so, he wanted to avoid drawing attention to himself so he could use the element of surprise to his advantage.

The door popped open, and he slipped into the seat and found the key in the ignition. Heavy equipment didn't have unique keys but used universal keys. One key started them all. Nathan breathed a sigh of relief. He didn't have time to hot-wire the thing.

The helicopter was already starting to descend.

He started up the excavator, which rumbled to life, the sound competing with the helicopter rotors. He noticed a few looks coming from the men holding Erin, Celia, and Holly. The excavator started forward slowly, and Nathan steered toward the beam of light from the helicopter while maneuvering the levers to lift the boom high.

Bullets pinged the cab. One hit the glass and merely chipped it. If only he could reach over and safely grab the women with the bucket and carry them to shelter. Gunfire continued from all angles, and Nathan might need to escape the excavator before someone climbed up here and yanked him out. Several men still surrounded the women and suddenly rushed them to the right and out of sight.

A new landing spot for the helicopter? The chopper's lights had moved in that direction as well. Nathan headed toward the light slowly crawling across the ground, but this time the helicopter beat him to the punch and landed. He couldn't let it take off with the women. He ground his molars and accelerated, heading directly for the chopper. Then he maneuvered the boom to reach out and forward.

As soon as the blades of the helicopter connected with the raised bucket, Nathan grabbed the keys, climbed down, and dashed away from the equipment. Metal twisted behind him. The concussive force of an explosion shoved him forward. Face in the dirt, he knew he'd achieved at least one goal. The helicopter was toast.

The excavator too, but . . . *lives were at stake.*

He scrambled back to his feet and sprinted behind the giant tires of the dump truck, his gun ready.

Sirens resounded in the night, echoing through the trees and off the mountains.

Finally.

Except the henchmen had another plan of escape. Their vehicles circled around and accelerated toward the one road out of here. Still, he couldn't be sure they wouldn't somehow escape before law enforcement arrived. Nathan climbed into the dump truck near the exit and started it up with the same key. The truck bounced and lumbered as he backed up until it blocked the path out.

The three fleeing vehicles swerved to a stop. He'd effectively cut them off. But his initial dread that they would use the women as hostages remained in play.

He climbed from the truck and aimed his weapon as he approached the vehicle holding the women. "Police. Get out of the car and *slowly* put down your weapons."

Another helicopter approached the area. This time it must be SWAT. Someone to help. Nathan didn't lower his weapon, trusting backup had finally arrived.

The helicopter landed and men in tactical gear rushed forward.

Relief flooded Nathan. But until he held Erin in his arms, he wouldn't trust that it was over. Not yet.

The mobsters in all three vehicles got out, their hands lifted. Holly and Celia also got out, though Celia stumbled forward and collapsed. Seeing the blood on her shirt, Nathan rushed to help her. "You're hurt."

"Don't worry about me. Erin. He took Erin. Find her."

FORTY-EIGHT

rin bit back the pain. Finn's fingers dug into her arm as he hauled her forward.

"You're hurting me."

"Keep up if you want to live." He jabbed the muzzle of his gun under her rib cage for emphasis.

"I can't move as fast as you." Nor could she see all that well, despite the bouncing beam of his dim flashlight.

Fear strangled her. She'd often tried to imagine how terrified Missy must have felt as the stranger carried her away. This time, Erin was the person being abducted, only she wasn't a child. If only she could find a way to escape. Run and hide.

"That night years ago, what did you do with my friend? What happened to Missy?" She'd wanted answers, and now was her chance to get them. But the rawness of the spoken words cut her heart open.

"I delivered the wrong child, and I paid for it. I've got you this time."

"Is she . . . is she dead?" Of course she was gone. Erin knew that, but she had always held on to an ounce of hope that somehow Missy had survived.

DEADLY TARGET

"Don't ask questions you don't want to know the answers to."

At his words, she stumbled. He kept her upright and squeezed tighter, igniting pain.

A fallen tree blocked their path, but rather than going around, the man shoved her forward, up, and over. He was especially skilled at keeping his tight grip despite her every movement. Erin took that to mean he knew if she got free, then she had a chance of hiding in the woods, especially with the arrival of law enforcement. They must have reached the copper mine by now.

Mom would get the medical attention she needed.

While the huge excavator was rolling toward the helicopter, the henchmen argued between themselves, finally realizing their only escape was in the vehicles. Just a couple of them had planned to ride in the helicopter along with the women—getting them out of the county and state and to the more familiar bustle of Boston, where it would be easier to hide in plain sight.

But Nathan thwarted their plan.

Thank you, Lord. Tears had emerged when she realized Nathan was the one driving the excavator, preventing the helicopter from taking them away. If they had been taken, they might never have been found.

But Finn McPherson had opted not to join his partners in crime and instructed the others to leave as planned. She suspected he hoped law enforcement would give chase, while Finn escaped with Erin.

He jabbed the gun under her rib cage again as he continued rushing her through the woods. Earlier Finn had been on his cell and called someone to help him get Erin out of here.

"Why are you doing this? You don't need me anymore. It's over. I don't know anything about money either."

"You're a loose end that I meant to take care of twenty years ago. I can always come back for your mother, but my father wants you. Nothing will hurt the old man Byrne more than to watch you die, and us getting the money he buried in that mine will make it hurt all the more."

"I don't even know my grandfather. I never met him. I didn't know anything about ties to you. Whatever you call yourselves. My death will be meaningless."

He yanked her around. "See, that's what you don't understand. Your death is the end of his legacy."

"You're wrong. *My life* is the end of his legacy. I work for good instead of evil. Mom too, even though she was born into a crime family. She chose a different life." Erin stopped walking, resisting as he tried to yank her forward. "And you can choose a different life."

He flashed his teeth in a twisted snarl, then shoved her to the ground, pressing his booted foot into her back. Her face pressed against needles, and she breathed in the earthy scents of pine and decay. She risked a glance up and caught the end of the gun, still pointed at her, while he peered through a small set of binoculars. Looking for his ride?

Her head pressed against the ground, Erin heard thumping as if someone was running through the woods. Someone was coming for her.

She had to distract Finn. "Why not choose a new life, Finn?"

"Stop talking." He dug the heel of his boot deeper into her back.

She grunted, gritting her teeth against the pressure.

He was right when he said she didn't understand. She could never understand.

A shadow moved in the darkness, then a form slammed into Finn, knocking him to the ground. Erin rolled away as soon as his boot released her. A gunshot blasted too close, but she continued to move and shuffled behind a tree. Heart pounding, she peered around it.

Finn was the one facedown on the ground now, releasing a

string of curses. Nathan finished putting the mobster's wrists in handcuffs even as his gaze searched the woods.

She stepped from behind the tree. "Nathan."

He exhaled, his relief clear in his demeanor.

She rushed forward and into his arms, pressing her face into his shoulder. "You did it, Nathan. You saved us."

"It's okay. It's all over now."

Erin pulled away. "He was waiting on someone to meet him. I think he was taking me back to the area near the train tunnel by the old warehouses. You need to get whoever is waiting on Finn."

Nathan shook his head. "I'm not leaving you again." Lifting his cell, he contacted Jack and then Trevor, informing them that he had apprehended Finn McPherson and instructing them to grab the man he'd planned to meet and where they might find him.

Shouts and flashlights filled the woods. Alex emerged from the trees, gasping. "You got her. So . . . glad . . . you got her."

Alex glared down at Finn as more law enforcement officers appeared and took Finn into custody, then ushered him through the woods.

"Jack's heading for the old warehouse district near the train tunnel, along with a contingent of deputies. All the roads are blocked," Alex said. "No one is getting away." He eyed Erin, dipping his chin as if to make sure she would be all right here alone with Nathan. "You okay?"

With Nathan's arms still around her? "Never better."

Alex nodded. "Good. I'm going to catch up with Jack, then."

"Be careful."

Alex took off through the woods.

Nathan tugged her closer and gazed into her eyes. "I'm so relieved it's finally over. You don't ever have to worry about your past catching up to you again, Erin."

"I'm sorry I didn't tell you about what happened before. I

should have trusted you. But Mom had warned me never to tell anyone what happened that night. As for the larger story behind it, I didn't know—not until I recognized her in that article you sent. Honestly, I understand. Mom was protecting not only me but also those around me. It's the same reason your father told you not to tell anyone."

"I figured that out." He hugged her tighter.

She could stay in his arms forever and hoped he would never let her go. But that wasn't reality. Erin buried her face in Nathan's chest. She listened to the strong, steady beat of his heart. The security, the stability she'd been searching for had been there waiting for her all along.

And she wanted another chance with him. He was a hero. *Her* hero. But he was also a detective and the son of a detective. And now that he knew the truth, that *she* was the granddaughter of a crime boss, would he want another chance too?

FORTY-NINE

At the hospital, Nathan stood with Henry in the hallway down from Dad's room.

Henry angled his head, a look of respect in his eyes. Not that Nathan had never seen that before, but a bright spark of admiration shone there too. "You did good work, Nathan." He clapped him on the back. "Like father, like son. I wouldn't have expected anything less."

"Thank you." Nathan took the words to mean that he and Henry were good again, despite Nathan stepping into the fray when Henry had told him to stay out of it. Still, Henry understood that Dad had put Nathan in an impossible situation.

"Now, get out of here and go check on her."

"You don't have to tell me twice."

Nathan left the hospital, relief welling and overflowing on so many fronts. Dad was talking. He was himself again. He needed a little therapy, sure, but he was well on his way to recovery. But his hospital room had gotten crowded with cops—the locals in Montana and from his district back East, and a few federal agents as well, taking statements. Asking more questions to figure out the whole convoluted mess.

A few reporters were waiting around too. Everyone wanted to get the big story.

Dad had pieced it together, aside from a few stray bits.

Lieutenant Sullivan had been the man waiting for Finn near the abandoned tunnel—not by any real choice. But he had a half brother, Paul, whom no one knew about who had joined the rank and file of the McPherson crime family, and he was feeling the pressure to redirect Newt. If Cara Byrne was going to be found, the McPherson clan would be the ones to do it. But do one thing for a crime family and you have to keep bending to their will. So Sullivan had no choice but to follow the McPhersons to Montana. He did it under the guise of checking on Dad, but his goal was to find out if he was talking and how much he knew.

Dad had already figured out most of it and would have told Nathan everything if he hadn't been shot by Ricky Flannagan, who hadn't expected his bomb planted in the dam to malfunction.

Nathan tried to embrace the fact that he'd hit a home run and Dad was there to watch, in a manner of speaking. But the game wasn't over yet. There was still the matter of winning Erin's heart. Winning her back before she ran again.

He'd seen that skittish look in her eyes. The same one he'd seen before when she broke things off with him.

He drove from Bozeman back toward Grayback County, more specifically Stone Wolf Ranch, where Erin and Celia were staying for the time being.

On the drive, Nathan thought back to the story Dad had shared.

Dad had been investigating the murder of a thirty-seven-year-old college professor—Kevin Cobbs. An ordinary enough guy, except for the fact his grandfather had gone into WITSEC thirty years before. Kevin hadn't been in contact with his grandfather in that long, at least. The investigation reminded Dad of the articles Dwayne had shared about the crime family boss,

Collin Byrne, whose daughter had disappeared. Dad worked Cobbs's case and at the same time looked into the missing woman in the articles for Dwayne. Dad had failed to follow through while Dwayne was still alive and felt he owed him.

Dad had been in law enforcement long enough that he had plenty of connections and learned that Kevin Cobbs's grandfather, Jacob Cobbs, had also been murdered—down in South Carolina, where he lived under his WITSEC identity as Jason Cain.

Mr. Cobbs/Cain wasn't a member of a crime family but thirty years or so ago had the unfortunate luck to have witnessed the murder of Ryan McPherson committed by Collin Byrne, and Cobbs gave his testimony in return for a new identity. His testimony put the crime boss in prison. But not before Collin Byrne warned his daughter, Cara, to disappear if she wanted to live because the McPhersons would come for their revenge.

Cara fled to Wisconsin and changed her name to Celia Jones. Only a few years later her true identity was discovered and a child was abducted—but it was the wrong child. Missy had been taken instead of Erica, all due to that pink hat.

Finn McPherson, Missy's abductor, had hoped to kill Cara and Erica in a most spectacular way to hurt Collin. Frustrated that the women had eluded him for too many years, Finn decided to kill anyone associated with his brother's murder. Kevin Cobbs was targeted because Finn believed he knew where his grandfather had moved, and Finn beat it out of him and murdered his grandfather. The man had stood by, watching Ryan's murder and doing nothing to prevent it, and then had the audacity to assist in putting Collin Byrne in prison and out of Finn's reach.

Brotherhood of psychopaths.

Then Finn finally found Celia and Erin and would have followed through with their murders, except his imprisoned father, crime family boss Jamie McPherson, got wind of money hidden in a mine and warned Finn off from killing anyone until they got the money first.

What they didn't understand was that the money wasn't buried in the mine—why would it be? Nathan chuckled to himself.

The money had been *invested* in the mine. Turned out that Collin hadn't sent his daughter off empty-handed, and she left having memorized bank account numbers and codes to be used at the right time—and not in a way that would draw attention to herself. Celia had the chance to start a new life far from the organized crime mentality. She believed she had invested wisely in the copper mine through a shell company created to protect herself and Erin.

As for Collin Byrne, he was still serving time in prison.

Nathan was just glad it was over, especially considering those innocents who died because they got in the way. Missy, for one, and then more recently Ian Sandfield and his mother, Lena. Kevin Cobbs and his grandfather Jacob.

Finally, Nathan turned onto the drive up to Stone Wolf Ranch, hoping—praying—that Erin was still there and that she would be happy to see him. He'd exchanged a few texts with Terra, begging her to make sure Erin was there when he arrived.

He slowly pulled around the circular drive and parked behind a USFS vehicle. Looked like Jack and Alex were here too. Great. That's all he needed—an audience, because he had no intention of letting them distract him from his purpose. From his mission.

Nathan climbed from his vehicle and jammed his sweaty hands into his pockets and headed for the front door.

Erin stepped out onto the porch and pulled the door closed behind her. She rushed forward and he thought she would jump right into his arms, but she hesitated.

"Nathan . . ." She sounded anxious.

He couldn't find the words. He'd planned them all out in

his head, and now they were just gone. So he reached for her, wrapping her in his arms and pulling her tight against him. She came willingly and lifted her chin, her lips. That was more than enough invitation and he accepted. He would kiss her until they were both breathless.

It was now or never.

God help me to convince her . . .

Nathan pulled his heart back—he didn't want to overwhelm her—and gently eased out of the kiss. She gasped, like he did, and he thought her heart was beating as fast as his.

This moment was everything to him. The past and the future. The present.

"Erin, please don't go."

"Shh." She pressed her finger against his lips. "Think about what you're saying, Nathan. Think about who I am. Now that you know who I really am."

"What?"

"I'm the granddaughter of a . . . of a . . ."

"And I don't give a rip." He pressed his lips against hers again, then lowered her in a romantic dip. It was all he could think to do. "Can you give us another chance? I . . . I love you," he whispered against her lips, still holding her in that position. "I'm not letting you up until you say yes."

She smiled and giggled, her lips brushing against his. "Yes, Nathan. I love you too. I was afraid you wouldn't want a second chance with me. But I had hoped something good could come out of all this, and I think . . . I think a second chance with you is the silver lining."

Nathan wouldn't argue with her. But Erin back in his life—now *that* was a gift from God.

Laughter and clapping drew them apart and they saw that Terra, Jack, and Alex watched from the porch.

Erin's closest friends ran forward and hugged them both, and then Nathan knew he'd truly saved the day.

Want More from

ELIZABETH GODDARD?

Keep Reading for a Preview of Book 3 in the

ROCKY MOUNTAIN
COURAGE

Series!

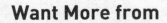

ONE

Her world was spinning out of control. Correction. Not her world—her *body*.

But what else could Mackenzie Hanson expect while in the grip of a colossal gyrating octopus? A cephalopod built from a jumble of plastic and metal parts, and powered by a smelly, backfiring motor. All of it quickly bolted together to be ready for patrons visiting the traveling carnival.

She imagined a tentacle flying off. How safe was she, really?

Her stomach grew queasy with the spinning and rocking motion.

Sky. People. Balloons. Asphalt. Sky. People. Balloons. Asphalt.

Over and over and over.

Mackenzie squeezed her eyes shut.

But for the brief time she'd kept them open . . .

She might have been hallucinating. Could centrifugal force cause hallucinations?

She thought she'd seen . . . No. It was only someone who looked like Julian.

Even with the mere thought of seeing him, her heart rate

skyrocketed. The ride wasn't helping. She squeezed her eyes tighter as if that would protect her from the G-force conspiring against her.

Screams erupted. Laughter too. Loud rock music pounded through her bones as her stomach dropped to catch up with her body being flung by octopus tentacles. She clung to the safety bar that kept her secure, or prevented her from escape. She hadn't decided which.

All she wanted was to get off the giant rolling octopus. Now!

A hand squeezed her shoulder. "Are you all right?"

That her friend—her *date*—William could even speak while the ride car continued spinning added to her anxiety. Mackenzie shook her head.

"I thought it would be fun." William's voice sounded tight. "Just hang on. It'll be over soon."

But the ride wasn't over soon. In fact, it continued far too long.

Was the operator distracted? Flirting with a girl much too young for him? Had he left to use the facilities? Mackenzie recalled enjoying this crazy, exhilarating fluttering of her stomach as a kid. Things had certainly changed.

Finally, hydraulics hissed and shifted with the decrease in the motor's rumble. Her heart calmed with the knowledge that torture by cephalopod was coming to an end.

Keeping her eyes closed, she leaned back and breathed in the malodorous exhaust from the ride's overtaxed motor.

An image popped into her mind.

Glasses. Dark hair. A forest-green jacket.

Julian Abel.

It couldn't have been him. But if she'd imagined him—why? She hadn't seen him in well over a decade, and she'd locked those memories in a vault and thrown away the proverbial key. Why was he breaking out of the crypt today?

"See, I told you it would be over soon." William's sarcasm demanded a smile.

A smile she had to force along with an incredulous chuckle. "What was I thinking to let you talk me into this? I'm too old for this kind of thing."

William pressed his larger hand over her smaller one that still clung to the safety bar.

"Too old?" He quirked a brow. "I beg your pardon."

She caught him looking at her and dropped her hand from the bar, breaking free from his touch.

"Saying you're too old is the same as saying *I'm* too old," he said.

"Well, if the shoe—"

"Fits. I know the idiom. I've got one for you. You're never too old to have fun."

"More accurately, you mean to say that you're never too old to learn."

"To *learn* to have *fun.*"

Her laugh was genuine this time. "Good one."

Now let me out of this cage.

"Mackenzie, you're young, vibrant, and beautiful, and the world is your oyster, as the saying goes." Reassurance filled William's tone. And his eyes.

Unpleasant shivers crawled over her. Was this how claustrophobia felt? Because right now, the space was growing smaller next to William. She exhaled as their turn to disembark from the car arrived. Perfect timing for an escape. The bar pinning them released. Mackenzie couldn't get out fast enough and hopped to the ground.

And to freedom.

She headed straight for the clearly marked exit from the fenced-off area. William followed closely, his hand against the small of her back. She searched the area around the ride, hoping he didn't catch on to her wariness.

Seeing Julian had been a hallucination. Nothing more.

Music, grinding motors, screams, and laughter filled the air along with the aroma of buttery popcorn and fried pies. Unfortunately, she also caught the pungent odor of an overflowing garbage can as they walked.

"How about we grab a soda and cotton candy?" William asked.

What are you, seven? She smiled for his sake. He was trying so hard. Too hard. "That sounds like a plan."

"Good. No more wild rides tonight." He grinned and led her through the crowd toward the end of a long line for the food truck that featured loaded fried pickles, hot dogs, greasy fries—glorious carnival junk food.

William held her hand, and she didn't have the heart to do anything but go along with it. What was wrong with her? He was handsome and thoughtful. He was just . . . not for her.

"Agreed. No more wild rides." Calliope music drew her attention as they waited in line. "The carousel would be nice." *Then maybe just take me home.*

To make matters worse, he'd driven all the way from Lansing to the Upper Peninsula for the weekend, just to see her. She kept a condominium in the quaint town near Lake Michigan for weekends and summers.

"So you're heading back on Monday for the semester?" she asked.

"If I could teach something as"—he lifted his shoulders— "how can I put it? Clandestine as you, then it would be fun teaching in the summer. But I forget, you can't really talk about your work."

She offered a smug grin. "Yeah . . . it's on a need-to-know basis." And wow, she enjoyed teasing him a little too much.

They'd met on the job, and he repeatedly asked her out until she finally agreed to a date.

One date. Which had somehow turned into a weekend

event since his parents supposedly owned a nearby summer lake house. *I never should have agreed to a date, much less an entire weekend.*

She was as trapped in this date as she had been riding the octopus. She had to grit her teeth to make it through and somehow let him down gently. Although . . . maybe he was feeling every bit as uncomfortable as she was.

While they moved forward in the line, Mackenzie took in the carnival activities. The growing crowd was beginning to shift from adults and younger children to older teens as the evening deepened. If Julian had actually been at the carnival, she probably wouldn't even have recognized him. They'd been kids when it happened.

William cleared his throat. He'd been paying attention to her on their date, and she'd been distracted. "I admit, I'm not good company for you this evening."

He shrugged. "You don't seem to be a carnival kind of person. And to be honest, neither am I. But I thought it might be fun. I saw it when I got into town, so made the suggestion."

"Oh, it was a great idea. We tried." She offered a grin. He really was a nice guy. Why couldn't she get into him? She'd thought that she'd be married and have at least two kids by the time she was thirty-two. Instead, she kept relationships at a distance.

They continued inching forward in the line, and she almost suggested they skip it and grab something from a drive-thru.

William leaned closer. "Instead of the carousel, why don't we walk on the beach?"

Just what she didn't need to do with William. Things could get . . . romantic. More personal. More awkward. "It'll be too dark for that."

Disappointment surfaced in his gaze. Oh no. She'd hurt him.

Fortunately, it was their turn at the counter and William

stepped forward. "What'll you have?" He didn't even look at her.

"Dr Pepper."

Someone bumped into her.

"Hey!" a kid yelled.

She turned to see the boy in line behind her glowering at the man in the dark-green jacket who cut through another line and disappeared in the crowd.

Julian? She had to know.

"Hey!" she echoed the kid as she left the line and followed the guy's path, hoping she would catch sight of him again. Weaving back and forth, dodging bodies left and right. She had to see for herself. Though finding Julian would prove that she hadn't hallucinated earlier while on the ride. But she really hoped that she'd been seeing things.

The crowd thickened as she kept her focus on the back of his head twenty or so yards ahead. He glanced over his shoulder, then turned around to walk backward and look at her. To hold her gaze.

Julian Abel.

Also known to her as *4PP3R1710N*.

Or rather, *Apparition*.

He had one of those boyish faces that obviously never seemed to age.

She hadn't imagined him, after all. He'd been watching her while she'd been on the ride.

Her stomach dropped as if she was being tossed and turned all over again.

He *couldn't* be here. And yet there he was, staring at her. *Why* was he here? He had that knowing look in his eyes, and it stopped her in her tracks. Right in front of a young boy who barreled forward, smashing sticky caramel-covered ice cream all over her rarely used date-night blouse. Okay. Her brand-new blouse.

The boy was around six, and his eyes filled with tears. His mother crouched to console him. "It's all right, sweetie. We'll get another one."

"Oh, I'm so sorry." Mackenzie hated that she'd made a child cry. She could have avoided this mishap, but she'd been too focused on finding Julian instead of watching where she was going.

The mother glared at her and dragged her son away.

William approached in a huff, somehow managing to hold two sodas and two cotton candies in his large hands. She immediately relieved him of one of each item and took a few sips of the Dr Pepper while she searched the crowd for Julian.

His gaze froze on her caramelized shirt. "Mackenzie, what's going on? Besides being covered in sticky syrup"—he lifted his dark eyes to her face—"you . . . you look like you've seen a ghost."

Julian had taken off. She'd seen a ghost, all right. A ghost that was very much living and breathing. And here, of all places. Here in Michigan at this carnival, and that look in his gaze left no doubt he'd deliberately tracked her down.

"Let's get out of here." Without waiting for agreement, she headed through the growing crowd toward the exit, wariness creeping into her bones. While she rushed forward, she scanned ahead, searching for the man who'd ruined her life. Correction. She'd ruined her own life. And that past had been sealed so it was no longer in the public record.

It had essentially ceased to exist.

But Julian's appearance tonight was a reminder that her mistakes were right behind her.

She felt like she was on the ride again. Couldn't escape fast enough.

"Wait. Hold up." William tossed his drink and cotton candy in the garbage and gripped her arm, stopping her. "Please, what's going on?"

"Not here." She ground out the words. And with them, she'd said too much.

She shrugged free, pitched her cotton candy and soda as well, then took off running. She had to get away from the carnival and the feeling that Julian was watching her. He was everywhere watching her.

And he was fully capable of being everywhere.

She weaved through the vehicles and dodged a few too. Finally, gasping for breath, she approached the shiny new Lexus. William's car. Not hers. She focused on the Ferris wheel in the distance. The lights and screams and laughter. A couple of blocks away, Lake Michigan waves rolled against the shore. Comforting and soothing. She longed to be there.

If she'd gone walking on the beach tonight, would Julian have followed her there too?

What did he want?

His face grim, William unlocked his car and opened the door for her.

"Thank you." She slid into the taupe leather seat, and he shut the door.

Once he was in the driver's seat, he started the vehicle and the quiet hum of the engine proclaimed power in complete contrast to the cranky motors of the traveling carnival rides.

"You wasted your money at the carnival. I'll make it up to you."

"You can make it up to me by telling me what happened back there. Something spooked you. What aren't you telling me?"

"Can we please just get out of here?"

In response, William steered slowly through the parking area, then turned onto the street. Mackenzie owed him something. Though not an explanation of what happened tonight, she definitely owed him the truth. But words failed her as images of Julian staring at her shuddered through her. A slow pounding started in her head, matching the palpitations of her heart.

To his credit, William didn't press her further.

Now that she had a moment to catch her breath, though, she could share at least something with him. "I saw someone I knew a long time ago. I was just surprised to see him, that's all."

"He must have made some kind of impression on you to upset you so much."

"It's complicated."

His lips pursed.

At the corner ahead, she spotted a man. Glasses. Dark hair. Green jacket.

He stepped into the street at the crosswalk and jogged forward to cross two lanes. A vehicle heading north in the opposite lane seemed to speed up.

Watch out!

All her muscles tensing, she gripped the seat. Julian suddenly stopped as if in shock. Mackenzie closed her eyes and gritted her teeth.

The next few moments held excruciating sounds. A thump. A speeding car.

William sucked in a breath and swerved to the side. "Did you see that? Someone just got hit by a car. It's a hit-and-run. Call 911!"

He jumped out and ran across the street, failing to close the car door behind him.

Other vehicles stopped. People rushed forward. Curious onlookers and those who actually cared. Mackenzie called for emergency services and learned that someone had already called. Help was on the way.

She wouldn't jump out of the car to join the gathering crowd. She could offer no help. The two of them—she and Julian—should never be seen together. Instead, she wanted to curl into herself, but with the door wide open, the gruesome scene was framed perfectly for her to witness every minute.

ELIZABETH GODDARD

Moments later, sirens rang out and lights flashed. Emergency vehicles—law enforcement cruisers, a fire truck as well as an ambulance—arrived on the scene.

She caught a glimpse of medics kneeling next to the body. What could she do? Nothing. Except, well, she could pray. She closed her eyes, but tears sprang up instead of heartfelt words to God.

She started to cross her arms, but her shirt remained sticky, so she thrust her hands into her jacket pockets. In her right pocket, she felt something that hadn't been there before. Mackenzie tugged it out.

A business card for HanTech—short for Hanson Technologies—her father's brainchild. And on the back? A QR code.

What is this?

Using her cell, she scanned the code.

An animated image popped up. Mackenzie gasped.

Freda Stone, her favorite character from Knight Alliance, the MMO—massively multiplayer online video game—she and Julian had played together as kids, whirled around with her sword.

"You're vulnerable to deadly attacks. They're taking the stronghold!"

Mackenzie watched the short graphic again.

And again.

Dread squeezed her insides until she couldn't breathe.

A warning. This was why Julian had bumped into her. To hand-deliver a warning important enough that he'd sought her out in person but had still kept his distance.

Important enough that he'd taken a huge risk.

Deadly attacks . . .

She eyed the emergency vehicles and the nausea from the ride returned.

William climbed back in and shut his door, then stared at the steering wheel, a haggard cast to his pale features.

"Well?" she asked, the question barely a croak from her tear-clogged throat.

"He was breathing when they put him on the gurney."

She slumped with a long exhale. Julian had survived. But for how much longer? He'd communicated with her without leaving a digital trail. He was that scared. And she should be too. She shouldn't go see him in the hospital and instead should stay away.

He would want that.

William said nothing as he drove her back to the condo only a mile away and parked.

She shifted in the seat. "Listen—"

"I know what you're going to say," he huffed. "'Thank you, William, but I don't want to see you anymore—at least on a personal level.' I know, because that's what I was going to say, only to you."

Okay, well, she deserved that. And despite sharing his sentiment, rejection always stung. "Um . . . I was going to say that I need to get to Montana."

"Montana?" Suspicion flashed in his eyes. "Just like that?"

"Just like that. Something has come up, and I need to cancel our weekend—except, well, you already canceled it. It's okay, William. We're still friends. Colleagues. And I agree, it wasn't working." And never would, because as tonight proved, she could never escape.

He slumped back, and oddly, relief flashed over his features. Then he smiled. "At least now we know."

She returned his smile. Sometimes one date was all it took. "Yes, we do."

"What's in Montana?"

"Family." *A brother who warned me to stay far, far away.*

Acknowledgments

'm so grateful for all the many writing professionals and dear friends who the Lord has put in my path along this journey. Writing a novel takes more than one person. I want to thank all my writing friends who have supported and encouraged me and, most importantly, believed in me along the way. There are too many to name, but I want to give a shout-out to Lisa Harris, Sharon Hinck, Shannon McNear, and Susan Sleeman—you guys are my virtual officemates who are there in an instant to hold my hand and give me guidance. To brainstorm and tell me when something isn't working, and to pray for me when the days are long and life is overwhelming. I couldn't do it without you!

Special thanks to my experts: Richard Mabry, MD—Doc, you always make yourself available to answer questions and direct me in writing credible medical scenes. Wesley Harris, you've been so helpful in keeping me on the straight and narrow when it comes to police procedures. Even so, we both know that mistakes will be made, and that's all on me.

I'm a fortunate writer to have landed at Revell and in the hands of one of the most amazing publishing teams. I'll always be grateful to Lonnie Hull DuPont, who saw something in my proposal and worked with me to get it right. Rachel McRae, you are a gem and such a huge blessing to so many. I'm so honored to work with you and grateful that God chose to bring us together in the publishing world. Specials thanks to Amy Ballor, who keeps my words grounded in reality! Karen Steele and Michele Misiak, you are an amazing marketing and publicity team, second to none! And thanks to the art design team for the fabulous covers that exceed my expectations—it all starts with your work and drawing the reader closer to take that first peek inside.

Agent Extraordinaire, Steve Laube, you have been an incredible blessing in my writing life, and I thank God every day for letting me catch your attention at conferences!

No writers can spend the time it takes to write a story worthy of publishing without the commitment and support of family, and words can't describe how much I both love and appreciate you—Dan, for believing in me well before I could write a decent chapter! And to my children, Rachel, Christopher, Jonathan, and Andrew—thank you for letting me write.

Thank you, Lord—you put this dream in my heart and you made it happen. You are my All in All.

Elizabeth Goddard has sold over one million books and is the *USA Today* bestselling author of more than fifty romance novels and counting, including the romantic mystery *The Camera Never Lies*—a 2011 Carol Award winner. She is a Daphne du Maurier Award for Excellence in Mystery and Suspense finalist for her Mountain Cove series—*Buried, Backfire,* and *Deception*—and a Carol Award finalist for *Submerged.* When she's not writing, she loves spending time with her family, traveling to find inspiration for her next book, and serving with her husband in ministry. For more information about her books, visit her website at www.ElizabethGoddard.com.

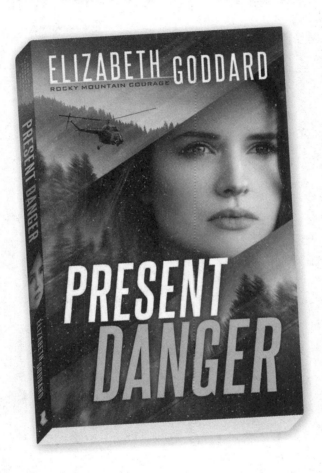

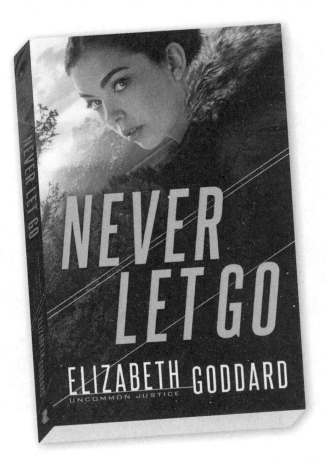

DON'T MISS BOOKS 2 AND 3 IN
THE UNCOMMON JUSTICE SERIES!

"Unique and intriguing romantic suspense that will have your heart racing. Goddard's fast-paced storytelling combined with emotional depth will keep you guessing until the very end."

—Rachel Dylan, bestselling author of the Atlanta Justice series

Revell
a division of Baker Publishing Group
www.RevellBooks.com

    RevellBooks

Avai able wherever books and ebooks are sold.

CONNECT WITH ELIZABETH

at **ElizabethGoddard.com**